Branded

A Novel by Neva Bell

For my bestie Jill

She just wanted a short story
about witches and werewolves

Chapter One

"For the love Chelsea! Could you drive any slower?!"

My twin sister ignores me. A pleasant smile on her face as she gazes out the windshield of the used Jetta we share.

"I know you can hear me."

She glances over at me, the sweet smile still on her face. "I'm not getting a speeding ticket because you're in a rush to get to the meeting."

"A speeding ticket? Are you kidding me? You're going forty in a fifty-five."

"Maybe you should have offered to drive."

I cross my arms and pout. "Maybe so."

Chelsea chuckles. "Chloe, calm down. Elliott isn't going anywhere."

"This isn't about Elliott."

She raises her eyebrow. "Oh no?"

I smirk. My sister knows me too well. Lying to Chelsea is impossible.

"If you get pulled over, just tell the cop you're me," I suggest.

"You know that won't work. Remember when you told the principal you were me so you wouldn't get detention?"

I groan. "How could I forget? Two extra detentions and I was grounded for three weeks when Mom and Dad found out."

I'm not sure how Chelsea and I haven't been able to pull off the "parent trap." We're physically identical in every way. Ice blondes with equally cool blue eyes, we stand at 5'6" and weigh exactly the

1

same. Our body frames are slightly different because of our physical activities. Chelsea loves ballet and yoga; I prefer rock climbing and cardio kickboxing.

"Do you think Elliott is as hot as the older girls say he is?" I ask, cat fully out of the bag.

"I don't know if anyone is as hot as they say he is."

Chelsea has a point. The way the older girls talk, Elliott is an Adonis, a gorgeous specimen of a man. Their eyes get hazy when they talk about him. I can't wait to see him for myself.

Chelsea makes a right turn onto Maple.

"Where are you going?"

"We have to pick up Rory."

I sigh loudly, but say nothing.

Chelsea met Rory Taylor on the first day of kindergarten and hasn't looked at another boy since. Over the years, she and Rory have been married several times. I was Chelsea's maid of honor in all of those backyard weddings. Most of the ceremonies were officiated by our next door neighbor Bruce, but our cat Tabby filled in every now and then. Snack cakes and lemonade were the standard menu.

Five minutes later, my sister's red-haired and freckle-faced boyfriend climbs in the backseat.

"Evening ladies," he says as he buckles his seatbelt.

Chelsea looks at him in the rearview mirror. "Hey babe!"

Rory pulls out a small box from his pocket and hands it to my sister. "Happy twentieth birthday!"

Chelsea blushes. "Aw! You didn't have to get me anything. And besides, my birthday isn't until tomorrow."

I try not to roll my eyes at Rory's goofy grin.

"Well, I may not see you tomorrow, with it being Branding Day and all."

2

Chelsea opens the box to find a beautiful pair of peridot earrings, our birthstone. "These are gorgeous Rory!" she gushes.

She unfastens her seatbelt, squeezes through the center of the front seats and plants a kiss on his lips.

I'm too preoccupied to poopoo their display of affection. Rory's casual mention of "Branding Day" makes my stomach drop. I look over at Chelsea. Her eyes gleam, completely smitten with Rory and his gift. She has no reason to be nervous, her future is clear.

Everyone knows Chelsea will have a beautiful white dove tattooed on her right shoulder tomorrow. I know exactly what this dove will look like because I've seen it on my mom's right shoulder for as long as I can remember.

The dove's feathers will be outlined in silver and its blue eyes will shine brightly. Perched on a snow-covered branch, it will span from the top of Chelsea's tanned shoulder to the bottom of her shoulder blade.

"Normal" people will see it and ask Chelsea where she got such a detailed and life-like tattoo. They'll marvel at how the dove's beautiful eyes project love and peacefulness. She'll make up a story about how she got it while we were traveling in Europe. Believable enough.

"Chloe? You okay?" I hear Chelsea ask.

I shake myself out of my thoughts. "Yeah, fine." I perk up a bit. "Let's go already!"

As Chelsea pulls out of Rory's driveway, she and Rory talk about the agenda for the coven meeting. I, of course, didn't bother to read the agenda that was emailed to all of the witches in my coven. I have to sit through the meeting no matter what, so why not be surprised?

I tune the two of them out as I think about tomorrow morning and the tattoo I'll be getting. Twins, even identical ones, can never get the same brand. One will get a dove, and the other will get a hawk. No one knows why. The popular theory is the universe is balancing itself out. Whatever.

3

The Vegas odds are on Chelsea being the dove. Which means an equally beautiful black hawk with piercing black eyes will be tattooed on my right shoulder. The hawk will be in full flight, ready to swoop in on its prey. Instead of love and peacefulness, my hawk's eyes will project strength and fearlessness.

Next to each other, the dove and hawk are each other's opposite. Yet somehow, they belong together.

There has been chatter about which brands we will get since Chelsea and I were babies. There wasn't much debate. It was clear from a relatively young age that my angelic sister will be the dove. She has always been the peaceful, passive one. The one who was easier for my parents of the same temperament to handle.

"Such a soft heart," is how everyone describes Chelsea. I don't want to know what they say about me.

My mom discouraged conversations about Branding Day and any theories about our future tattoos. "Que sera, sera," she would say. "For all we know, Chloe will be the dove and Chelsea will be the hawk."

My mom talks a big game, but there is something in her eyes leading me to believe she agrees with all of our relatives. I certainly do.

"You excited to get your brand?" Rory asks from the backseat.

I play it off like I wasn't just worrying about it. "It will be what it will be," I say, mimicking my mother's words of wisdom.

"She's more excited about meeting Elliott," Chelsea teases.

"Ah," Rory says. "The infamous Elliott. How cool would it be to 'read' someone's skin? Do you think he'll learn all of your secrets?"

I snort. "God, I hope not."

Elliott is not only a hottie, he is a Reader - a warlock who can "read" a witch's skin to determine which brand she should receive.

"It's so unfair. You ladies get to have all the fun," Rory pouts.

4

"If you want," I tell him, "you can come over tomorrow and have Elliott give you a tattoo. Maybe you can get something manly like a dragon."

Before he can respond to my jab, Chelsea cuts us off. "We're here," she announces. She pulls into the parking lot of an inconspicuous brick building in a run-of-the-mill upstate New York suburb.

No one would guess two hundred witches and warlocks use this building to convene for their monthly meetings.

Chelsea

"I'm worried about Chloe," I whisper to Rory after we take our seats in the meeting hall. The room is full tonight, Elliott is a big draw.

"Why?" he asks.

"She's scared to death about tomorrow."

Rory crinkles his nose. "Chloe? Scared?"

I nod. "She won't admit it, but she doesn't want a hawk brand."

Rory considers this a moment. "I wouldn't want to be a hawk either."

Before I can respond, our coven leader Samantha steps up to the microphone at the front of the room. Samantha looks nothing like the witches in horror movies. She is a petite, strawberry blonde who prefers khakis and floral print to tight black dresses.

When Samantha's mother retired from the coven leader position eight years ago, Samantha was the unanimous pick to take her place. She is smart and incredibly talented. Samantha's not nearly as powerful as the Verhena, the Supreme Leader of our kind, but she's the most skilled witch I've ever met.

Samantha clears her throat and the room calms. "Good evening everyone. Thank you for coming tonight. As your agenda noted, we have two witches turning twenty tomorrow. Chloe, Chelsea, will you stand please?"

5

I feel my face redden. Chloe, who's sitting a few rows up with our parents, shoots up immediately. She grins and waves at everyone. I, on the other hand, barely manage to stand and give a small head nod before sitting right back down.

Samantha smiles and continues as Chloe takes her seat. "Our youngest coven members asked me a few questions during our youth session. I thought it would be cute to let everyone hear what they are curious about."

We all say "aww" as three little ones walk toward the microphone, two girls and a boy. None of them can be older than five.

One of the little girls, a cutie with brown hair and big brown eyes goes first. "Do good witches get a dove and bad witches get a hawk?"

Her question hits me in the gut. I know this is Chloe's biggest fear about being a hawk.

Samantha smiles. "No Lily, that's not what the brands mean. The brands help you decide which kind of magic is best for you. Have you used magic yet?"

Lily nods her head. "I use it when I play Barbies."

The crowd laughs. Chloe and I did the same thing when we were young. We made Barbie walk around, get dressed and get in the Barbie Corvette without laying hands on her. Although we weren't supposed to, we also used our powers to do chores when Mom and Dad weren't home.

"I see," Samantha continues. "When you turn twenty, you will get your brand. Witches branded with a dove use their magic for things like healing, protection, and preservation of nature. Hawks use their magic to defeat other beings - both natural and supernatural. They are on the front lines of any good versus evil war. They are our gladiators."

A man in the crowd raises his hand.

Samantha points to him. "Yes, Burt?"

6

"Why do you think there has been a recent increase in the number of hawk brands given?"

This is a question we've asked in my own household.

Samantha sighs. "Well Burt, it's hard to say. For decades we saw a decrease in the hawk brands, likely because of our peace treaty with the werewolves. My guess is the untimely passing of Barbara Sheep caused the uptick in hawk brands."

Rory leans into my ear. "Untimely passing? That's an interesting way to describe murder."

The thought of werewolves sends shivers down my spine. The older members of our coven talk about the risk the werewolves in the west serve, but our people have been separated for generations. The wolves stay west of St. Louis, and witches stay east of St. Louis. Anyone who passes the boundary line takes their lives into their own hands. This simple truce has stood the test of time.

Well, until a year ago. Our coven doesn't talk much about Barbara Sheep anymore. When she was murdered last year, the leader of the werewolves insisted it was not an act authorized by him. He claimed a pack of rogue werewolves was responsible. Our leader, the Verhena, chose to believe him.

The little boy steps up next to ask his question. "Why don't boys get brands? Doesn't seem fair."

This makes the crowd chuckle again.

"You paid him to ask that question, didn't you?" I tease Rory, remembering his sulking in the car.

He smirks. "Maybe…"

Samantha takes a few minutes to explain that witches are a matriarchal society and women are our leaders. "The nice thing about not getting a brand Jacob, is you get to choose what kind of magic you want to learn when you go off to Leviston. Won't that be fun?"

Jacob brightens. "I get to pick?"

Samantha nods. "Yes. When a female witch goes to Leviston, her classes are determined by her brand. But when you go to Leviston, you tell them what you want to do."

I think back to my campus tour of Leviston a couple months ago. The campus is gorgeous. Tucked away in the dense woods of northern Vermont, where it gets unbearably cold for many, the small college campus looks like any other small college from the outside.

"My mom is a dove, but my dad went to hawk classes. So I'm not sure which to pick," Jacob says with a frown.

Samantha tussles his hair. "You have plenty of time to decide."

Rory and I haven't talked about the type of magic he will practice once we get to Leviston. I'm hoping he'll follow me on whichever path I must take, but I don't want to pressure him.

In a way, I'm glad fate will decide which path is right for me. It would be a huge decision otherwise. The only bad thing is Chloe and I will be on different paths no matter which brand I get.

When I was younger, I worried about Chloe and I being separated once we get to Leviston. I hate when she and I are apart for more than a day or two. Our cribs were side by side as babies. Even now, we can have our own bedrooms, but we insist on sharing.

Luckily, hawks and doves have a lot of interaction at Leviston. They attend the same basic magic courses, but are separated for advanced classes. Doves will never use the combat spells taught to hawks, just like hawks won't need the advanced nature spells doves utilize in their practice.

The final question from the young coven members is a cute one too. The second little girl, her brown hair in pigtails, asks if getting your brand hurts.

"Mine didn't hurt at all," Samantha answers. "I wish Elliott could have made it tonight, because he would have told you all about the process."

There is a soft murmur from the crowd.

Samantha puts her hand up. "Sorry everyone, but Elliott couldn't make it tonight." Samantha makes eye contact with me, then Chloe. "He wants me to assure Chloe and Chelsea that he is on his way. He will be at your home tomorrow morning for your brands."

"Chloe is not going to be happy about this," I murmur to Rory.

Sure enough, a few hours later, Chloe is complaining about Elliott's absence.

"I can't believe he didn't show up! The coven meeting dragged on and on. Had I known Elliott wasn't going to be there, I would have skipped it."

We're both laying in our beds with the lights off.

I yawn. Chloe is right, the meeting lasted forever and I'm tired. "He probably had something important going on. Besides, you'll see him in the morning."

Chloe doesn't respond. I'm about to fall asleep when she whispers, "I'd love to see a dove on my shoulder tomorrow, so I can be like you and Mom."

Her confession is not a total surprise, but I'm dismayed all the same. I hate to see my sister hurting. In her mind, the hawk brand will cement her feelings about being an outsider in our family. The only hawk in a house full of doves.

"You never know. You could be the dove and I'll be the hawk. Or maybe we'll be the first twins ever to have the same brand."

Chloe chortles. "Yeah right Chelse. We both know what's going to happen tomorrow." She pauses for a second, then moans, "I don't want to be like Aunt June!"

I can't help but laugh. Aunt June is our only relative who is a hawk. She's my dad's oldest sister and a little off her rocker.

"Oh Chloe! Aunt June isn't the way she is because she's a hawk! She's just weird!"

I try to come up with the most awesome hawk I can think of. It takes me a minute because there aren't nearly as many hawks as there are doves. Our elders say it used to be a fifty/fifty mix, but like Samantha was saying tonight, the number of hawks has decreased over time.

I finally think of the perfect thing to say. "What about Helen Borren? She's a hawk."

"Oh... Do you think if I'm a hawk I'll get the chance to meet her?" Chloe asks, a twinge of excitement in her voice.

My sister has been in awe of Helen Borren our entire lives. She frequently pretended to be Helen when we played outside as kids.

I smile in the darkness, proud of myself for giving Chloe a reason to feel good about her fate. "I'm sure you will."

I expect Chloe to go on and on about Helen Borren. Telling me for the hundredth time how Helen Borren single-handedly fought off three werewolves who crossed over into our territory. How Helen is the most powerful witch of her generation.

Instead, she lays quietly in her bed. I'm not sure if she is lost in thought or sleeping. I don't disturb either. I consider my own brand. Rory and I are both pretty sure I'm the dove, and I hope to goodness we're right. The thought of being a hawk terrifies me. I don't think I'm cut out for the kind of training and strength necessary for hawks.

But Chloe is. She's always been the strong one, both mentally and physically. She may look as fragile as I do, but the truth is she fears nothing.

I stay awake as long as I can in case Chloe wants to talk more. Eventually though, my eyelids are heavy and I give in to sleep.

Chloe

I'm so anxious, I wake up before the alarm clock. I roll over and see Chelsea sleeping peacefully in her bed three feet from mine. I'm a smidge jealous of her. I'd love to know exactly what my future will look like. She'll get her dove brand, go off to Leviston, marry Rory, and have a beautiful family.

10

I, on the other hand, have no idea what the future holds for me. Yes I'll be going to Leviston too, but I will be on the hawk path. No one I know has taken the hawk training in the last twenty years. I have no idea what to expect.

Plus, I'm not excited about Leviston. A witch-focused college seems like a good idea in theory, but I'd rather go to a traditional school. A college filled with magic and supernatural abilities sounds like an adventure, but it's not. From what I saw at orientation, Leviston will involve a lot of lecturing and homework.

The only promising thing about Leviston is the exposure to more warlocks. The boys in our local coven aren't anything to write home about, so I'm hoping Leviston has better options.

I had boyfriends throughout high school, but my relationships never lasted long. I don't see the point in getting involved with an average guy. He would never really understand who I am as a person. This isn't *Bewitched*. I won't find a Darren who will fall in love with me and accept my abilities. Any witch who has tried a long-term relationship with a non-witch has failed, horribly.

It's not like any of the regular boys I dated held my interest anyway. I was often more daring and adventurous than them. They were only interested in making out. While I won't deny I enjoyed it immensely, none of the boys were challenging enough for me. Maybe I'll find my match in one of the hawk classes.

It's common for witches to meet their future partners at Leviston. In fact, my parents met there. Mom was in her second year when she volunteered to give a campus tour to incoming freshmen. As luck would have it, Dad was one of the new students in her group. It was love at first sight.

I jump when the alarm starts its annoying and shrill ringing. Chelsea rolls over, slams her hand on the snooze button and smashes her face in her pillow.

"I hate that stupid thing!" she whines.

Our bedside alarm is the only thing Chelsea has ever hated in her life.

I giggle. "Rise and shine sleeping beauty."

Chelsea opens one eye and looks at me. Suddenly, she sits straight up and throws off the covers. "Chloe! It's Branding Day!"

She jumps out of her bed and starts tugging on my blanket.

"Hey!" I protest. "Quit!"

"Get up! Let's go! We have to get ready."

Despite my moodiness, her excitement is infectious. "Alright, alright."

Chelsea smiles widely as she drags me to the bathroom across the hall. We stand side by side in our bathroom, each in front of the sink we assigned ourselves as kids. Mom and Dad think it's funny we won't use the other's sink, but it makes perfect sense to us. We even stood on the bathroom counter one day and painted our names above the mirror in "our spots." Chelsea wrote her name in pretty pink script, and I wrote mine in purple block letters.

Chelsea grins at me in the mirror. "Do you want to go first when Elliott gets here?"

I shrug my shoulders. "Doesn't make a difference to me. Although I would like to catch a glimpse of him."

Chelsea giggles. "Of course that's your main concern."

I finish brushing my teeth and spit into the sink. "Can you blame a girl? I'm not tied down like you."

Mom makes bacon and eggs for breakfast, but the only one who eats more than a few bites is Dad. Mom tries to calm our nerves by telling us about her own Branding Day. We've already heard the story ten times, but she means well.

Like us, Mom received her brand shortly before she left for Leviston. Her path was decided and she was happy about it, for the most part.

"Being a hawk might have been fun," she muses, although I think she's only saying that to make me feel better.

When Dad met Mom all those years ago, he decided to follow her on the dove path because he fell head over heels for the "cute blonde girl" leading his tour.

"Would you have taken the hawk path?" I asked him one day a couple years ago. "If you hadn't met Mom?"

He considered my question, his dark brown eyebrows furrowing. "Probably not," he admitted. "I'm not a hawk kind of guy."

Dad is a sturdy man, but he has a docile demeanor. While he physically fits the bill of male hawks I've seen, he is more of a peacemaker than a warrior. Same with Mom. Chelsea and I inherited her lean, athletic physique, but her specialty at Leviston was healing potions, not battle strategy.

After breakfast, we sit in the living room pretending to watch TV. *House Hunters* is on, but none of us is paying much attention to it. I keep glancing at the clock and catch my sister doing the same.

When the doorbell rings, all four us stand up simultaneously, then freeze. No one quite sure what to do.

Dad makes the first move. "I'll get it," he says and heads for the front door.

I sit back down on the couch. "You can go first Chelsea. I'll wait."

"Are you sure?"

I smile. Chelsea looks like she is about to burst at the seams. "Yes. I don't think you can wait a minute longer."

Chelsea breathes a sigh of relief. "Thanks." Then walks toward the front of the house.

I'm tempted to run down the hall when I hear an unfamiliar deep voice greet my dad and Chelsea. Elliott is here! I resist the urge to catch a peek of him and remain seated. I don't want to interfere with Chelsea's Branding Day.

But four hours later, I'm fidgeting like crazy. What is taking so long? I want to sneak in our front room and see what's going on, but Chelsea and I agreed to wait until we've both had our tattoos to

13

look at our backs. Mom and Dad try to keep me entertained, but they're as nervous as I am.

I stand when I hear footsteps coming around the corner. Chelsea is beaming as she enters the room.

"All done! Your turn Chloe."

I make a circle around her, hoping her blue tank top isn't covering her new brand. To my chagrin, the tattoo is concealed by a huge white bandage.

Chelsea giggles as I sigh. "I knew you'd try to peek!"

"Did it hurt?"

She shakes her head. "Not at all. Remember, one of his powers is to calm and heal as he tattoos."

"Yeah, doesn't mean I want to be poked with a needle for four hours."

Chelsea smiles. "I think you'll be fine as soon as you meet Elliott."

This peaks my interest. "For real? Is he hot?"

Chelsea blushes.

Damn! Elliott must be really hot for Chelsea to notice him. She's usually completely blinded by her love for Rory.

When I step into the front room, I see why Chelsea was blushing. Elliott is wiping down a padded massage table with a hand towel. Black tribal tattoos cover his sun-kissed arms. He is wearing a black t-shirt and ripped blue jeans. A black baseball hat covers his dark hair. I don't need to see his face to know he's gorgeous.

I play it cool when he turns my way, hoping he didn't notice me checking him out.

He extends his hand to me. "Hi. I'm Elliott. I'll be branding you today." He says it so casually it makes me chuckle.

I return his handshake. His hand is warm and his shake is firm. "Chloe. Nice to meet you."

Elliott smiles and dimples appear in his cheeks. "You ready?" he asks as he arranges items on a silver tray. Unfortunately, I get no clue about my pending brand because he has both white and black vials of ink in his hands.

I stand tall and square my shoulders. "Yes."

Elliott gives me another beautiful smile. Damn this man is fine. And his hands are going to be all over my back. I get goosebumps thinking about it.

My smile falters when I see the tattooing equipment. I've never been a huge fan of needles. In fact, Chelsea used to hold my hand when we got shots at the doctor's office.

My concern must be written on my face.

"Don't worry," Elliott assures me. "You won't feel a thing. I promise."

I take a deep breath. "Okay, let's do this."

I pull off my t-shirt and walk over to the table in my bra and cutoff shorts. I hope Elliott will give me a good onceover, but he doesn't. I lay flat on my stomach and turn my head toward him as he sits in the chair beside me.

"Do you want to know which brand I'm giving you, or do you want it to be a surprise?" he asks.

"I want to wait. I promised Chelsea I would."

Elliott nods. "She said the same thing. In that case, you should look the other way."

I do as told and turn my gaze toward our front windows. The blinds are closed so no one can see inside. The neighbors would probably find it a bit strange if they saw me getting a tattoo in our living room.

Elliott begins softly running his fingertips down my back as he hums quietly. I wonder if he is humming some ancient witchy song that will make my skin "speak" to him, but then I recognize the melody. I can't help but laugh.

Elliott's fingertips stop. "What?"

I look over my shoulder at him. "Justin Bieber? Really?"

He grins. "Hey, *Love Yourself* is a great song."

I roll my eyes. "Whatever."

"No more interruptions," Elliott says in a stern voice, then cracks a smile.

I turn my head back toward the windows and lay still. Elliott trails his fingers down my back, then uses massage-like motions to knead the skin. I'm incredibly relaxed until he takes in a sharp breath. The motion of his hands abruptly ceases. He lays his palms flat on my back for what feels like an eternity. My once relaxed mind is now reeling. What is going on?

Stay calm Chloe, I tell myself. This is just part of the process.

But I'm all kinds of freaked out. Something feels wrong, off in some way.

Elliott takes his hands off my back and silently takes a seat on his stool. The ink vials clink and his equipment hums as he tests it. I wish I could ask him about my brand, but Chelsea will be upset if I don't wait. I consider asking him anyway and lying to my sister. His momentary pause while reading my skin has left a rock in my stomach.

Elliott stands and leans over my body. I shiver as his breath tickles my neck. He whispers in my ear, "It's going to be okay Chloe. Rest now."

I close my eyes and steady my breath. Despite my concern, I slip into a sleep-like state. I can faintly hear and feel Elliott moving around me, but it's hazy. It doesn't seem real. I don't feel any pain, not even a prick. Instead, my mind wanders and I have no sense of time.

I'm still out of it when Elliott gently nudges my shoulder. "Chloe, honey, it's time to wake up."

My first thought is – he called me honey! Woo hoo!

I roll onto my back and slowly open my eyes. As they adjust to the light and I creep out of my brain fog, I notice the sun has set and the overhead light is on.

"How long have I been asleep?" I ask in a raspy voice.

Elliott wraps his arm around my shoulders and helps me sit up. "A while."

He stretches his arms to the sky, his shirt lifting high enough for me to see a crow tattoo above his belt.

Nice.

When my head clears, I slide off the end of the table and do a quick stretch myself. I'm more alert as I grab my shirt. I stop short before putting my right arm through the sleeve for fear it will rub against my shoulder.

"Is it okay if I put my shirt on?" I ask Elliott.

"Yes. The skin is completely healed."

"One of the perks of a magical tattoo, right?"

Elliott smiles in response, but it doesn't meet his eyes. "There's something I need to…" He stops himself. "You know what? I'll wait a few minutes and let you and your sister enjoy the moment."

I don't like the look on his face. "No, tell me. What is it?"

Elliott takes off his hat and throws it on the table. "I don't know where to start." He runs his hand through his black hair. "Just go get your family and reveal your brand however you planned it out."

I step toward him. "You're scaring me. What's going on?"

Elliott shifts his weight. "Chloe, your life is about to change. A lot."

I relax, the tension in my shoulders easing. He probably says this to all of his canvasses. "I know. I've been waiting for this day since I was a little girl."

Elliott closes the distance between us and takes my hands. "You don't get what I'm trying to tell you, but you will in a few minutes."

17

I search his eyes for some sort of clue. The sense of doom I had when he was reading my skin is back in full force. "Something is wrong, isn't it?"

He hesitates. "Nothing is wrong, not exactly. Just unexpected."

A glimmer of hope rises in me. "Am I a dove too? Are Chelsea and I the first twins to get the same brand?"

Elliott opens his mouth to respond, but my mom interrupts him.

"You're done!" she exclaims from behind me.

Elliott drops my hands and steps back toward his equipment. I stare at Elliott a moment before turning to Mom. What was he about to say? His expression gives away nothing.

I shake the concern from my mind and smile wide for Mom. "All done!"

Mom grins and yells, "She's done!" down the hallway.

Chelsea comes running toward the front room and nearly knocks me over when she grabs me for a hug. "Are you ready? Are you ready to see?"

I return her infectious smile. "Hell yeah!" I chase her up the stairs and into our bathroom. We stand in front of our sinks with goofy grins on our faces.

"Can I go first?" Chelsea asks, her eyes gleaming.

I nod. "You got your tattoo first, you show first."

Chelsea turns her back to the mirror. "Will you take the bandage off?"

"Don't you want to see?"

"I'm too nervous. You look for me."

I laugh. "Okay."

I pick a corner of the bandage and start peeling it back. My heart pounds as I reveal more and more of Chelsea's skin. I know full well whatever her brand is, mine is the opposite. I'm essentially revealing my own brand by looking at hers.

18

I'm not surprised at all when I see the silver and white ink. All of our family and friends were right, Chelsea has a white dove on her shoulder.

"Chelsea, it's beautiful," I say with pure sincerity, genuinely happy for my sister. She wanted this more than anything.

Chelsea glances over her shoulder into the mirror. I see tears form in her eyes. "Wow," she says after taking it in. She looks up at me and smiles. "I'm a dove." Her smile falters. "Oh Chloe, I'm so sorry."

This is the amazing thing about my sister. Her dream has just come true, and all she can think about is me.

I hug her. "Don't be sorry Chelse. This is the right thing." I don't tell her there's a piece of me hoping I'm right about both of us being doves.

Chelsea pulls away. "Your turn! Let's see it."

I turn my back to the mirror, take off my shirt, and wait for my sister's reaction. All I hear is a gasp. I look over at Chelsea, her eyes wide as saucers. Her expression gives me hope. I am a dove too!

I look over my shoulder and my jaw drops open. I meet my sister's eyes.

"Oh my God," I say before turning back to my reflection.

There's no way this is happening.

"What's going on in there?" Mom asks from the hallway. "Can we come in?"

Chelsea and I stare at each other, shell-shocked. She moves toward the door and opens it. Mom comes bursting in.

"Oh girls! We're so excited! We can't wait to," she stops mid-sentence when she sees my back.

Dad pushes in behind her. "Let me in. I want to see."

Mom turns toward him, disbelief and fear on her face. "Steven?" His name comes out like a question.

19

Dad stares at my back silently, not showing any emotion. He spins on his heels and walks out of the bathroom. "I'll call Samantha. She'll know what to do."

Mom takes one last look at my back before following after him. "Are you sure that's a good idea? You know the danger she'll be in now..." her voice trails off.

Chelsea reaches out and grabs my hand, both of our faces pale in the mirror.

"It's going to be okay," she says, her voice barely more than a whisper.

A tear slides down my cheek. As much as I didn't want to see a black hawk on my shoulder, I'd give anything to have it now.

I've only seen my brand in pictures. Never in real life. A gorgeous white hawk with wings expanding from shoulder to shoulder. Its feathers outlined in gold ink. Beautiful, but fierce blue eyes that leap off the skin. It is as equally stunning as it is powerful.

The brand of the Verhena.

I squeeze Chelsea's hand. "I'm screwed."

Chapter Two

Chelsea

The look on Chloe's face is killing me. Her knees are pulled tight into her chest and she's rocking back and forth.

We are hiding under a makeshift tent in our room like we did when we were kids. Huddled together under a quilt draped over our beds, I attempt to console her.

"You should be excited. Do you know how special this is?"

She scowls at me.

I clear my throat and try again. "I know you're scared Chloe, but it will be okay. I promise." I can't help but notice how much I sound like our mother.

"Was it okay for the last girl?" Chloe asks, dripping with sarcasm.

I frown. She's got me there. "That was an odd situation. It won't happen to you."

Chloe stops rocking and glares at me. "The wolves tore her to pieces Chelsea!" Seeing me flinch, she softens her tone. "They'll come for me now. I might as well have a giant target on my back instead of a white hawk."

I touch her shoulder. "The wolves came after Barbara because her stepbrother told everyone during a podcast that she was the next Verhena. He outed her to the world. No one is going to do that to you. We all know we have to keep your identity a secret until you have all of your powers."

Our bedroom door cracks open.

"Girls?" our mom asks tentatively.

I pull back the cover of our tent. "Down here."

Mom smiles and crawls under the quilt with us. "I haven't seen you girls do this for years."

"I've started my confinement right away," Chloe grumbles.

Mom frowns. "You won't be confined."

"Really?" Chloe spits back. "So I can just go on about my life like nothing has changed?"

Mom sighs. "Not exactly. Precautions will have to be taken."

For the first time in years, I see my sister break down. Her head in her hands, she begins sobbing.

"Oh sweetheart," Mom says as she pulls my sister in for a tight hug.

Tears fill my own eyes as I watch my mom and sister cry together. I can't imagine how my parents must be feeling. I'm not even sure how I feel about Chloe being the next Verhena. It's an odd combination of pride and fear.

After a few minutes, Chloe calms down. Mom momentarily leaves the tent for some tissues and we all dry our eyes.

"How long will it take for her powers to come in?" I ask.

Mom shrugs her shoulders. "It's hard to say. There's only been one Verhena in my lifetime, and she's in her eighties now. She came to a coven meeting years ago, but I haven't met her personally."

I turn to Chloe. "Do you feel any different?"

She is staring into space, but answers my question. "I don't feel more powerful, if that's what you mean."

"It's not instantaneous," Mom explains.

"Duh," Chloe says, "or Barbara Sheep would still be alive."

I shiver every time someone mentions Barbara's name. I heard a rumor that the wolves mangled her body so badly, she was unrecognizable.

"Maybe the wolves aren't looking for the next Verhena," I hypothesize. "They know she will be watched like a hawk."

Chloe snorts. "No pun intended."

Mom and I give her a "really?" look.

"Sorry," she apologizes weakly before tucking her knees into her chest again.

I don't mind my sister's attitude. If anything, it shows me the Chloe I know is still in there.

"Did Dad talk to Samantha?" I ask Mom.

She nods. "Yes. She said we cannot tell anyone else, not even the members of our coven."

I'm surprised. "Seriously? We can't tell the coven?"

Mom's eyes are soft. "We have to be careful Chelsea."

Chloe and I exchange a glance, both of us disturbed by Samantha's directive. If we can't trust our own coven, who can we trust?

Wait a second... "Can I tell Rory?"

"Of course you can," Chloe responds at the same time my mom says, "No."

Before we can discuss it further, there's a knock on the door.

Dad leans his head in. "Ladies?"

Mom throws the quilt back this time. "Over here honey."

Dad chuckles, then stops when he sees Chloe curled up like a ball. "Chloe..."

She looks up at him in response.

"Elliott needs to speak with you."

Chloe tucks her chin back on her knees. "I'm not leaving this tent."

"He needs to talk to you," Dad presses. "As the Reader, it's his job to provide you with information."

"About what?" Chloe asks.

Dad rubs his temples. I have never seen him this distraught. "I don't know exactly. He wouldn't tell me. I'm guessing there is a protocol he has to follow."

"I'm not getting out of this tent," Chloe repeats.

I move the quilt and stand up. "Fine. Elliott will have to come up here." I extend my hand to Mom. "Let's go Mom."

She takes my hand and I pull her to a standing position. Chloe remains still as we exit the room. I shut the door behind us and we make our way downstairs to the kitchen.

"How is she?" Dad asks as we take seats at our circular, honey-colored wooden table.

"Not good, she's scared. Hell, I'm scared," Mom admits.

Dad nods. "Me too. I was not prepared for this." He turns to me. "How are you holding up?"

How am I holding up?

I just found out my sister is going to be the leader of our kind. She'll likely be taken somewhere far away for extensive training. I may not see her for long periods of time. She will stay at the Verhena's super-secret compound doing whatever it is the Verhena does.

Selfishly, I am disappointed. Not because I want to be the Verhena. No way. Chloe is my twin, my other half. A part of me will be gone if she's taken away from me.

Instead of saying all of this, I simply tell my dad, "I'm okay."

For the first time all day, I check my cellphone. I have two missed calls from Rory and a text asking, "Well???"

I sigh. "Mom, are you sure I can't tell Rory?"

Dad answers for her. "You can't tell him. Not yet."

"He won't tell anyone," I plead. "He loves Chloe as much as we do." Well, maybe that's a bit of a stretch. Rory and Chloe don't always see eye to eye, but they're like siblings. Rory would never do anything to hurt my sister.

24

Mom pats my hand. "We know. But for now, we have to keep it between us. You'll be able to tell him soon."

I type "It's a dove!" into a text and hit "send." After some thought, I send another message. "Hey, it's going to be crazy here tonight. I probably won't be able to call you until tomorrow morning. I love you."

I get a quick response. "Woo hoo! So happy you got a dove. Love you too Chelse."

I smile. Rory would have acted excited even if I got a hawk. Would he be terrified of the hawk training? Absolutely, but I know in my heart of hearts he would have weathered the storm with me.

I put my phone down and tune back into my parents' conversation.

"Where do you think they'll take her?" Mom asks Dad, concern furrowed in her brow.

"Where will *who* take her?"

Dad turns to me with a grimace. "The Guard will be here any minute."

My pulse races. The Guard?

Chloe

Elliott laughs lightly when he sees the tent arrangement. It takes him a minute, but he manages to squeeze his large frame in between our twin beds.

When he's settled, he says, "Wow, this may be a first for me."

"First time in a girl's room?"

He grins. "No. First time in a girl's tent."

I stretch my legs as far as I can and lean back against Chelsea's bed. "There's so much I can say, but I'll let it go."

"That's probably for the best."

25

The light banter with Elliott eases my mind a little, but he's here for a reason. "Rumor has it you need to speak with me."

Elliott nods. He put his hat back on, but it doesn't hide his chocolate brown eyes. "I've been trained to tell you a few things."

"Okay. Can I ask a few questions first?"

"Of course."

Of all the questions floating around in my brain, which do I choose first? I pick the one shouting the loudest. "Why did you give me this tattoo?"

I don't want this damn tattoo. I want to be a normal witch. Well, as normal as a witch can be.

The amusement is gone from Elliott's face. "I gave you the tattoo my reading told me to give you."

"What exactly did my skin tell you?"

"It's hard to explain." He pauses. "When I touch someone's skin, I get a sense of who they really are. Not the person they try to be, or the person we think they should be. The real woman. Who she is now and who she can become. A vision of the bird that is right for her literally flies through my mind. I see it clear as day."

I think back to the moment Elliott was reading my skin and chills run through me.

"Is that why you stopped during my reading? You saw the white hawk?"

"You sensed that?"

"Yes."

Elliott picks at the skin on the palm of his hand. "I've never seen the white hawk before. It took me by surprise."

"Because you never guessed I'd be the Verhena?"

He shakes his head. "No. I never thought I'd give the Verhena tattoo." He meets my eyes. "I wasn't sure I could do it."

"Wait, didn't you give Barbara her tattoo?"

26

Elliott cringes. "No. My dad did."

Seeing I've hit a nerve by asking about Barbara, I change the subject. "What do you have to tell me?"

Elliott straightens up. "Some of it you probably already know. First, you cannot share this with anyone unless you are one hundred percent sure they will take the secret to their graves."

I nod. "I know. Our coven leader told my dad we can't tell the rest of our coven."

"She's absolutely right. This is the kind of thing people love to gossip about. The news will spread like wildfire."

The shock value alone of me being the Verhena is enough to get people yacking. No one will believe it.

"Second thing," Elliott continues, "your tattoo is different than the other magical brands."

I snort. "No shit."

He smiles. "Obviously, right? What I mean is, as you become more powerful, your tattoo will change."

"Really?"

"Yes. I've never seen it myself, but your tattoo will fill in with more gold as your power increases. It's a gauge of how much stronger you're getting."

Fascinating. "My hawk will eventually be completely gold?"

"Not completely gold. At least I don't think so. The feathers on the current Verhena's brand are golden from the tip to about one-third of the way up the feather. Your hawk will remain mostly white, but more gold will slowly fill in."

I'll be checking my back day and night to see if it's changing. "This is so weird."

"Yes, it is," Elliott agrees.

"In sum, don't tell anyone about my white hawk; and my tattoo is a power barometer. Got it. Anything else?"

Elliott frowns. "This is the part you're not going to like."

My stomach drops. "What?"

"I had to call the Guard."

My body tenses. "The Guard? Why?"

"I'm sorry Chloe, I had to. I was told to call the Guard immediately when and if I give the Verhena tattoo."

"The Guard is coming here? To my house?" It feels like an elephant is sitting on my chest.

"Yes, they will be here soon."

"Do my parents know?"

Elliott nods.

Holy shit. The Guard. This is so bad. The Guard is the witch equivalent of the Army Rangers, the Navy Seals, and the Green Berets. They are called in when the shit has hit the fan. The fact that they are coming to my house drives home how much danger I'm in.

I pull my legs back into my chest, fighting tears. "You got it wrong. Your vision was wrong."

"Hey, don't." Elliott reaches out and puts his hands on my shoulders. I refuse to meet his eyes. "You are the Verhena. I know you don't think so, but you are."

I'd love to believe what he's saying, but I can't. I'm bullheaded and stubborn. I defy authority for fun. How can I possibly be the leader our people need?

Tears spill from my eyes. "You don't know me Elliott. I'm not the Verhena."

"Look at me," Elliott commands. I hesitate, but give in. I gaze up at him, his face gorgeous despite the stern expression. "My reading was right. You are strong. Smart. Compassionate. Everything we need our next Verhena to be. I know you can do this."

28

"How do you know?"

"I just do. My reading for you was the strongest I've ever had. I saw things I don't usually see with the others."

Elliott drops his hands and sits back. I feel colder without his warm touch.

"Like what? What did you see?"

He is conflicted. "I shouldn't have mentioned it."

"But you did. What did you see?" I press.

"I can't tell you."

"Seriously? You can't do that to me! Tell me!"

Elliott sighs. "I don't know if it was a vision, or if it was my subconscious. It's not reliable."

What the hell is this man talking about? I have enough on my plate without having to worry about Elliott seeing my untimely demise and not sharing the details with me.

"Elliott, tell me. I have to know."

His face flushes. "It's kind of ridiculous."

"All of this is ridiculous."

Elliott starts to say, "I saw," then stops himself.

This is so frustrating. "Come on Elliott. Just tell me."

He opens his mouth only to shut it again.

I'm about to go nuclear on him when he speaks, a look of determination on his face. "To hell with it. This should explain it."

Elliott leans toward me. His hand slides behind my neck and pulls my face to his. Before I realize what he is doing, his soft lips are on mine. It is a gentle kiss, but it sends electricity surging through my body.

Elliott pulls back. "I'm sorry Chloe. I don't know what I was thinking."

I smile. "I have to say I'm a little disappointed."

29

He shakes his head, embarrassed. "It was wrong of me. I'm sorry."

I shift my weight. "I know you've got more than that."

Elliott looks shocked when I press my mouth on his lips, still wet from our kiss. There is hesitation on his part at first, but then he gives in. He wraps his strong arms around my body and pulls me in closer.

The connection is instant and strong. I get lost in his kiss. No longer worried about werewolves or the Guard.

Too soon, Elliott pulls back. "Not now. Not here."

I pout as he shifts away from me.

"I want this. Trust me, I want it badly. But now isn't the time."

"I understand." I curl up again. I don't know if I'll ever leave this spot.

Elliott reaches his hand out and takes mine. "I hope you do. So much is about to change for you. You'll be going through extensive training and you need to focus."

What he's saying is right. This isn't the best time to be messing around. His rejection still hurts though.

Elliott rubs the top of my hand with his thumb. "This might make you feel better - my brother is a member of the Guard."

"Really?"

"Yes. They call him Tank."

I laugh. "Big guy, huh?"

"You could say that. His real name is Frank."

"Will he be here? At my house?"

Elliott nods. "Yes. He's the commander of this District."

"Why isn't he a Reader like you?"

"I am one of three children," Elliott explains. "We all have the ability to read skin, but there isn't a need for three Readers right

30

now. So Frank joined the Guard. His ability to read skin makes him very valuable to them."

Before I can ask any more questions, I hear a car pull into the driveway. My stomach rolls again. I won't be able to eat for a week.

Elliott crawls out of the tent. "I think they're here."

"Do I have to get up?" I whine.

"I think so. Tank and his buddies won't fit under your tent." Elliott grins. "Although I'd like to see them try."

I hesitate. I have to get up, but once I do, my entire life will be different. I look over at Elliott, who is standing at my bedroom window.

"Is it them?"

"Sure is."

"How many?"

He smiles at me. "Three, and my brother is one of them."

I try to smile back. "That's nice."

Sensing my trepidation, Elliott walks over and extends his hand. "Come on. You can do this."

I sigh, but give him my hand. He helps me up and pulls me into a hug. I wrap my arms around him and lean my head on his chest. He's so warm and inviting. I don't want to let go.

We pull apart when the doorbell rings.

In the coming months, I will evaluate my life in two phases: pre-doorbell and post-doorbell.

Chapter Three

Chelsea

My parents and I exchange a glance when the doorbell rings. All of us nervous about the arrival of the Guard.

When Chloe and I were five or six, members of the Guard came to a coven meeting to introduce themselves and answer questions. The only thing I remember about their visit was they were terrifying. None of them said or did anything in particular to scare me, they were just huge.

I follow Mom and Dad to the front door as the bell rings for the second time.

"Impatient, aren't they?"

I glance over my shoulder to see Chloe and Elliott coming down the stairs together. My sister looks a little better than she did when I left her in our quilt tent, but exhaustion rests in her eyes.

My dad takes a deep breath before swinging the door open. I stand on my tiptoes trying to see our company over his shoulder.

"Hello," a deep voice says. "Is this the Miller residence?"

Dad clears his throat. "Yes, yes it is. Come in."

I was expecting soldiers in camouflage carrying machine guns. Instead, three bulky men wearing khaki pants and Under Armour polo shirts step into our house. They look like an Under Armour ad with their matching outfits, except they are wearing different color shirts. The first man to walk in is in red, followed by blue, then green. All three have huge arms and army-style haircuts in common.

My family is frozen in place, mesmerized by the Guard members. Chloe stands at the bottom of the steps eyeing the men suspiciously.

Elliott steps forward and grabs the hand of the man in red. "What's up Frank?"

Frank gives Elliott a "man hug" as they clap each other on the back.

"Good to see you little brother," Frank says.

Dad raises an eyebrow. "You're brothers?"

"Yep," Elliott answers. "This is my older brother, Frank. He is the commander in this District."

I search Frank's face for a resemblance to his younger brother. They both have dark eyes and dark hair, but that's about it. Frank is at least three inches taller than Elliott and looks like he spends every waking hour in the gym. He has no visible tattoos and doesn't look like the kind of guy who would grow his hair out. I can't tell if he has dimples like Elliott because he hasn't smiled yet. Based on his current demeanor, I won't hold my breath.

"They call him Tank," Chloe chimes in from behind us.

We all turn to look at her. She holds her place by the steps, defiance in her eyes.

Frank walks over to her. "Are you Chloe?"

Frank makes my sister look like Tinkerbell. I am terrified of these three men, but per her usual, Chloe is unfazed.

"I am," she answers.

"I need to see it," Frank says.

The two men behind him step closer.

"Well, that's awfully forward of you Tank." Chloe smirks. Already messing with him.

"Chloe..." Dad warns.

"Your brand. I need to see it," Frank repeats.

Chloe rolls her eyes and takes off her shirt. She turns around and shows Frank the beautiful white hawk on her back. The man in blue gasps, but regains his composure when the man in green elbows him in the rib cage.

Frank's eyes gleam as he stares at the tattoo. "May I touch it?"

Chloe looks over her right shoulder. "Double checking your brother's work?"

I have no idea what she means, but Frank does. "You can never be too careful."

"Have at it," Chloe tells him.

Frank steps forward and places his fingertips on Chloe's back. She stiffens when he trails his hands down her skin.

"Is Frank a Reader too?" I whisper to my mom.

"Sure looks like it," she murmurs back.

Chloe stands awkwardly as Frank presses his palms flat on her back. Frank closes his eyes as his hands remain motionless. After a moment, he steps back.

"You can put your shirt on," he tells Chloe.

Elliott shifts his weight. "What do you think?"

"You're right. She's our next Verhena."

Elliott, who'd been holding his breath while Frank read Chloe's skin, looks relieved. Chloe looks crestfallen.

Frank turns to my parents. "Sorry if I've been rude. As Elliott mentioned, my name is Frank." He points to the man in the blue shirt. "This is Thomas." Then he points to the man in the green shirt. "And this is Matthew."

Matthew is a mountain of a man. His bulkiness reminds me of Goldberg, a wrestler we used to watch on TV when we were kids. Despite his straight face, his blue eyes are kind.

Thomas is tall like the other two, but leaner. His big brown eyes look at nothing, but see everything at the same time.

Dad steps forward and shakes all of their hands. "My name is Steven. This is my wife Fran. You've already met our daughter

35

Chloe." Dad puts his hand on my shoulder as he continues. "And this is Chloe's twin sister Chelsea. Elliott gave her a dove today."

I momentarily shrivel when the three men turn to me, but relax as soon as they turn their attention back to Chloe.

"Steven, is there a place my men and I can speak with Elliott privately?" Frank asks.

Dad nods. "Absolutely. Let me show you to my office in the basement."

"Well that's rude," Chloe complains when the men have exited the room. "They're supposed to be here for me, then they convene by themselves."

Mom laughs. "Magical or not, all men have their faults."

"You know they're talking about me," Chloe huffs.

"Of course they are," Mom says with zero doubt.

Mom walks behind Chloe, places her hands on Chloe's shoulders, and pushes Chloe along to the kitchen. "Let them have their powwow. Let them think they're in charge. Then you can crash the party and show them who's boss. In the meantime, let's get something to eat."

Chloe and I sit at the kitchen table while Mom whips up some pancakes.

Trying to cheer Chloe up, I say, "I don't think you have to worry about your safety around those guys."

She shrugs her shoulders. "Werewolves can tear a man limb from limb, even if those limbs are huge."

Mom drops her spatula on the floor. "Chloe!"

"Just sayin'," she responds with her casual nonchalance.

Visions of Barbara Sheep cornered in a dark alley flow through my mind. I shiver.

Mom brings over a big plate of pancakes, steam slowly rising off of them. "Dig in."

36

We do as told and fill our plates. I haven't eaten anything since breakfast and I'm starving.

"You know," I say between bites, "the guy in blue looks a lot like Jason Mamoa. Am I right?"

Chloe's eyes light up. "Ohhh, you're right! He does have that dark and mysterious thing going on."

"You can be his Khaleesi," I joke.

"What is a Khaleesi?" Mom asks.

"It's from *Game of Thrones*," I explain.

Chloe puts more syrup on her pancakes. "The guy in green looks like the Incredible Hulk."

We giggle.

"I bet he looks good when his shirt rips open too," Mom says with a grin.

"Mom!" Chloe protests. "Gross!"

Mom winks. "Just sayin'."

Before we can go any further with our assessment of the Guard, Dad walks into the kitchen.

"Frank wants to see you," Dad tells Chloe. When he notices our plates, he asks, "Leave any pancakes for me?"

Chloe slides her plate toward Dad. "Why can't they come in here?"

Dad takes Chloe's fork and sits down. "They want to talk with you privately."

Chloe pushes her chair away from the table, a scowl on her face. "Let's go Chelsea."

My parents turn to look at me.

"What? They want you Chloe. Not me."

"I don't care what they want. You're coming with me."

I hesitate, but Chloe is insistent.

"I'm not going down there without you. Let's go."

Chloe

Seeing these big men crammed in my father's office is comical. Frank occupies my dad's seat behind the desk and is flanked by Matthew and Thomas. Elliott is sitting in one of the two chairs across from Dad's desk.

When we walk in, Elliott jumps up and offers Chelsea his seat.

I give him a quick smile. Such a gentleman. I put my big girl face on when I sit down across from Frank.

"We need to speak with you privately," Frank says as he watches Chelsea take a seat.

"Anything you have to tell me, you can tell my sister."

"No," he answers.

"I'll just…" Chelsea starts to get up, but I put my hand on her arm.

"Sit Chelsea," I say softly to her. I turn back to Frank and harden my tone. "My sister stays, or I go."

Frank's jaw tightens. "This is confidential information. We cannot have any third parties in here. In fact," he turns to Elliott, "you need to leave as well."

Elliott shrugs. "Alright, I'll be upstairs." He winks at me as he leaves the room. My heart flutters.

Frank ruins the moment. "Don't think for a second I don't know what's going on between you two." Frank is using his booming voice again.

I roll my eyes.

Chelsea leans over. "What's going on between you and Elliott?"

"Nothing," I whisper back. "I'll tell you later."

"Your sister needs to leave," Frank interrupts.

"She's not leaving."

For a second I think Frank is going to slam his fist on the desk. He'd probably break it in half if he did. "Enough of this. Chelsea, go."

"I told you. If she goes, I go," I repeat.

"What don't you understand?" he asks irritated.

"What don't *you* understand?" I shoot back. Before he can respond, I continue. "This is my house. This is my future. You are here to protect me. If I say I want my sister here, she stays here. If you can't handle that, then you and the other Under Armour models can leave."

Frank crosses his arms over his chest. "So that's how it's going to be, huh? You're taking charge?"

I smile. "Yes, I am. If I tell you to jump, you jump. Right?"

I think I'm being a badass, but quickly regret being snarky when Matthew shifts his weight and Thomas frowns. Neither pleased with my attitude.

Frank sighs. "We're here for your protection. I don't think you understand how important it is for you to remain anonymous for a while. No one can know about your brand."

"I get it. I don't want you to think I'm going to be a pain in your ass, but I need my sister here. I will follow your advice. I will do what you tell me to do, but Chelsea is with me. Always."

Frank leans back in his chair. "Fine. Every Verhena has an adviser. Chelsea can be yours."

Chelsea and I exchange looks. She shrugs her shoulders. "Sure. Why not?"

With that issue resolved, Frank moves on. "Who knows about your brand?"

"My parents, Elliott, you guys and our coven leader."

"Who is your coven leader?" Frank asks, brow furrowed.

"Samantha."

He relaxes. "Ah, Samantha. She's a good leader."

Chelsea and I say, "Yes, she is," in unison.

A small smile crosses Frank's lips. As quickly as it appears, it is gone. "No one else?"

"No, but we have to tell Chelsea's boyfriend Rory."

Chelsea gives me a grateful look. It would be incredibly difficult for her to keep this from Rory. They tell each other everything.

Frank is frowning. "Why?"

"Rory is practically family. He will know something is up."

"And you trust him?"

"Completely," I answer without hesitation.

Frank rubs his chin. "Let me run a background check. If it comes back clear, you can tell him."

I nod. "Sounds fair."

"We need to talk about the coming weeks and how to keep you safe," Frank continues. "It's going to be months, years really, until your powers have matured. Even then, you're going to want our protection."

This is all too much. I can hardly think past tonight, let alone the amount of security I may or may not need for the rest of my life.

"You are scheduled to leave for Leviston in a couple weeks. We intend to follow you there and set up a security detail."

I'm surprised when Chelsea interrupts. It's not like her. "Chloe can still go to Leviston?"

"Yes."

"Is that safe for her?"

"It will be before she gets there."

Chelsea's eyes are intense. "How? How can you keep her safe at Leviston?"

40

Frank shifts his weight, disarmed by my usually sweet-tempered sister's change in attitude. I myself am almost brought to tears by her concern. If the situation were reversed, I would be pushing Frank just as hard.

"We already had a plan in place," Frank explains. "It was no secret a new Verhena would be branded in the next year or so."

"Because of Barbara?" I ask.

Frank, like Elliott, grimaces. "Yes, because of Barbara. Our current Verhena is getting older and is ready for her replacement. We all thought it would be Barbara, but obviously that came to a bad end."

I can't help myself and ask something I probably shouldn't. "Were you in charge of guarding her?"

Frank shakes his head. "We weren't, but other members of the Guard were."

"What happened?" Chelsea asks, her eyes no longer burning holes through Frank.

"As Chloe pointed out earlier, while the Guard is here to protect the Verhena, she can do as she pleases. I think a part of it was a false sense of security. We haven't had any trouble with the wolves in years. Barbara didn't think she was vulnerable. It's my understanding she insisted on going out to a bar. When she got there, she climbed out of the bar's bathroom window and into the alley."

"Falling right into the hands of werewolves," I finish.

"Exactly."

We are all quiet for a minute.

"I don't want this," I finally say to no one in particular.

Chelsea reaches out her hand and gives mine a quick squeeze.

"Too bad," Frank says, zero pity in his voice. "You are the next Verhena. You have to live up to that privilege."

"She will," Chelsea promises. "She just needs time. We all do."

41

Frank is unmoved. "I understand everyone is upset, but we don't have time to wallow in whatever angst you feel. We have to be prepared at all times."

I don't like his tone with Chelsea, or the smug expression on his face.

"Yeah, and are we prepared now?" I ask, pissed off. "Wolves could be outside my door as we speak."

"They're not," Matthew says, face emotionless.

I shoot him a look. "How do you know?"

"I've been patrolling your house for a week. No wolves here."

My mouth drops open. "A week?"

Frank nods. "We patrol and investigate the homes of all girls before their Branding Day. If the wolves are following Elliott waiting for the next Verhena, we'll be ready."

I sit back in my chair. I've been watched for a whole week and didn't know it. Should I be impressed or creeped out?

"No wolves are aware, at least not yet, that Chloe is the next Verhena?" Chelsea asks.

"Correct. We have not seen, or heard, from any wolves since Barbara's attack."

"Maybe they're not as smart as you think they are," I speculate.

"Possibly, but we can't make that assumption. It's true Barbara was an easy target, the whole world knew who she was and she wasn't careful. On the other hand, the wolves attacking her is a clear indication they are coming after us," Frank reasons.

I don't like the thought of werewolves stalking me. "I thought their leader insisted they don't mean us any harm."

"He has. However, it seems the leader's son may be going his own way and trying to take over the pack."

Chelsea sighs. "He thinks if he can defeat us, he will win loyalty."

42

"Exactly right," Frank confirms.

The thought of a werewolf/witch war terrifies me. Especially if I'll be the leader of this mess in a few years.

"What do we do now?" I ask.

"Go on about your life as if you received a black hawk tattoo. You will go to Leviston next month just as you would if you were not the Verhena. It is critical you appear to be a normal witch attending her first year of school. You cannot stand out in any way."

"How am I safe at Leviston? The werewolves know we go to school there."

"Leviston has strong wards against the wolves. They've been in place for years. Even if the wolves get through the wards, there are guards everywhere on campus. We can discreetly increase our numbers while you are there."

"Will she have personal security?" Chelsea asks.

"Not exactly." Frank shifts his weight. "We..." he gestures to Matthew and Thomas, "will be on campus with you. We will take positions as teachers in the physical training facilities. Not everyone knows this, but members of the Guard begin their initial training at Leviston as well. We will go through your training as seamlessly, and invisibly, as possible."

"What about the extra stuff I'll need to know as the Verhena?"

Frank smiles. "We'll have it covered."

"Will I meet the Verhena?"

"Not yet. We can't risk it right now. The wolves could be watching her."

"What am I supposed to do until it's time to leave for Leviston?"

Frank shrugs. "What are your plans for the rest of the summer?"

I frown. "We were supposed to go to Jones Beach and spend some time on Long Island, but I guess that's out."

Chelsea turns to me, surprised. "Why?"

43

"I can't go to the beach with this tattoo on my back."

Understanding sets in. "Oh…" Chelsea's disappointed face mirrors my own. We planned this trip months ago. A last hoorah with our friends from high school. We were really looking forward to it.

I frown at Frank. "I'm homebound, aren't I?"

"Not necessarily. You can run errands, go to the mall, etcetera. But we'll be with you. Maybe not right next to you, but with you."

"What about her security while she's home? Will someone be staying with us?" Chelsea asks.

Matthew raises his hand. "I will. I look the most like your family."

I smile. "I guess you'll be my cousin on steroids?"

He smiles back. "Something like that."

Frank throws Matthew a stern look. "This is serious business. You are not here for fun."

Matthew clears his throat. "Sorry Frank."

Frank turns back to me. "I need you to promise me you won't do anything stupid or careless."

I huff. "I'm twenty years old. By definition I'll do something stupid or careless. I just won't do anything that puts my life at risk."

This placates him. "Fine. We'll work out the details with your parents." Frank stands, my cue to leave.

Frank's voice stops me before I reach the door. "Oh…and Chloe?"

I turn around. "Yes?"

"No personal calls with my brother."

"What?" I demand. How did he know I planned to get Elliott's number?

"It's possible my brother is being watched. You two can't have a personal connection."

44

"So what if he is being watched? He's not allowed to date me? What difference would it make to the wolves?"

"It may not make a difference to the wolves, but it makes a difference to me."

"I can't have a boyfriend?"

"You can, but you shouldn't."

This is too much. He has no right to dictate my personal life like this. "Are you serious?" I hiss.

Frank crosses his arms over his broad chest. "Think it through Chloe. If the wolves find out you are the Verhena, the first person they'll go after is my brother, or any other guy you decide to date."

I'm about to tell him that's ridiculous, but I pause. He's right. The wolves will go after my loved ones.

"What about my parents? Are they in danger?"

Frank softens when he sees I've put two and two together. "We'll have someone watching them at all times. They'll be okay."

I sigh. "This is so messed up."

Chelsea consoles me as we walk upstairs. "It will be okay. It seems hard now, but it will get easier."

That's my sister. Always thinking positively.

Chapter Four

Chloe

I listen half-heartedly as Frank fills my parents in on our new house guest and the plan to send me to Leviston. My parents are wearing brave faces, but the stray glances between them, and the way my mom gently clears her throat before she asks Frank questions, lets me know they are scared.

"I should move out. Stay somewhere else," I suggest.

"Absolutely not," my dad says at the same time Frank says, "No."

"Come on you guys. It's the safest way."

"No," Dad says again firmly. "You're staying here." I am all too familiar with this tone. It's the same tone that denied me a belly button ring and a date with a guy in college when I was sixteen.

I glance around the room. I can see there is no winning over this crowd. I sigh and walk away. I'm tired of listening to safety plans. I wander off to see if Elliott is still around. Despite Frank's warning, I hope Elliott hasn't left without saying good-bye.

To my relief, I find him packing his equipment in our front room.

"Hey, how'd it go?" he asks with a smile.

I shrug. "Okay I guess."

Elliott starts folding his table. "Things are going to be weird for a while, but they'll level out."

"I'm not so sure about that."

He chuckles. "It will. I promise."

He's so damn cute. It's too bad I can't pursue this any further. I break the bad news to him. "I'm not supposed to talk to you anymore."

Elliott finishes folding the table and leans it against the wall. He walks over to me. "I figured Frank would say that. But I'm a step ahead of him."

I raise my eyebrow. "Oh yeah? What's the plan?"

"I'll call you on Frank's phone."

"Huh?"

"Frank's my brother. What's weird about me calling my brother?"

"True. There's one problem though. You think Frank's going to hand over his phone so we can chat? Plus, he'll have to track me down every time you call."

"I hate to be the bearer of bad news, but Frank is going to be on you like white on rice."

I groan. "Great."

Elliott wraps his arms around me and holds me tight to his chest. "He's not so bad once you get to know him."

"He hates me," I mumble against his shirt.

Elliott squeezes me tighter. "He doesn't hate you. Give it some time."

I close my eyes and lean into him. He smells amazing.

"You know," Elliott says after a moment, "there's nothing wrong with a brother visiting a brother either, right?"

I'm beaming now. I look up at him. "You're a genius."

"I wouldn't say that, I just know I want to see you again."

His eyes twinkle, a smile on his face. Elliott is about to lower his mouth to mine when I hear a deep voice clear his throat.

"Time for you to go little brother. You've been here too long already. Could look suspicious."

Elliott laughs as he pulls away. "I tattooed twins today Frank. Of course it will take longer than normal. Especially when one of them is very needy," he says, winking at me.

48

"Whatever," I tease back.

Elliott grabs his equipment and heads for our front door. I'm bummed when it sinks in that I won't see him again for a long time, if ever.

As he's about to leave, Elliott turns back to Frank. "I'll call you soon."

Elliott and I exchange a glance, then laugh.

Frank looks back and forth between us like we're crazy. "What's so funny?"

Elliott shakes his head. "Nothing." He gives me a warm smile before stepping out the door. "Later Chloe."

Frank shuts the door before I can respond.

"Hey! That was rude," I protest.

"Get used to it," Frank says, walking by me. "I'm not known for my charm."

I snort. "Me neither."

Frank pauses for a moment and turns to me. He looks me dead in the eyes. "I want what's best for you. Sometimes, you won't like it."

He walks away, leaving me to process his honesty.

Chelsea

"Rory, I can't go to Long Island without my sister. I'm sorry."

Rory is over at our house, begging me for the tenth time to go on our trip.

"She wants us to go," he argues.

He's right. Chloe has told me over and over again I should go on the beach trip, but I can't do that to her. She's disappointed enough as it is. She doesn't need me coming home with a tan, full of stories about the fun I had.

I sit down next to Rory on our couch in the basement. "I wouldn't have a good time. I'd feel too guilty."

Rory sighs. He's disappointed. "Fine."

This is awful. No matter what I do, I'm hurting someone's feelings.

I run my hand through his red hair. "I'm sorry. It's just weird right now."

Frank ran his silly background check on Rory and gave me the go ahead to spill the beans. Rory was as shocked as we all were when I told him Chloe is the next Verhena.

"Chloe? Are you sure?" he asked me more than once.

Rory pulls me in for a hug. "I was really looking forward to some alone time with you."

"I have a backup plan."

"Oh yeah?"

"How do you feel about a few days away? Just the two of us in New York City?"

His eyes light up. "Seriously?"

I nod. "It's not the beach, but it can still be a romantic getaway."

"Absolutely!" He leans in and gives me a sweet kiss. "I love you Chelse."

My heart warms. "I love you too."

We snuggle together and turn on a movie. I'm glad I came up with the idea of going to New York City. Not only will I get some quality time with my boyfriend, we'll get out of the house for a little while. Poor Rory has been stuck in the house with me for the last two weeks.

Rory chuckles at something in the movie, but I missed the funny scene. I'm too busy worrying about Chloe. She'll be okay here by herself, right?

Chloe's been a basket case and I'm doing all I can to cheer her up. Her future doesn't look anything like she thought it would. She's still going to Leviston, but it will be a completely different experience than she anticipated.

"No parties. No boys. No fun," she whined the other day.

"It can still be fun," I told her. "There will be plenty of chances for you to let loose."

She rolled her eyes. "Yeah right. I'll be training all day, every day. And worse, I'll have the Guard watching every move I make."

I couldn't argue with that. The Guard is already watching every move she makes. Mine too. It's unnerving. A member of the Guard is not only living in my house, but trailing me wherever I go.

"Creepy," Rory said the first time we noticed a Guard member at the same restaurant as us.

Now Rory makes it a game. He times how long it takes to spot the Guard member watching us behind the scenes. He'll even go so far as to yell, "gotcha!" when he spots the Guard.

Rory's been amazing through all of this. Making me laugh at what would otherwise be a dreadful experience.

I surprise him with a kiss on the cheek.

He smiles. "What was that for?"

"For being awesome."

He squeezes my shoulder. "I can't wait until our trip. I'll have you all to myself."

I giggle. "Aren't you sick of me yet?"

Rory leans down and kisses my lips. "Never."

Chloe

The last three weeks have been the most boring weeks of my life. I've only left the house a handful of times. It's weird being followed. I don't always see Frank, but I know he's there. I keep

51

waiting for him to jump out and yell "boo!" when I'm not expecting it.

My cousin, aka green shirt guy, aka Matthew, has blended in well with my family. In fact, my mom likes him way more than she should. I can't help but think she's picturing his shirt tearing open over and over again.

I hide away in my room most of the time reading books, watching TV, even drawing occasionally. It's just so damn boring.

I'd love to talk with Elliott, but Frank and I don't interact as often as I thought we would. He's always lurking around somewhere, but he and I can't be seen together in public until we're at Leviston.

As much as I didn't want to go to Leviston before, I'm chomping at the bit to go now. I need out of this house. I have everything packed and ready to go. I had to buy myself new clothes because my brand has to be covered at all times, including workouts. It sucks not being able to wear a tank top, but I guess that's better than being dead. Although I'm not living much of a life lately.

Samantha, our coven leader, has come over to the house a few times to visit me. She is helping me with new spells, things the coven hasn't taught us yet. Each witch has his or her own specialty and Samantha's is her "green thumb." With her help, I've learned cultivation spells. I can now grow a tomato in three minutes. What I will do with that skill, I have no idea.

Samantha also showed me a basic combustion spell. When I'm powerful enough, I'll be able to shoot fire from my fingertips. Right now though, I can't do much more than warm up a bowl of soup.

I want to learn more magic, but Frank insists I wait until I get to Leviston. If I could, I would teach myself spells behind his back. But I don't have much to work with. It's not like I can go on YouTube and watch witch videos. Trust me, I've tried. Everything online is hokey, fake witches pretending they know magic.

The videos make me laugh because normal people believe all the movie clichés about witches, which are all wrong. The biggest mistake I see is a magic wand. Witches don't need magic wands. Once you know your stuff, the spells aren't required either. All you have to do is mentally envision what you want to happen.

It's exactly one week before we head to Leviston and Chelsea skipped town to go to New York City with Rory. Not having Chelsea around sucks, but I can't blame her for bailing out. I would if I could.

I emerge from my bedroom around noon. I find my "cousin" watching ESPN in the family room.

"What's up?" I ask Matthew as I flop onto the couch.

"Same old, same old," he answers with a grin.

I like Matthew, he's more laid back than Frank.

"Are we going anywhere today?" he asks.

"Bored like me, huh?"

"I hate to say it, but yes. I'm not used to being inside this much. I'm usually out on patrol," he explains. "I suppose it beats the alternative."

"Oh, I don't know. Getting attacked by wolves could be interesting."

He chuckles, then returns his attention to the television.

I'm sure Matthew would give the werewolves a run for their money. He's built like a ton of bricks and from what I hear, is one of the best fighters in the Guard. Poor guy is probably as desperate to get out of here as I am.

When *Sports Center* cuts to commercial, I tell Matthew something I should have said a long time ago. "Hey, thanks for doing this. It's not flashy or exciting, but it means a lot to me."

Matthew blushes, not used to getting praise. "No problem. This has been my easiest job yet." He pats his stomach. "I've gained ten pounds. Your mom is awesome."

I smile. "Yeah, she is."

I'd love to add, "She's nice to you because you're so damn hot," but I keep my comments to myself.

I stand up. "I'll leave you to your ESPN."

"Chloe…wait."

I turn around and Matthew hands me a cellphone. When I give him a questioning look, he explains, "Elliott's number is in there."

I'm shocked. "Are you serious? I can call him?"

Matthew nods. "Just for a few minutes. And don't worry about Frank. Frank's the one who got this burner phone for you."

"A burner phone?" I examine the phone. Looks like any other cellphone to me.

"It's a disposable phone. It can't be linked to you because it's registered in a fake name. Frank said this is the only way you are allowed to call Elliott."

I roll my eyes. "Well at least I have Daddy's permission."

Matthew chuckles. "Indeed. He sees how bored you are. You need some cheering up."

I give Matthew a quick hug. "Thank you for this! I'll bring the phone back in a few."

I run up the stairs like a kid with a new toy. I get to call Elliott!

Matthew already typed Elliott's number into the phone, so all I have to do is hit the dial button. I pace around my room as I wait for the call to go through. I feel like I'm going to bust as I listen to the ringing.

And then he answers. "Hello?"

"Elliott?" I can barely get his name out.

"Chloe?" he whispers. "Is that you?"

"Yes! Can you talk?" I hope he isn't in the middle of branding someone.

"How are you calling me right now?" he asks.

"I'm on a burner phone."

"Does Frank know about this?"

Really? He's worried about Frank?

"Yes, he knows."

Elliott hears my disapproval and laughs. "Sorry. I had to make sure you won't get in any trouble."

"Ha ha," I say dryly. "You don't know what I've been dealing with here."

"Hey, I grew up with the guy, remember? Seriously though, is he being good to you?"

I throw myself on my bed and lay on my back. "Actually, I haven't seen him at all. Just Matthew."

"You and Matthew aren't getting too close are you?"

I snicker. "Please. And compete with my mother? I don't think so."

"Ugh. There's an image I didn't need in my head."

"Yeah, it's kinda gross." I change the subject. No one needs to think about Matthew and my mom getting busy. "Where are you today?"

"Home. I have the day off."

"Where is home?"

"Burlington, Vermont."

I roll onto my stomach and prop myself up on my elbows. "Oh, you're close to Leviston then."

He laughs. "Yes ma'am. Not far at all."

"That's good. Really good." I'm practically drooling.

What the hell is wrong with me? I meet a man once, kiss him a couple times, and I'm acting like a total goober. This is not me at all.

"I've thought about you a lot since I left," Elliott says into the phone.

My heart flutters. "You haven't been busy rubbing on other girls?"

"Well, maybe a little. But just for branding purposes."

I chuckle. It feels good to laugh. "Sure, sure. I bet you say that to all the girls."

"Been keeping yourself busy?"

I sigh. "I'm bored out of my mind."

"I wish I was there to entertain you." He's flirting now and I love it.

"Me too. I'm sure we could find all kinds of fun ways to pass the time."

"Maybe I'll hop in my car and drive down there."

I smile. "That would be amazing. You'd have to get past a few men in Under Armour first."

Elliott laughs. "What is up with those shirts anyway? Don't they realize they look ridiculous?"

"Careful now. Your brother could be listening."

"True. He'll probably kick my ass the next time I see him."

"Nah, I think you can take him," I tease.

"Seriously? Have you seen the guy? He'd pick me up and throw me through a wall."

Now I'm laughing too. "No worries. I'll be your personal nurse."

"Hmm…I think I'd like playing doctor with you."

"Yes, you would."

There is a knock on my door and Matthew peeks in. "Time's up Chloe."

I nod my head. "Okay Matthew, I'll be out in a second."

Matthew closes the door to give me some privacy.

"I have to go Elliott."

"I heard." He sounds disappointed. "Are you really okay?"

"Yeah. I'm just bored. And a little scared. At least I'm safe here. Who knows what will happen when I get to Leviston."

"My brother is super smart. He'll make sure you're safe."

"I know," I say halfheartedly.

"You know what's weird?" Elliott asks before we hang up.

"My whole life?"

Elliott chuckles. "Well sure. But I'm talking about me. I hardly know you Chloe, and I can't stop thinking about you."

I know exactly how he feels.

Chapter Five

Chelsea

Rory whistles. "This place is great Chelse! One of the perks of being the Verhena's twin, huh?"

I wish I shared his enthusiasm.

Chloe and I moved into our new apartment at Leviston three days ago. Rory and I are unpacking the remaining boxes.

"It's alright."

"Alright? Alright? This place is fantastic."

Rory, like most first year students, moved into his dorm room today. It's barely big enough for his bed and desk. There is a communal bathroom down the hall with old showers and stall toilets. The walls are paper thin and music is playing at all hours. I don't know why, but I'm jealous.

I should love the apartment Chloe and I are in. It's on the top floor of a four-story brick building near the northwest corner of campus. We each have our own bedroom and bathroom, and there's a full kitchen and living room. The problem is, the rest of the building is filled with Guard members, not students.

"Does it freak you out to know you're being watched all the time?" Rory asks as he puts drinking glasses in a kitchen cabinet. He's referring to the cameras installed in our apartment.

"A little. Okay, a lot," I admit. "Someone is probably monitoring our conversation right now."

Chloe and I definitely aren't happy about the camera situation. Frank promised the cameras are only recording in the kitchen and main living areas. He swears there are no cameras in the bathrooms or bedrooms. I sincerely hope he's being honest. No one needs to see me in my skivvies.

Equally unsettling are the panic buttons scattered throughout the apartment. Most are hidden in everyday items like the remote control, a book and a soda can in the fridge, but there is a huge button in Chloe's room. Chloe joked that it looks like the giant red button in the Staples commercials, but Frank wasn't amused.

Rory looks over at me. "You alright Chelse?"

"This isn't what I thought college would be like." I get choked up. "For any of us."

Rory comes over and gives me a hug. "Chelse, it's going to be fine. You like to have everything planned out, but life throws you curveballs sometimes."

He's right. I'm not really upset about the apartment or the Guard. It has more to do with how different things are turning out than I thought they would.

Rory kisses my forehead. "It's still you and me Chelse. Always has been. Always will be."

I smile. "You're the best boyfriend ever."

"I know." He pulls away and makes a silly face at the camera in the kitchen corner. I smack his arm, but I'm laughing.

"What?" he asks. "They're probably really bored."

Chloe

My first few weeks at Leviston are hectic. Between classes, homework, and my additional Verhena training, I have no time to sit still. I am constantly running from one place to the next and have little to no social interaction with my classmates.

That being said, no one seems suspicious of me. Everyone is too busy dealing with their own issues. I can't help but roll my eyes when I hear my classmates complain about their busy school schedules. They don't even know!

The Verhena training is insane. I knew it would be intense, but I was not prepared for what Frank and company throw at me. Every day my training begins with Frank kicking my ass. Plain and simple. Yesterday he broke my arm. I put my arm out to catch myself as I fell onto the gym mats and Frank pancaked me. Luckily Matthew is a healer and was able to fix it in a jiffy.

"This is ridiculous!" I screamed at Frank after my arm was healed. "Why are we doing all of this combat training? When I have my full power, I won't have to lay a hand on anybody. I will blast the hell out of them with magic!"

Frank was not persuaded. "Last time I checked, you don't have your full power yet. In the meantime, you need to know how to fight."

"Fine." I stomped my foot. "No more breaking my arm though! That shit hurts!"

Frank laughed, but then beat me up again. I'm getting better at dodging him, although my bruises don't show it.

After Frank uses me as a personal punching bag, I have magic training. I am learning new things in my regular classes, but these extra training sessions focus on advanced strength and combat spells.

When I walk into the gym today, Frank has a surprise for me.

"Dean Lucas is coming in for your advanced magic session. She is going to be your primary instructor for a while."

"Dean Lucas?"

Frank nods. "She has amazing magical abilities. She's very well-rounded. Not nearly as powerful as the Verhena, but the most powerful witch at Leviston."

I let this sink in. "Wait a minute. Did you tell her about me?"

"Of course."

"What do you mean 'of course'? You've been drilling it into my head since day one that I can't tell anyone who I am, yet you can tell whoever you want?"

Frank clenches his jaw. "This is different. Dean Lucas had to know. How do you think we got an entire apartment building on campus to ourselves?"

I narrow my eyes. "You asshole. It wasn't your information to share."

"Seriously? I'm an asshole?"

"Yes," I hiss.

"I'm keeping you safe," Frank insists. "I have done everything in my power to pull this together for you. I am getting you the best training possible. And I'm an asshole?"

"I don't know Dean Lucas from Adam. Just because you trust her, doesn't mean I do."

Frank opens his mouth, then abruptly shuts it. To my surprise, he says, "You're right. I shouldn't have told her without running it by you."

Did he just say I'm right about something?

After we stand awkwardly for a few seconds, I say, "Well, what's done is done. Next time, ask me first."

Frank nods. "I will."

Dean Lucas is much livelier than I expected. I figured she would be a stuffy woman in a suit. Instead, she shows up in sweatpants and a t-shirt.

"Hello!" she beams when she walks in the gym. "Nice to finally meet you Chloe!" she says as she shakes my hand.

Dean Lucas is a short woman with a round belly and auburn hair. She exudes a positive energy, but also has an air of confidence.

"Word on the street is you're a powerful witch," I say with a grin.

She laughs. "Relatively speaking, I suppose I am. Most witches have one or two areas they excel in. I am a jack of all trades, so to speak. Although I'm not nearly as powerful as you will be one day. You will be a master of all the known spells."

"What are we going to work on?" I ask her, ignoring the awe in her voice.

She smiles. "Let me show you one of my favorites."

We step outside and into the humidity. I can't wait for the cooler weather to set in.

Dean Lucas looks around for a second, then points to a tree. "You see the squirrel over there?"

I follow her gaze and see a gray squirrel running up the trunk of an elm tree. "I see it."

"Watch this," Dean Lucas says with a grin.

Without warning, the squirrel stops mid-run. It's frozen in place, its whole body stuck in an awkward position.

"Are you doing that?" I ask Dean Lucas with wide eyes.

"Yep." She starts a countdown, "Three…two…one..." When she reaches one, the squirrel takes off again as if nothing happened.

"Wow!" I gush. "That was amazing!"

Dean Lucas shrugs her shoulders. "It's okay. Once you get the hang of it, you'll be able to hold people and objects in place for a lot longer."

"Really?"

"No doubt in my mind."

A week later, with Dean Lucas's supervision and the fire skills Samantha showed me back home, I'm able to freeze a person in place for a couple seconds, then singe them with a mini spark.

"Nice work," Frank tells me after practice.

"Thanks!"

Of course Frank can't just leave a compliment sitting on the table. "Pretty soon, you'll be able to light a candle."

"Ha ha. Very funny. Can I go now?"

"In a second. I have something for you."

I follow Frank to a corner of the gym and he hands me a cardboard box.

"What is this?"

"Journals."

"Journals?"

He takes the lid off the box. Six books are stacked one on top of the other. I turn my nose away when a musty smell hits me.

"These are the journals of the previous Verhenas. Your predecessors. I think you should read them."

"Um, okay."

I walk back to my apartment, drop the box in my closet, and promptly forget it exists.

A few weeks later, I lie to Frank and tell him I read the journals every night.

"Good! Any valuable information in there?"

"Uh, yeah," I lie. Before he can ask me for details, I scurry off for my training with Dean Lucas.

The truth is I haven't opened a single one. My free time is minimal, and I need a few hours in my day when I'm not worrying about being the Verhena. I don't like being dishonest with Frank, but he wouldn't understand.

Guilt must enhance magical power because my training session with Dean Lucas is awesome. I run all the way home to tell Chelsea about my breakthrough.

I burst through the front door. "Chelsea!"

"In here!" she yells back.

I follow her voice to the living room and find her and Rory doing homework.

"What are you guys up to?" I ask in between breaths.

Chelsea looks up from her book and smiles. "I'm reading the next chapter for our potions class. This week is illnesses and maladies."

"Sounds thrilling," I say, still catching my breath.

Chelsea is excelling in our potions and healing classes. The professors love her.

"Guess what?!" I'm so proud of myself, I'm practically bursting at the seams.

Chelsea giggles at my excitement. "What?"

"I started a fire today!"

"You did!? That's great!"

Rory looks up from his book. "What's going on?"

Chelsea playfully shakes her head at how oblivious Rory is, but fills him in. "Chloe started a fire today!"

"With my bare hands," I add, holding my hands out for them to see.

Rory smiles. "You're making great progress."

"Let's see your back," Chelsea says. She checks my brand every time I make progress to see if my feathers are filling in with gold. I pull up my t-shirt and she walks over to examine me. "There's more gold today! I swear!"

"For real?"

She nods her head vigorously.

I make a break for my bathroom mirror and take a peek. "You're right! There is more gold!"

I walk back into the living room and hug Chelsea. "It's happening! I'm becoming more powerful."

Chelsea grins. "We have more good news. Rory is going to be Professor Steller's research assistant!"

Rory stands to take a mini bow as we clap for him. "Thank you! Thank you!"

65

"That is amazing Rory. Professor Steller is the best teacher on campus."

Rory's eyes are wide. "He is so smart. I was in awe during his lecture yesterday about the history of the conflict between the wolves and witches."

As was I. That little "conflict" is something I have to get personally acquainted with.

"Crazy how love ends up starting a war, right?" Chelsea adds.

I frown. "Yeah, the war was really our fault, wasn't it?"

"It appears so," Rory agrees.

I think back to Professor Steller's lecture. He was reading from our textbook like it was a dramatic play, motioning with his hands and adding flair to the story.

"In the late 1800s, Eleanor Wiley, a witch from New York, bought a ticket for a Trans-Atlantic boat ride from New York City to London. It was during this voyage that she met Alexander Groome, a werewolf and her future lover. The two spent a month together in London before travelling home. Upon their return to the United States, Alexander confessed to Eleanor that he was not just any werewolf, he was the leader of the Eastern pack.

Eleanor was shocked by the revelation, but it didn't change her feelings for him. However, Alexander was not done confessing. Alexander admitted to Eleanor that he was in fact married and planned to return home to his wife.

Fueled by her fury, Eleanor killed Alexander. Eleanor's local coven tried to help her cover up the crime, but they were ultimately unsuccessful. The murder of their pack leader and the subsequent attempt to cover it up enraged the werewolves and ignited a brief, yet bloody war.

After three years of brutality, both sides came to a truce. The wolves retreated to the west, and the witches promised to stay in the east." Professor Steller snapped the book shut and concluded, "And that ladies and gentleman is why you cannot travel to California."

"What I don't understand is the textbook said wards were placed over the boundary line to stop the wolves from crossing into the east, right?" Chelsea asks us.

Rory nods. "Yes."

"If that's true, how did the wolves cross into the east to kill Barbara?"

"Well," Rory explains, "I talked to Professor Steller after class yesterday and he said wards don't last forever. They lose strength over time. If a ward is not recharged, it loses its power. The original wards between the east and west were placed long ago. After about fifty years or so, we stopped renewing them."

I interject. "We dropped the ball?"

Rory shrugs his shoulders. "Yes and no. The pure amount of time and energy it would take to maintain the boundary line didn't make sense given that both sides were voluntarily upholding the agreement."

"Until now," Chelsea says.

"Right. Until now. Professor Steller believes most wolves want to keep the truce. He thinks whoever killed Barbara did so without the authority of the pack leader."

Interesting. "Maybe so, but we can't take our chances."

Chelsea reaches out and squeezes Rory's shoulder. "You're so smart."

He leans in and gives her a quick kiss.

"Blah!" I jump up from the couch. "I'm hitting the shower."

After my shower and a quick dinner of macaroni and cheese (a girl needs to carbo load), I sit down to read our potions homework. Just as I'm getting into cures for the stomach flu, there's a knock at the front door.

I look through the peephole to see Frank. "What's up?" I ask when I open the door. "Here to beat me up some more?"

Frank smiles. We get along now. I think being able to punch me in the face helps him deal with me.

"I wanted to bring you a burner phone."

I light up. "Is it time for an Elliott call?"

"Yep. Here ya go. There's thirty minutes on it. Use them wisely."

I give Frank a high five. "You're awesome."

"Tell me that tomorrow during combat training."

I run to my bedroom and close the door. Rory and Chelsea are out, but I want my privacy in case they come home. And I don't want the Guard listening to my conversation from the cameras in the living room.

I've talked to Elliott once a week since I moved to Leviston. The conversations have been a bit like getting-to-know-you sessions. Elliott is easy to talk to and he makes me laugh. It's nice to have something to look forward to that doesn't involve magic or combat training.

"Hey baby," Elliott says smoothly when he answers.

I love hearing his voice.

I tell Elliott about my day and starting a mini-fire. I also tell him about my tattoo.

"Awesome!" Elliott always acts so excited when I tell him about my small milestones.

Then he tells me about his day. "I branded another girl with a hawk today. I think she's terrified."

We both laugh.

"My last three out of four brands have been hawks. Think it's because of the issue with the werewolves?"

"Probably," I say. "I hope it doesn't come to an all-out battle. That would be awful."

"I'm sure it won't," Elliott assures me. "Neither side wants to repeat history."

I sit down on my bed. "Our professor told us about the conflict yesterday."

"Ah, yes. Hell hath no fury, as they say."

"No doubt. I think Eleanor lost it a little bit." I pause for a second, then add, "I can't imagine ever being that upset with a guy. Well, except for your brother. I'd like to take a knife to him a few times."

Elliott laughs. "Frank's harmless."

"Easy for you to say! He didn't break your arm."

"True." There's a few seconds of silence, then Elliott asks, "Is it safe for me to assume you've never had your heart broken?"

I consider this. "No. I've been sad after a breakup, but never heartbroken." I don't tell him I've ended every relationship I've been in. I don't want to scare him off.

"Have you ever been in love?"

"No, I guess not. You?" I'm not sure I want the answer to this question, but he asked first.

"Yeah, once."

I twirl a strand of hair around my finger. "Who was it?"

"A girl I dated a couple years ago."

"What happened?"

"She didn't like that I travel so much."

"To give the branding tattoos?"

"Yep."

"Oh, that stinks. I'm sorry." I try to envision this girl. The girl who Elliott was in love with.

"Hey, I'm over it. Plus, if she was still around, I wouldn't be talking to you."

"Her loss. My gain." I make light of it, but I'm still thinking of his ex. Is this what jealousy feels like?

"Enough about my love life. Let's talk about yours."

"There's not much to tell. I've never been in love, remember?"

"How is that possible?"

I lean my head back on the headboard of my bed. "I haven't met someone I had those kind of feelings for."

"You've never had a boyfriend?"

"I didn't say that," I correct him. "I said I've never been in love."

"How many boyfriends then?"

"Define 'boyfriend.'"

Elliott laughs. "A boyfriend is someone you went on more than ten dates with."

"Hmmmm… I've had five boyfriends."

"Five? And none of them did it for you?"

"Nope."

"What was wrong with them, if I may ask?"

I smile. "They just weren't, I don't know, special. I never had butterflies in my stomach or felt like I wanted to be with them every moment of every day. If they were around, great. If they weren't, that was fine too."

"I see." Elliott pauses and I can tell he has another question.

"What?"

"Can I ask a really personal question?"

I'm pretty sure I know what's coming. "Sure, why not?"

"Are you a virgin?"

I laugh. Yep, I knew he was going there. "No, I'm not."

70

He lets out a sigh of relief. "Okay good. I can't handle that kind of pressure."

I laugh again. "Don't want to be the first, huh?"

"Hey, I'd gladly take on the challenge if you asked me to."

"I'm sure you would."

"Do you have an embarrassing personal question for me? I think I owe you one."

"I don't think so. I mean, is there anything I need to know? Any weird fetishes I should be aware of?"

"Nope. Well, there is the whole truffle butter thing. Although I'm not quite sure I completely understand it."

I laugh out loud. "Calm down Lil' Wayne."

"Yeah, I don't know what that means."

We joke back and forth a little more. I wish he was with me and I tell him so.

"Me too. I talked to Frank and he thinks I should be able to come see you this weekend."

I sit straight up. "What?! You're just now telling me this?!"

"I wanted it to be a surprise, but as you can see, I couldn't keep it to myself."

"Oh my God!" I start bouncing on my bed. "You're really coming here? For real?"

"Are you jumping on the bed?" Elliott asks, laughing.

"Yes! I'm so excited! I can't wait until the weekend!" I flop down on the bed, out of breath from jumping.

"I'm glad you're happy. I was worried you'd tell me not to come."

"Are you crazy? Why would I say that?"

"Because it's so soon. I'm worried you'll think I'm a nutcase."

"Oh please. I have the market cornered on nutcase."

71

After the phone dies, I run across the hall to Frank's apartment. He opens the door in nothing but gym shorts and flip flops.

"Put on some clothes! Jesus!" I accost him.

He smiles. "Got tickets for the gun show?" Frank lifts his arms and flexes for me. He looks like a contestant in a body building competition.

"Ugh! Gross!"

He deflates. "Gross? Really?"

I roll my eyes. "Get over yourself. You know you're freaking hot. But you're like a brother and no girl wants to see her brother flex it out."

Frank considers this. "Fair enough. Now, what do you want?"

I hop up and down in the hall. "Elliott's coming!"

Frank shakes his head. "Couldn't keep his mouth shut, could he?"

I give Frank a big hug. "Thank you so much!"

He pats my back in return. "You've been working hard and deserve a break."

Frank mentioning my hard work reminds me of my tattoo.

"Hey look! My feathers are filling in." I lift my shirt up to show him.

He makes a disgusted face. "Put your clothes back on! Jesus!"

He promptly shuts his door and leaves me standing in the hallway with my shirt pulled up over my head.

Chapter Six

Chelsea

"Excited about this weekend?" Rory asks.

Rory and I are walking around campus hand-in-hand. Orange, red and yellow leaves canvas the lawn.

"Yes! It will be nice to get away."

Elliott is coming to stay with Chloe for the weekend, so Rory and I rented a small cabin about half an hour away to give them space.

Rory squeezes my hand. "It has been a little crazy, hasn't it?"

"I'm getting used to it. I love the school work."

He leans down and kisses my forehead. "I'm looking forward to having you to myself for a few days."

"Even with the Guard in tow?" I ask softly.

Rory nods and smiles. "Even with the Guard in tow."

Rory was less than pleased when I told him Matthew will be traveling with us this weekend. At least Matthew is staying in the cabin next door and not with us. It's strictly precautionary to make sure we are safe while off campus.

What was once the subject of humor and pranks has become tiresome and old. My parents are feeling the strain of the constant security as well, but we're all tolerating it.

We continue down the sidewalk and greet our classmates as they walk by. There aren't many of us on campus, so we recognize most of the people as they pass. One of them is my Curing classmate Arial.

"Chelsea!" she exclaims when she sees me.

Arial is a tiny thing with wavy, beach blonde hair. She is a nice girl, if not a bit high strung.

"Hi Rory," Arial says in her singsong voice when she walks up to us.

Rory nods his head at her. "Arial."

Arial turns her attention back to me. Her eyes are bright and her smile is wide. "I heard you're going to be Professor King's research assistant."

"That's right," I say, returning her smile.

Professor King is our Curing professor and my personal hero. Her healing powers are amazing and I can't wait to learn all I can from her.

"Well it's no surprise!" Arial beams. "You are so far above and beyond the rest of us it's crazy. I'm so happy for you!"

"Thanks. I appreciate it."

"Maybe you can be my tutor."

I laugh. "You don't want me as a tutor. And besides, you're pretty good at it yourself."

Arial grins. "Well, gotta run. I'm meeting someone for dinner."

I wave good-bye as Arial runs off.

"She's a ball of energy," Rory observes.

I laugh. "That's putting it mildly."

We start walking again, no particular destination in mind. Just enjoying the fall air.

Rory entwines his fingers in mine. "So here we are. Both of us with great apprenticeships, doing well in school..." he pauses dramatically, "and madly in love."

I giggle. "Doesn't get better than this, does it?"

"We'll graduate. Head back home where you can open your own holistic healing practice and I'll get a job as a college professor. It's going to be incredible."

74

I see the true happiness in his eyes, but Rory knows me and sees the hesitation in mine.

"What? What is it Chelse?"

We stop and face each other. I look up at him, a small frown on my lips. "It's just…well, I may not be able to go home anymore."

His forehead creases. "Why not?"

I stammer. "We don't know where the Verhena's headquarters are, but I'm pretty sure it's not our hometown."

Rory throws his hands up in frustration. "Seriously? We have to follow Chloe around now?"

"I'm her Advisor Rory, I have to."

"You're her Advisor in theory, not in practice."

He has a point. I don't even know what the Verhena's Advisor does.

"I'm sure in a couple years Chloe will need an actual Advisor, and I agreed to be that person."

Rory stands speechless. He's upset and I understand why. This whole Verhena business is changing all of our plans.

I take his hand. "Remember when you were telling me that sometimes life throws you curveballs?"

He doesn't respond. Instead, he stares down at the ground.

"Hey, look at me."

It takes Rory a moment, but he meets my eyes.

"You can still be a professor. And I can still be a holistic healer." I cradle his face in my hands. "And we'll still be together. That will never change."

His eyes soften. "You're right Chelse. I'm sorry."

"Besides, we may be putting the cart way before the horse. For all we know, Chloe gets to pick where her headquarters is located. You know she'll want to go back home."

He lifts an eyebrow. "You sure about that?"

I smile. "I know for a fact her Advisor is going to advocate hard for it."

Rory laughs. Crisis averted.

Chloe

Elliott is coming tonight!

I've been fidgeting all day long and could hardly sit still during my classes. The nervous energy proved helpful in my combat training. I managed to kick Frank in the face. Take that G.I. Joe!

"Nice!" Frank said, blood flowing from his lip. "Those power and strength spells are definitely working."

If only I knew how to conjure up the perfect outfit for my date with Elliott.

"You need to calm down," Chelsea tells me as she flops onto my bed. "You've been running around like a maniac for the last four days."

I hold up two pairs of jeans. "Which do you like better?"

Chelsea eyes my options. "The skinny jeans with a pair of heels."

I nod in approval. "Agreed."

Chelsea pats the bed next to her. "Sit."

I put the extra pair of jeans back in my closet and sit down.

"What's going on?" she asks as she scans my face.

I bite my bottom lip. "I'm nervous."

Chelsea laughs. "You like this guy, huh?"

"Yeah," I admit. "I do."

She pulls me in for a side hug and I rest my head on her shoulder. "He likes you too Chloe, or he wouldn't bother to come see you."

"I'm worried I'm going to mess it up."

"How would you mess it up?"

I shrug my shoulders. "This whole situation is crazy. It's a lot for someone to handle."

"Elliott knows exactly what he's getting into. He's the one who gave you the tattoo, remember? He was the first person to know you're the next Verhena. And he didn't run out of the house screaming."

"You're right. It's just…" I pause.

"It's just what?"

"I like him Chelsea. It scares me."

"Awww. My little Chloe is falling in love," she says in a singsong voice.

I smack her arm, but I'm laughing. "Get out of here. Shouldn't you be in the car with Rory?"

"Rory *and* Matthew."

"Don't tell Mom," I joke.

Chelsea makes a gagging noise. "Yuck."

I give Chelsea a hug before she leaves. "Have a good time."

She squeezes me back. "Don't forego the pleasure because of the potential pain."

"Did you read that in one of your romance novels?"

She smiles. "Maybe."

I'm putting the finishing touches on my hair when the doorbell rings. I'm in my skinny jeans and red heels with a black cowl neck sweater. I'd love to show more skin, but I don't want to overdo it.

I give myself one last look and fix a smear in my red lipstick. Even though I want to run, I walk as casually as possible to the front door. Summoning my inner sexiness, I swing it open.

And there he is. Elliott. He's wearing ripped blue jeans with a brown leather jacket and white Nike high tops. He's ditched his hat and has his black hair styled with the perfect amount of hair gel. He looks better than I remembered.

"Hi," I manage to get out.

He leans in and kisses my cheek. "Hey." Chills run up my spine as he whispers, "You look fantastic," in my ear.

I'm weak in the knees, but invite him inside for a tour of the place. As he walks by me, I see a small gym bag swinging in his hand. My heart flutters. Does he plan to stay the night with me?

"Is big brother watching?" Elliott asks, pointing at the ceiling.

I follow his gaze toward one of the cameras in the living room.

"Yep. Frank's probably up there right now. Hi Frank!" I wave at the camera for good measure.

Elliott laughs. "That's so creepy."

I crinkle my nose. "It is, isn't it?" I reach out for his bag. "I can take that for you."

"Nah, it's kinda heavy. Where's your room? I can throw it in there real quick."

The butterflies in my stomach are going ballistic, he is definitely staying with me tonight!

I walk Elliott down the hall and secretly thank God I cleaned my room earlier. On our way, I point out the guest bathroom and Chelsea's room.

"This is it," I say when we cross the threshold into my room. "I haven't had the chance to finish decorating yet."

Elliott does a 360 degree turn. "Looks great to me."

"Chelsea and I painted the walls last week."

"I love the paint color. Very serene."

"Thanks. It took forever to pick it. Do you know how many grey paint options there are? This one is called 'After the Rain.'"

Elliott smiles at me and I feel myself blush. I'm blathering on about paint colors. Someone please stop me!

He walks over to my picture wall and looks at the pictures Chelsea and I hung of our family and friends. The silence in the room is killing me. I'm afraid Elliott will hear my heart beating like a drum in my chest.

"I just got this bed set last week," I tell him.

He glances over at my grey comforter with soft yellow flowers. "Nice. I like it."

I bite my lower lip when he turns away. Way to go Chloe! You pointed out the bed!

I fumble with something to say. "There are no cameras in here," I blurt out.

Doh!

"Good to know," Elliott says with a grin. His dimples are showing and I have to look away.

Thankfully, the doorbell rings before I can die of embarrassment.

"It's probably your brother," I guess as we walk down the hall.

I'm right.

"You look nice," Frank says after looking me over.

Before he can add an insult, I ask "What do you want?"

"Are you two going out tonight? If you are, we need to plan accordingly."

Elliott is as surprised by this question as I am. "Is it possible for us to go out?"

Frank nods. "It's possible, but you won't be able to show any signs of affection."

I roll my eyes. "Good grief Frank."

"It has to look like we're out as a group. My brother is in town and we're getting a bite to eat."

"Are you hungry?" Elliott asks me.

My stomach wants to scream - Yes! Feed me already! But I simply say, "Yeah, a little."

"Do you want to go out?" Elliott is talking to me like Frank isn't there. I like it.

I shrug my shoulders. "Sure. Although we'll probably have to sit at opposite ends of the table."

I was joking, but Frank isn't when he says, "Probably not a bad idea."

A couple hours later, Elliott and I are laughing as we walk back into my apartment. We went out to a small Italian restaurant off campus and had the best dinner. Frank, Thomas, and a few of the other Guard members came with us. It was nice to sit back and relax with the guys who protect me 24/7. Some of them were "on duty" but the others let loose a bit. I got to hear more about them and their personal lives.

Any casual observer would think we were a large group of friends having a good time and catching up. I did my best not to stare at Elliott or to throw him too many glances.

Frank had me sit across from Elliott as opposed to next to him. Which was a good idea because I don't think I would have been able to resist touching him in some way. A small shoulder nudge or a careless whisper could give it away.

"Home sweet home," I say as I kick off my heels. "Want anything to drink?"

"Nah, I'm good," Elliott responds from the living room.

I grab a bottle of water out of the fridge and take a deep breath before leaving the kitchen to calm myself down.

Elliott is checking his phone when I walk into the living room. He's taken off his leather jacket, his tattoos and tan skin stand out against the plain, white T-shirt he's wearing. The muscles in his arms flex as he types and his tribal tattoos move with them.

"Hey, sorry," he says, momentarily looking up from his phone. "I swear after I respond to this message I'm turning my phone off."

I move past him to sit down on the couch. "No biggie. Take your time."

A minute later he puts his phone down and walks over to me.

"Want to watch a movie?" I ask.

I know it sounds lame, but what am I going to do? Whip out the UNO cards?

"Sure. Whatcha got?"

I get up and walk over to the built-in shelves next to the TV. "All of our movies are over here."

Elliott walks up behind me and presses his body against mine. Instant heat courses through my veins. "Where? Here?"

He kisses the back of my neck and I melt into him. I put one hand on the wall to steady myself and the other on the back of his head. Elliott leans further into me and explores my body with his hands, all while continuing to kiss my neck.

A small moan escapes my lips, but I get distracted when I see one of the cameras in the corner of the ceiling.

I turn to face him. "Not here." I motion my head toward the camera and he follows my eyes.

"Ah, yes. The eyes in the sky."

I take Elliott's hand and lead him down the hallway to my bedroom.

I wake up the next morning with a weight on my chest. What the hell?

I smile when I realize it's Elliott's arm. We are spooning in my bed, snuggled underneath my new comforter. Streams of sunshine seep in through the blinds and cover us with rays of light.

I trace the pattern of his tattoos with my fingertips and relish the moment. I don't want to ever get out of this bed. No more practice. No more spells. No more worries about werewolves. Just us.

After a few minutes, Elliott stirs. He leans in, presses his face into my hair, and inhales deeply.

"I love how you smell," he whispers.

I giggle. "That's awesome because I need a shower."

Elliott lays flat on his back and stretches his arms and legs. "Room for two in there?"

I get out of bed wearing nothing but his white t-shirt and head for my bathroom. "It's a stall shower, but I think we can make it work."

"I've always enjoyed a challenge." Elliott stands up and I'm once again dumbstruck by his body.

I'm surrounded by muscular and fit men all day long, but they have nothing on Elliott. The tan skin, the tattoos, the lean muscle… And he's standing here naked in all of his glory in my bedroom.

"Wow, I feel really overdressed." I pull the t-shirt over my head. "There, now I fit in."

Elliott grunts as he moves toward me. "You lost your chance at a hot shower all by yourself."

"Damn," I say, feigning disappointment.

After our shower, we spend the rest of the day hanging out in the apartment. The TV is on, but we don't pay much attention to it. We're too busy talking and sharing more about ourselves. I almost feel like a normal girl. Almost.

Elliott confirms Chelsea's suspicions. "Your sister is right. Your tattoo definitely has more gold in it."

"Really?"

"Yes. You don't notice it because you see it every day. But I can tell the gold has come in bolder and thicker."

I pull my shirt down over my head before we head out for another group dinner.

"How is Chelsea handling all of this?" Elliott asks as he laces his Nikes.

"What do you mean?"

"This has to be hard on her."

I pause. This probably has been a lot for Chelsea, and I haven't asked her one time how she's doing.

"I think she's doing okay." I look down at my hands. I feel awful. Chelsea has been so selfless and I've never thanked her for it.

"Hey…" Elliott scotches over next to me. "I didn't mean to upset you."

"It's not you. I just realized I'm not a very good sister."

Elliott pulls me in with his arm. "You're a great sister. You have a lot going on right now."

"That's no excuse."

"I'm sure Chelsea will forgive you."

"Yeah, I know." And she will forgive me, without hesitation. Because that's Chelsea.

"Alright then." Elliott jumps up. "Ready for another testosterone filled dinner?"

I grin. "You know it."

Saying good-bye to Elliott sucks. A lot.

"I'll get you more burner phones tomorrow," Frank promises as we watch Elliott drive away from my living room window.

This does little to ease the ache in my heart. I wish I could go with him. Jump in his car and get out of here. Leave all of this behind.

But Elliott and I both have obligations. Duties to uphold.

"One day things will calm down," Elliott told me before he left, "and we'll be together."

I hope he's right.

Chelsea and Rory return home from their trip about an hour later. They're all lovey dovey. Same old, same old. When Rory leaves, I talk with my sister in her bedroom. Unlike my grey walls, she has chosen a pale purple with white trim.

"How was your trip?"

She unzips her suitcase. "Amazing! How was Elliott?"

Hearing his name pains me, but I play it off. "He's great. We had a really good time."

Chelsea smiles. "Good!"

I pick at my blue fingernail polish. "Hey Chelse, are you doing okay?"

She gives me a questioning look. "What do you mean?"

"I know this isn't the experience you had in mind when we talked about coming to Leviston."

Chelsea puts an armful of clothes in the hamper. "Some of it's exactly what I thought it would be. The classes. Meeting new people. Being with you and Rory. The only things that are different are this apartment, which is fantastic, and the muscular men who watch my every move. The last part is weird, but it's not awful."

"Are you sure? I mean, if you want to, you can move out." I don't want Chelsea to leave, but I don't want her to feel trapped either.

Chelsea smiles. "Don't be ridiculous. Miss out on this little adventure? Never."

I stand up and give Chelsea a hug. "I love you sis."

Chelsea is surprised by my show of affection, but hugs me back. "I love you too Chloe."

84

The next couple months fly by.

Halloween is an interesting time at Leviston. There aren't frats and sororities because Leviston is so small, but we have one giant party everyone is invited to. Chelsea and I had a blast dressing up like the Doublemint Twins in mint green polo shirts and white tennis skirts.

Thanksgiving and Christmas were different than normal, but we made it work. Mom and Dad came to our apartment for the holidays and brought all of the Christmas decorations with them. Members of the Guard spent the holiday meals with us, which required three times more food than usual. We rang in the New Year with our boyfriends by our sides and kisses all around.

January is usually a rough month for me because nothing exciting is happening. This year, however, I'm too busy to be bored. My magic has improved exponentially. I'm no longer allowed to practice my fire skills indoors for fear I'll burn the training facility down. With Dean Lucas's help, I can freeze people and objects for a solid two seconds. The gold in my tattoo has spread noticeably. My white hawk is becoming more beautiful with each passing day.

Frank is working on reaching out to fellow witches who can help me learn new skills. This is easier said than done because he has to be one hundred percent sure the witches who meet with me won't reveal my identity.

Chelsea is doing great too. Her healing powers are a sight to see. Our Curing teacher told us compassionate people are the best healers, and this is true of Chelsea. Helping others is her nature.

Rory is his usual uber-genius self. He is constantly pouring over text books and rambling on and on about witch history. I should be listening closely to what he's saying, but after classes and my workouts, I'm ready to veg on the couch and watch mindless TV.

It's the Friday before Valentine's Day weekend and the nervous energy is back. Elliott is coming tonight and I want to hit the fast-forward button to make him get here sooner. I haven't seen him since New Year's Eve and I've missed him every single day. The weekly phone calls just aren't enough anymore.

"What are you and Rory doing for Valentine's Day?" I ask Chelsea over breakfast.

"He told me on the phone earlier to pack a bag. He's picking me up in a little while. I have no idea where we're going."

"Somewhere warm maybe?"

Chelsea sits down at the table with a bowl of Frosted Flakes. "I don't think so. My guess is he's taking me back to the cabin we went to in the fall."

"It's not Miami Beach, but I'm sure it will be nice."

"I really don't care where we go as long as we go together."

I make Chelsea giggle when I pretend to gag myself with my spoon.

An hour later, Rory stops by to pick up Chelsea. He barely says "hi" before insisting Chelsea get her things.

"I don't want to hit traffic," he whines.

I give Chelsea a good-bye hug. "Have fun!"

She squeezes me back. "When will Elliott be here?"

"He's supposed to show up around 7:30."

"Is he staying the whole weekend?" Rory asks as we walk toward the front door.

I'm beaming. "Yep. I get him until Sunday afternoon."

"Well, we won't be back until Sunday night. You'll have the place all to yourself," Chelsea says with a grin.

I smile. "Yeah, I know."

Rory shifts his weight and gives me a pointed look. "Aren't you going to be late for training?"

It's clear Rory is trying to get rid of me. "I'm heading that way soon."

Rory turns to Chelsea. "Let's hit the road."

"Okay." Chelsea gives me another hug. "Tell Elliott we said hi."

"Will do."

I watch Rory and my sister walk down the hallway toward the elevator. Chelsea laughs about something and takes Rory's hand. She looks at him like he's the most handsome man in the world. I don't get it, but he makes my sister happy. That's all I need to know.

Rory glances over his shoulder and catches me watching them. He smiles awkwardly and puts his hand up to acknowledge me. Chelsea turns to see what he's looking at, and when she sees me, waves good-bye. I return her wave, then scurry to get my workout clothes on. Rory was right, I'm going to be late.

Chelsea

We're twenty minutes away from campus when I realize I left one of my bags on my bed.

"Rory, I forgot my toiletries bag. We need to turn around."

He gives me a sideways glance from the driver's seat. "Do we have to go back? Can't we stop at Walgreens?"

"The thing is, that bag has all my bathroom items in it and I don't want to buy new stuff."

I leave out the fact that his Valentine's Day gift is in the missing bag too. I really want to give him the brand new watch I bought him. Rory loves watches and I think he's going to love the Tag Hauer I picked out.

"C'mon Chelse. We'll stop at a drug store and get you some things. We're only going to be gone two days."

I pout. "Please Rory?"

I'm shocked when I see agitation cross Rory's face. But as quickly as the annoyance appeared, it is gone.

87

He smiles at me. "Sure, let's turn around."

"Thank you," I say, rubbing his shoulder with my left hand.

"Be quick about it okay? I want to get to the cabin at a decent time so we can go out to dinner tonight."

"Okay." I dial Matthew's number, who's following in a car behind us, to let him know we're turning around.

The trip back to campus is bizarre. Rory seems annoyed, but when I engage him in conversation, he smiles and responds. Why is he acting like this?

Then it hits me.

He's going to propose!

He's anxious to get to the cabin because he wants to pop the question. Which is why he wants to be sure we get to dinner tonight.

I smile to myself and relax into my seat. I'm feeling much better by the time we pull into the parking lot of our apartment building.

"Want me to go up with you?" Rory asks.

"No. You stay in the car. I'll run in to get my bag and be right back down."

"Be quick," he tells me again.

I close the car door and jog up to the apartment building. I try to disguise my giddiness. I don't want Rory to know I've figured out his big plan.

Matthew rolls down his car window and yells, "How long will you be?"

"Not long at all!" I yell back. "Stay in the car. Two minutes. Tops!"

Matthew nods and rolls his window up.

I forego the elevator and take the steps to the fourth floor. I'm winded but excited as I reach our apartment door and burst through it. I'm giggling to myself as I picture Rory down on one knee.

Will he propose at the restaurant? Or the cabin?

Will he have a long speech prepared? Or will he get right to it?

None of it makes a difference to me. I'm going to say "yes."

I'm on cloud nine as I jog into the living room. Then I smell it. A rustic, woodsy smell. It's not a bad smell per se, but out of place in our apartment.

Something is wrong. My excitement kept me from sensing it sooner. I turn for the front door, but it's too late.

Standing in our living room are three men. All in black jeans, black boots and leather jackets. I step backwards involuntarily and bump into the wall.

"Chloe…we've been waiting for you," growls the tallest man. He has salt and pepper hair and hasn't shaved in a while. His eyes gleam like emerald gemstones.

The other two men are younger. One with a bald head and the other with spiky black hair. Like the older man, their eyes shine an unnatural emerald green.

I don't have to ask who they are or what they want.

They are werewolves. And they think I'm Chloe.

I summon all of my strength. "Wanted to meet the Verhena face to face, huh?"

All three growl in response. The hair on my arms stands up. My heart is in my throat. Where is the Guard? Why aren't they here?

As if reading my mind, one of the younger wolves, the bald one says, "Don't bother screaming. We shut the power off to the building, so the cameras aren't on. And by the time your security gets here, you'll be dead."

The three men approach. I wait for them to transform into their Were forms, but they remain human.

The tall man speaks again. "Are you going to beg for your life?"

My mind is racing. I could tell them I'm not Chloe, but what good would that do? They'll kill me anyway. And maybe, just maybe, if they think they've killed Chloe, they'll leave campus and

Chloe will be safe. I have to keep up the charade. I know exactly what Chloe would say if she was facing these men.

Standing tall, my chin held high, I channel my sister. "Fuck you."

Chapter Seven

Chloe

Frank lets me off the hook today.

I arrive at the training facility to find him dressed in khakis and a camo green Under Armour polo shirt.

"What's up? Where's your workout clothes?" I ask.

Frank smiles. "No workout today. Just a quick lesson with Dean Lucas."

"For real?"

"I don't want to beat you up the day my brother comes to town. A black eye isn't sexy."

I punch his arm. "You're gross."

Dean Lucas promises to keep our session brief, but tells me, "I have something new to show you."

I watch in amazement as Dean Lucas puts her hands on the cinderblock wall of the gym and starts climbing. It's like the woman has glue or suction cups on the bottom of her feet. When she makes it all the way to the top, she crawls across the ceiling.

"Holy crap!" I exclaim, my head tilted all the way back so I can watch her crawl upside down. "You gotta show me how to do that!"

Dean Lucas teaches me the spell and shows me the best way to position my body as I climb. After learning the hard way that the gym mats aren't as forgiving as they look, I don't dare climb higher than a few feet.

"Good job Chloe," Dean Lucas says when I'm too worn out to climb anymore. "You are picking up on new skills quickly. You're getting more powerful by the day."

"Do you think Dean Lucas is right?" I ask Frank as we walk back to the apartment. "Am I picking up on skills quicker?"

Frank nods. "You are. The stronger you get, the easier new skills will be for you. It's like compounding interest."

I crinkle my nose. "What?"

"Compounding interest." When I continue to look at him like he's talking a foreign language, he laughs. "It's a money thing. I'll explain it to you someday."

"No thanks." My focus shifts to Elliott's visit. "Are we going out to dinner tonight?"

Frank shrugs. "I'm sure the guys will be game, but that's really up to you."

Before I can tell Frank I definitely want to go out, something catches my eye. Rory's car is in our parking lot.

"Why are Rory and Chelsea here? They left a while ago."

"I don't know. I haven't heard anything from the other guys."

An odd feeling washes over me. My muscles tense and my heartbeat accelerates. I jog over to Rory's car. He's staring up at the apartment and jumps when I knock on his window.

He rolls his window down. "Hey Chloe. Back from practice already?"

"Yeah. Short day today. What's up?"

Rory licks his lips. "Chelsea forgot a bag. She'll be back down in a minute."

I glance over at Matthew's car. Frank is hunched over the driver side door, the two men having a conversation. I assume Frank is getting the same story I am. I look up at the apartment windows and my stomach lurches. Something is wrong. Very wrong.

I take off for the building entrance, Frank yelling behind me. I don't stop. I run up the steps two at a time. I have to get to Chelsea. My fears are confirmed when I find our apartment door standing open. Chelsea would never leave the door open. She worries too much about someone sneaking in behind her.

My senses are on hyper drive as I run into the apartment. Everything is moving in slow motion. An earthy smell, like dirt or trees, assaults my nose.

"Chelsea!"

I round the corner to our living room and come to a halt. I gasp when I see three men, three werewolves, standing around a lump on the floor.

"What the hell?" the oldest one asks, looking at me, then back down at the floor.

I'm struggling to process the scene. Where is Chelsea? I have to find her.

"Shit!" one of them exclaims. "We killed the wrong one!"

Did he just say "killed"? My breath gets caught in my throat when I realize the lump on the floor is a body. My vision starts to swim when I see blonde hair.

"No…" I whisper.

I faintly hear Frank yell, "Chloe! Wait!" behind me, but it doesn't register.

No way that's Chelsea. She's probably hiding in her bedroom. Locked away in her closet or under the bed.

I take a step toward the body, paying no mind to the three men about to pounce. They line up side-by-side, baring their teeth and growling, but they don't transition into their Were forms.

"Get her!" the oldest one yells before they all lunge toward me.

Without much thought or effort, I freeze them. It happens instinctively, just like Dean Lucas told me it would. The men are stuck in place as I continue to move past them. Out of the corner of my eye, I see Frank and Matthew are frozen as well. Frank's mouth hanging open and his hand reaching out for me.

93

It's an odd sensation to be the only thing moving in a room, but I pay it little mind. I hurry, not because I'm worried about the spell wearing off, but because I have to help the woman on the floor.

I drop to my knees beside her. She is face down in a pool of blood. Crimson soaking her beautiful blonde hair. The frame of her body is familiar, identical to my own. I choke back sobs as I roll her over to her side. Chelsea's vacant eyes stare at me.

A scream escapes my lips. "Chelsea! Chelsea! No!"

I cradle Chelsea in my arms, rocking back and forth as I cast every curing spell I know. I hold her close to me, alternating between chanting spells and begging God for my sister back. Despite my efforts, Chelsea's body remains lifeless in my arms. I bury my face in her hair, tears streaming down my face.

"Please Chelsea! Please! I need you. Please!"

The world remains frozen around me. It's just me and Chelsea. My beautiful, wonderful, caring and perfect identical twin sister. My best friend. My partner in crime. The best sister a girl could ask for. Gone. She's gone.

After an eternity of sobbing, I lay Chelsea on the ground and gaze at her angelic face. I close her eyes and wipe blood splatters off her cheek. I lower my head to her chest one more time, listening for even the faintest of a heartbeat. But reality is setting in. Chelsea is dead. Her innocent face covered in her own blood.

I look down at my hands. They are also covered in blood. Chelsea's blood. I feel a sudden and intense wave of fury rush through me. I stand up and turn toward the wolves. Their faces frozen in nasty grimaces, stuck in full attack mode.

I unfreeze everyone and watch as they fall back into step. They are instantly confused. They were running toward me, except I'm not there anymore.

"I'm right here," I say, voice raw from my sobs and screams.

All five men turn to look at me.

"Get back," I tell Frank and Matthew.

"Chloe," Frank starts to protest.

I put my hand up. "Get. Back."

Frank's eyes widen when he sees my fingertips. He grabs Matthew and pushes him toward the hallway. The wolves, oblivious to what is coming their way, charge toward me. I unleash all of the fury and rage building inside of me. The absolute terror on the wolves' faces is something I will always look back on with satisfaction.

Fire blasts from my fingertips like flamethrowers and within seconds the men are reduced to nothing but ash. The back wall of the living room explodes outward. Brick and glass shattering into tiny pieces, leaving the entire wall open and exposed to the outside. Wind and cold air blow into the apartment, whipping my hair around my face.

When I'm sure the wolves are dead, I fall to my knees. Frank rushes to my side and pulls me into his chest protectively.

"Holy shit!" Matthew exclaims, assessing the damage. Then a second later, "Oh my God! Chelsea!"

Frank squeezes me even tighter. "Matthew, try the curing spells."

"It's too late," I whisper. "She's gone."

More Guard members flood the apartment, the shock apparent on their faces.

"What the hell?" one of them murmurs. "Was there a bomb?"

Frank yells more orders. "Secure the area! Check to see if there are others! Get vehicles ready to move!"

There is a whirlwind of motion around me, but I stay in Frank's arms. I block out the noise, memories of my childhood with Chelsea playing in my mind. All the fun times we had together. Our travels. Our future plans.

What is my life without her in it?

"Someone call Elliott," I hear Frank say. "Tell him not to come here. Tell him to go home and we'll reach out to him."

Elliott! How silly that a mere fifteen minutes ago my biggest concern was what panties to wear tonight. I was so stupid. Flittering around my world like a school girl. Ignoring all warnings of danger. Oblivious to the havoc about to be wrecked upon my life.

"How did they know Frank? How did they get to us?" I whisper.

He sighs. "I don't know. I don't know what happened."

"I think I know what happened."

Frank and I both turn to see Thomas standing a few feet from us.

Frank's tone is icy when he responds. "Not now Thomas. We can talk about it later."

I pull away and look up at Frank. His ironclad "I'm the boss face" is on, but there are tears in his eyes.

"No," I insist. "I want to know."

To Frank's chagrin, Thomas walks over and sits down across from us on the floor.

"You know how I've been monitoring all of Chloe's and Chelsea's social media pages?" he asks Frank.

Frank nods.

"Well, literally five minutes before I heard the explosion, I was doing my daily check of Chelsea's Facebook page."

"And…" Frank prods when Thomas pauses.

Thomas's face contorts as he fights back tears. "I'm so sorry Chloe. I wish I would have noticed it sooner."

"Noticed what?" Frank insists.

Thomas clears his throat and regains his composure. "There is a post on Chelsea's page. It went up earlier this afternoon. It told everyone that Chloe is the next Verhena."

"What?" I ask in disbelief. "Someone outed me?"

"Yes," Thomas confirms. "The person who posted as Chelsea also expressed concern about the wards at Leviston. Even went so far as to say she was worried about leaving you alone this weekend because she doesn't think you are safe."

It's all too much for me to process. Whoever hacked into my sister's Facebook account not only outed me, they wanted me dead. Told the world who I am and made me appear vulnerable.

Frank strokes my hair. "We're going to figure out who did this. I promise."

I'm about to tell him it doesn't matter. Chelsea is dead. The damage is already done. But then I hear someone yelling my sister's name in the hallway.

"Chelsea!"

Oh my God…Rory.

I turn to Frank. "You have to let him in."

Frank nods. "It's okay," he says to his men. "Let him through."

Frank stands me up and I cling to him, worried I'll fall over on my wobbly legs.

Rory runs into the room. "Chloe! What is going…" He stops short when he sees Chelsea. "No…no….NO!"

The pain in his voice is raw. I break down and press my face against Frank's chest. He holds me tight, once again shielding me from the chaos.

Rory kneels next to Chelsea and picks her entire body up into his arms. He buries his face into her hair and sobs.

I pull away from Frank and slowly walk over to Rory. I kneel next to him and put my hand on his back. Saying nothing as he continues to cry. We stay like this for a few minutes. Both of us crying in anguish.

Suddenly, Rory lets go of Chelsea and she rolls onto the floor. I reach out to stop her body, but Rory pushes me hard on the shoulders.

I fall back onto my hands and grimace as pain shoots through my wrist. "Rory, what are you doing?" I ask stunned.

His face is twisted in fury. "You! This is all your fault!"

Frank and several Guard members make a move for Rory, but I put my hand up to stop them.

"I'm sorry." I'm fighting back another crying fit, but I deserve this. Rory is right. It is my fault.

Rory is pointing his finger at me. "They were supposed to kill you! Not her!"

I nod my head in agreement. "I know Rory. I know."

Rory is pacing back and forth. Fuming. "If I had known this was how it would turn out…"

He mumbles to himself, then gets down in my face. "You ruined her life! All of our plans!" I cringe away from him as he screams at me. "She was your prisoner here! She was your slave! You uprooted everything and expected Chelsea to go along with it!"

His words sting because they're true. "Please Rory, I'm sorry," I plead.

He backs away from me huffing. "Those dumbass wolves. They can't get anything right."

I nod. "I should be dead. Not her." I lower my head. "We didn't protect her. I should have kept her away from me. There never would have been any confusion."

Rory is doing his crazy pacing again. "I laid this out perfectly for them! All they had to do was show up!"

What did he just say? He laid it out for them?

"What are you talking about Rory?"

He waves his hands around frantically. "They messed it all up!"

I sit up straight. A harsh reality becoming very clear.

I put the puzzle together out loud. "You thought I'd be here alone because you and Chelsea were going out of town."

"Yes!" he exclaims. The Guard and I watch him unravel. "But then she forgot her stupid bag! And insisted we come back for it! It wasn't dark yet, so I thought we'd be okay."

I feel nauseous. It was Rory who posted on Chelsea's Facebook page. Rory who wanted me dead. Out of the way so he and Chelsea could live the life they planned since we were kids.

My stomach rolls again when I remember all of the times Rory talked about the wards. "You removed the wards, didn't you?"

He gives me a Joker-like grin, but doesn't respond.

"That's how they were able to get on campus," I continue, working everything out in my brain.

"Yes!" Rory admits. "I finally found what I needed from Professor Steller's materials. And I did it! I removed the wards!"

All the conversations I half-listened to between Rory and Chelsea about his work with Professor Steller were actually red flags I ignored. Rory's fascination with wards and removing them went well beyond the history of the werewolf/witch conflict.

"She's dead because of you," I whisper.

This pushes Rory over the edge. He lunges for me, arms outstretched and eyes raging. "She's dead because of you!"

Rory's hands latch on to my neck and squeeze. I pry at his fingers, desperately trying to loosen his grip. But I'm weak from the magic I used against the wolves. He glares at me, his wicked grin getting wider the harder he presses against my throat.

Before I can summon the energy to defend myself, Frank grabs Rory. Rory struggles, but it's useless. Frank's powerful arms envelope him. In a quick movement, Frank reaches his hand around Rory's chin and jerks hard. I wince when I hear the sickening sound of bone snapping. Frank lets go and Rory crumples to the ground like a rag doll.

I stare at Rory's lifeless body. I remember something my grandmother told me once – the worst thing about betrayal is it doesn't come from your enemies.

99

Guard members are running around like ants. Chilly, winter air flows through the room, yet I feel nothing but heat. My entire body burning from the inside.

This cannot be real. It has to be a dream.

Chelsea is dead.

Rory is dead.

I have killed three werewolves. Burned them to a crisp and destroyed the building in the process.

I lay back on the floor and stare at the ceiling. Frank's giant frame lumbers over me.

"Thank you," I manage to say.

"You didn't need his death on your conscious."

I nod, thankful I didn't have to be the one to kill Rory. Even if he was trying to kill me. Visions of all of those childhood weddings I participated in flitter through my mind. It's all too much for me to bear.

"I want to speak with Matthew."

Matthew comes over immediately and crouches down next to me. "Are you hurt Chloe?"

"No."

His look of concern remains. "How can I help?"

"I want to sleep."

Matthew has the ability to not only cure, but to calm. Matthew nods in understanding and takes my hand. I welcome the darkness.

$\int$

Chapter Eight

I'm running through the woods trying to catch Chelsea. She is wearing her light blue winter coat, her blond hair streaming behind her in the breeze. I yell to her, but she refuses to turn around. She just keeps running.

I'm thrown off balance by the uneven forest floor. Tree branches slap and cut my face. My feet get tangled in bulky tree roots. I am breathless, but she is so close.

I finally catch up and grab her shoulder. "Chelsea, wait..."

But when Chelsea turns around, it isn't Chelsea I've been chasing. It's Rory. And he's wearing his wicked grin.

"Gotcha now Chloe!"

I sit up in bed, a cold sweat dripping from my hair line. Gasping for air, I look around. I'm in a large antique bed, a white down comforter twisted around my legs. I panic when I realize I have no idea where I am.

"Frank!" I yell as loud as I can.

I nearly jump out of my skin when a female voice says, "He's sleeping sweetie."

I turn toward the voice. An elderly woman is sitting behind a small desk in the corner, her gray hair pulled back in a tight bun. A desk lamp illuminates the fine lines in her face. She sets down her pen, removes her glasses, and stands. She's wearing a white silk robe over white silk pajama pants, and of all things, white bunny slippers.

"Frank and the others are resting. It's been a long day."

I eye the woman suspiciously. Who is she? And more importantly, where am I? Glancing around the room, I see three doors to my right. Which one is the exit? To my left are long, floor length curtains. Presumably, there are windows behind them.

I assess the situation. I have to pass the woman at the desk to get to the doors. And what if I choose the wrong one? My only other option is to go out the window.

I kick off the down comforter and run for it. I rip open the voluminous curtains and gasp. I immediately take a step back, not believing my eyes. The windows are floor to ceiling in height, creating a giant wall of glass. There is no chance of me making an escape. I am high up over a city street. I look out over the skyline and recognize the landmarks immediately.

"I'm in New York City."

"Yes, you are," the woman confirms.

"How did I get here?"

The woman walks toward me, but stops when I take a step away from her. Sensing my fear, she sits on the edge of the bed.

"Frank and the Guard brought you here. You have been sleeping for a while now."

"How long is a while?"

"Twelve hours or so."

I cross my arms over my abdomen and give myself a hug. It's then that I realize I'm no longer in my bloodstained clothes. Instead, I'm in a soft pink t-shirt and black leggings.

"Whose clothes are these?"

"They're yours now."

I look down at my hands. The blood has been washed away. Matthew must have zapped me with one hell of a powerful spell if I not only slept through a wardrobe change, but also a bath.

I ask the most obvious question. "Why am I here?"

"This is the safest place for you."

"According to who?"

She shrugs. "Everyone, I suppose."

"I want to see Frank."

The woman stands and walks closer to me. "You will. Soon. He needs rest. The only reason he left your side was because I promised to stay with you until he comes back."

I step away from her. She seems nice, but I have no clue if anything she's told me is the truth.

"Who are you?" My intent was for the question to come out hard and bitter, but my tone has no effect on her.

"Perhaps this will explain." She turns her back to me and drops her robe. A beautiful white hawk with golden feathers covers her skin. It is identical to mine, except hers has more gold.

I gasp. "Oh my God. You're the Verhena."

For reasons I can't explain, I run to her and give her a hug. She chuckles as she squeezes me back.

"That's me. Well, until you take over."

When we separate, she tells me her name is Wilhelmina. "Everyone around here calls me Willa." She pats the bed. "You should lay back down, get some more rest. You've been through a lot in the last twenty-four hours."

"Did Frank tell you what happened?" I fight back tears.

Willa frowns. "He did."

"I need to call my parents."

"Matthew is with your parents. They know about Chelsea."

A tear rolls down my cheek when I hear my sister's name. I can't imagine what my parents are going through. "How are they?"

"Exactly how you imagine they are," Willa says honestly.

"I need to see them."

Willa hesitates. "Chloe, that's a dangerous proposition. The wolves are watching you and your family. Your identity is no longer a secret."

103

"Are my parents safe? Should they come here too?"

"Your parents are safe where they are. In addition to Matthew, six other Guard members are at your home. Nothing is going to happen to them. The wolves will never get anywhere near them. I guarantee it."

This makes me feel a little better, but then I think of Chelsea again. She's really gone.

I cry into my hands. Willa places her hand on my shoulder and a sense of tranquility washes over me. It doesn't take me long to figure out she's using a calming spell. I don't protest. Once I'm relaxed, I crawl under the covers and doze off.

When I open my eyes, I wake to find Willa still sitting at the desk. The only light in the room is the desk lamp. I lay quietly for a while, then break the silence.

"Have you ever lost someone close to you?" I ask her.

"Yes, I have."

"Does the pain ever stop?"

Willa walks over to the bed and sits down beside me. "It never goes away completely. It hibernates after some time. You go on about your daily life, find things to distract you. And then the grief springs up out of nowhere. As painful as it ever was. Then it hides away again."

"I can't go to Chelsea's funeral, can I?"

"No. You, Chloe, cannot go to your sister's funeral. It would be too risky."

I sigh. "I'll never see her again."

"That's not necessarily true."

I lean up on my elbows. "What do you mean?"

Willa smiles. "I said Chloe cannot go to the funeral."

"Okay..."

"What if I told you that one of my specialties is changing someone's appearance?"

"Really? Like a disguise?"

"It's more than a disguise. You will transform into a completely different person. I've already discussed it with Frank. If you want to go to Chelsea's funeral, he will go with you in a glamour of his own."

"A glamour?"

"My fancy word for disguise," Willa explains.

When she sees I've calmed down, Willa returns to the desk and hums while she writes.

"Did you tell my parents about Rory?" I ask a few minutes later.

"No, we didn't. We told your parents and Rory's family the wolves killed him. No sense in causing unnecessary upset or a dispute in the coven."

I start to protest, then close my mouth. Willa is right. Rory's family would be devastated, as would my own, if they knew the truth. They have enough to deal with, why add more pain?

Anger rises inside of me when I think of Rory and what he did. "He's the reason my sister is dead."

"Yes, he is one reason," Willa agrees. "But let's not forget the wolves carried out the act itself."

How could I forget?

"I want them all dead," I pronounce, malice in my voice.

Willa's pen comes to a halt. "Most of the wolves are good people. Only a small fraction of their population wishes us harm." She looks over at me right as I yawn. "We don't need to get into all of that now. You need more rest."

I'm about to tell her I'm fine, but that's not true. I roll to my side and gaze out the windows. The lights, the sounds, the people. All completely oblivious to my pain and anguish. I close my eyes and nod off.

I wake up to sunlight streaming in through the giant bay windows. I'm reminded of my first morning with Elliott, the two of us cuddled up together. How I ache for that now.

My mind fills with thoughts of Elliott. Does he know what happened? Will Frank let him come see me? Will he even want to?

I roll over expecting to see Willa, but Frank is now occupying the desk chair. He's bent over a stack of papers, no doubt reading the report about yesterday's events. I watch him for a few minutes as he reads the pages. His eyebrows furrow in certain sections. In others, he looks close to tears.

"Hi," I finally murmur.

Frank looks surprised, oblivious to my spying on him. A happier me would rejoice in the irony.

Frank puts his papers down and walks over to the bed. "How are you feeling?"

"Like crap."

He sits beside me. "Me too."

"She's dead," I choke out.

He takes a deep breath. "I know."

I lay on my back and stare at the ceiling. It has to be the most ornate ceiling I've ever seen. White tiles with beautiful, intricate patterns cut into them. Willa must be one rich witch.

"When is the funeral?"

He winces. "Tomorrow."

"How are my parents?"

Frank sighs. "Not good Chloe. Not good. They're worried sick about you."

"Can I call them today?"

"Yes. They've been asking to speak with you."

I sit up and give Frank a good onceover. "You look like I feel."

He cracks a small smile. "Things have been hectic."

"Did you get any sleep?"

"A little."

From the looks of it, very little.

"Am I safe here?"

Frank nods. "This is the safest place for you. This building is more secure than you can even fathom. Willa has all the latest technology. No one will ever get to you here."

I'm about to ask about the plans for my sister's funeral, but Frank continues.

"We should have brought you here in the first place." Frank runs his hands through his super short hair. Must be a family habit. "We thought the wolves would never look for you at Leviston. We were wrong. So wrong."

I put my hand up to stop him, but Frank keeps talking. "We were lulled into a sense of security. We thought everything was fine. We got lazy. We should have been on top of it. None of this would have happened."

Frank's about to break down. I don't know what I'll do if he cries in front of me.

I reach out and touch Frank's shoulder. "Hey. Don't. None of this is your fault."

Frank has tears in his eyes. "I should have brought you here the first night I met you. You'd be safe and Chelsea would be alive."

I grab Frank under the chin and force him to look me in the eyes. I repeat what Willa said to me a few hours ago. "Listen to me. The wolves killed Chelsea. Not me. Not you. The wolves."

Frank gets himself together and walks back over to the desk. He shuffles through his papers. "We confirmed Rory is the one who hacked Chelsea's account. We also spoke with Professor Steller and he advised us there are documents missing from his office. Likely the information Rory needed to take down the wards around campus."

Frank is back to business as usual, but I'm only half-listening. I'm not ready to get back into action. I want to hide away in this giant down comforter for the rest of my life. Let everyone else deal with this mess.

Frank catches my attention when he says, "Video surveillance on campus shows there were two more wolves."

"Two more?"

"Yes. They were in another vehicle two blocks away from the apartment building. As soon as the wall blew out, they bolted."

"Can you tell who they are?"

Frank frowns. "We're working on it."

"How? How are you working on it? Is there a werewolf database somewhere?"

Frank shifts his weight. "We have our methods. We can talk about that later."

Frank is keeping something from me and I don't like it. I'm about to tell him as much when a knock on the door interrupts us.

"Come in," Frank yells, thankful for the break in conversation.

A woman in her late twenties walks in the door furthest to my left. She is carrying a stack of towels and a basket filled with shampoo, conditioner and soap.

"Here's everything you'll need for a nice shower," she says with a warm smile.

There is nothing flashy about this woman, but she is pretty all the same. She dons a brunette pixie cut, and almond-shaped brown eyes dominate her face. She has a beautiful smile and full lips every woman would be envious of.

After what I've been through, I'm skeptical of everyone. "Who are you?" I ask.

"I'm Jessica. I work for Willa," she explains. "If there's anything you need, please let me know."

My stomach rumbles. "I haven't eaten in a while. Would it be possible for me to get something to eat?"

"Of course! We're having lunch in half an hour if you're interested. Willa ordered salmon."

I crinkle my nose. I've never been a seafood person.

Jessica laughs. "We can make you anything you want. Just tell me what you'd like and I'll take care of it."

"Can I have pizza?"

She nods. "We can handle that."

I eye the toiletries Jessica brought up for me. "I need to take a shower first."

Frank grabs his paperwork and heads for the door. "I'll leave you to it."

I call out to him before he leaves. "Don't think I've forgotten where we left off."

He rolls his eyes. "Wouldn't dream of it."

I throw back the comforter and stand up. "Do I have any clothes here?" I ask Jessica.

"Yes." She motions for me to follow her. "I'll show you where they are."

Jessica walks toward the middle door and pushes it open, revealing a large closet.

"Wow," is all I can say when I step inside.

It is painted a bright white with rows and rows of white shelving. Clothing racks are scattered throughout. A massive mirror stands in the back corner, its frame a chunky metallic silver. A cushy white chair sits in front of a vanity lit by four ornate light fixtures. One corner of the closet is filled with my clothes from Leviston. The rest of the closet, except for one other rack, is empty. The clothes on the second rack still have tags on them.

"Whose clothes are those?" I ask.

"When we found out you were coming, I bought you some things. I wasn't sure what you were bringing with you given how quickly you had to vacate your apartment."

All of the pieces of clothing Jessica bought for me are beautiful, and I'm guessing expensive too. The cotton on the sweaters is so soft I want to rub the sleeves on my cheek. Everything she picked is something I would buy for myself.

"Your undergarments and pajamas are in here," Jessica says, standing next to a built-in dresser.

She pulls out the top drawer and I see a pair of pink underwear with the word "Saint" written across the back in white letters. I walk over and pick them up.

Jessica smiles. "Those are cute."

"They're not mine," I whisper. "They're Chelsea's."

Jessica's eyes widen. "Oh."

I put the underwear back into the dresser and sit down on the chair in front of the vanity. "Where are the rest of Chelsea's things?"

"At your parents' house." Jessica looks scared to death. She's probably worried I'm about to break down. She may be right.

"Nothing was thrown away?"

"No. Everything went to your mom and dad's except for your clothing and other essential items."

I sigh with relief. "Okay." We sit quietly for a moment before I say, "I'm sorry Jessica. I didn't mean to freak you out."

"Oh my gosh! Don't apologize to me. You've been through hell."

I nod. "I really have."

110

The tears come again. Jessica rushes over and kneels in front of me. She gives me a tight hug.

"You don't know us yet, but we're all here for you," she whispers in a comforting voice.

"Thank you," I choke out.

Jessica stands and hands me a tissue from the box sitting on the vanity.

I wipe my tears and blow my nose. "I think I'll take my shower now."

"Sure thing. In the meantime, I'll order pizza."

The bathroom is even fancier than the closet. A huge soaker tub, a stall shower, double sinks with gold faucets, and tile flooring with golden brown hues. It's the type of bathroom you see in a showcase home.

If I wasn't so damned depressed, I'd be psyched.

I walk over to the double sinks. The countertop is beautiful – marble with golden flakes. When I look above the sinks, I want to see Chelsea's name written in pretty pink script above "her" sink. Instead, all I see is ornate wallpaper with streams of gold flowing through it.

I stand under the scalding hot water in the shower, trying to wash everything away. I sit down on the shower floor, curl myself into a ball, and let the hot water run down my back.

When my fingertips are raisins, I turn off the water and grab a towel. The wall opposite the shower is one giant mirror. Despite the amount of sleep I've had, there are deep purple smudges under my eyes. My wet hair hangs lifeless over my shoulders. I look lost. Broken.

I slip on the white bathrobe hanging from a hook in the bathroom and head for the closet. I search through the dresser until I find a t-shirt and a pair of cotton shorts. I grab one of my hoodies and pull it on over my head. I don't bother to fix my hair or try to look presentable. Seems like too much work.

111

I'm ready to go, but I'm not sure where I'm going. I open my bedroom door and peek my head out.

"Ready for lunch?" a voice asks.

I jump back, startled. I prepare myself for an attack, but stop short when I realize it's just Frank. "Jesus Christ! Are you trying to give me a heart attack?"

He frowns. "Sorry. I came back to take you to the dining room."

"I think I can figure it out," I say in a huff, my heartbeat slowing to its normal pace.

"I wouldn't be so sure about that. This is a big place. I'll get you a map after we eat."

"A map?" I ask as we make our way down a long hallway with white carpet and white walls. Scattered along the walls are photographs of colorful and exotic flowers. We pass two doors on the left, and two doors on the right. Assuming they lead to bedrooms, I don't bother to ask where these doors go.

We turn the corner and I come to a stop when I see two silver elevators. I raise my eyebrow at Frank. "Elevators?"

He hits the down button. "I told you this place is big."

Above the elevators are antique, brass floor indicators. The numbers go from one to twenty in roman numerals. I watch as the dial slowly moves from the number five to the number eighteen.

"We're on the eighteenth floor?"

"Yes."

"How many of these floors does Willa occupy?"

We step onto the elevator and Frank hits the "10" button. It glows a soft yellow when he pulls his hand away.

"All of them."

My jaw drops open. "All of them?"

"Yes," Frank confirms. "See why you need a map?"

"What does she need an entire building for?"

112

A chime sounds when we reach the tenth floor and the silver doors open. I am once again met with opulence. I step out onto white marble flooring. The walls are, of course, a bright white. Two black leather couches rest on a shaggy white rug.

How does Willa keep this place clean?

Frank walks off to the right. "This is where we meet for meals."

I turn to see a massive piece of glass held up by black marble pillars. The rectangular table is surrounded by twenty chairs covered in grey fabric. Despite the number of seats, there are only five place settings. Frank chooses the chair next to the head of the table and motions for me to take the seat opposite him.

Frank answers the question I asked him in the elevator. "This building is more than Willa's office and home. We, I mean witches collectively, bought this building a hundred years ago to be our headquarters. This is our White House, Pentagon, and barracks all in one."

"Why haven't I heard of this place?"

"It's top secret. Not many people know where it is."

Our conversation fades. I play with the edges of the cloth napkin in front of me. Frank and I are too lost in our own thoughts to make small talk. Our silence is broken by the chiming of the elevator.

"Chloe!" Willa exclaims as she exits the elevator. "You're joining us."

She squeezes my shoulders before taking the seat at the head of the table. Her gray hair is still pulled back in a tight bun, but she's changed into a flowing black dress.

She unfolds her cloth napkin onto her lap. "I think we're having fish today."

I shake my head. "I'm having pizza."

Willa smiles. "Sounds delicious. Unfortunately, I'm watching my weight."

"You look good to me."

"Thanks. I've lost forty pounds over the last twelve months."

"Really?"

"Yes. I'm afraid to say I got lazy in my old age."

"Well, you look fantastic," I say truthfully. I'm not sure how old Willa is, but from what I've heard, she may be in her eighties. But if I walked by her on the street, I would guess she's in her sixties, early seventies tops.

Willa clasps her hands together and sets them on the table. "There's something I want to talk about before we eat. I took the liberty of calling in a grief counselor."

Frank nods. "Excellent idea Willa. I'm sure the guys will appreciate it."

"I figured as much. There were quite a few upset men coming in last night."

I continue to play with the edges of the napkin. I hadn't thought about the members of the Guard who were on campus with us. They all liked Chelsea. Once again, I'm so focused on myself, I don't think about anyone else's needs.

Willa reaches out and touches my forearm. "Chloe, he's going to be in the library today and tomorrow if you want to see him."

"Okay." It comes out as a whisper.

"You don't have to go. I just wanted you to know he's available if you want to talk to someone. He was incredibly helpful to me when my daughter died."

Willa told me she lost someone close to her, but I had no idea it was her daughter. In fact, I didn't know Willa had a daughter. I assumed the Verhena wasn't allowed to have a family.

"What was her name?" I ask.

"Vanessa." Sorrow fills Willa's eyes. "She had cancer. I tried every curing spell I could find, but even I couldn't stop it."

I close my eyes, remembering all the spells I tried on Chelsea.

114

"I'm so sorry Willa," Franks says. "I had no idea. When did she pass?"

"Fifteen years ago. She was thirty-five."

I open my eyes when Willa pats my arm. "My husband got me through the worst of it, but the counselor helped a lot. If you decide to meet with him, and you like him, he can come back for as many sessions as you want."

Willa is married?

"Is your husband here?" I blurt out. I immediately regret my question, worried I'm overstepping my bounds.

Willa shows no sign of being offended. "Henry passed two years ago."

"Oh jeez Willa. I'm sorry."

A door in the corner of the room swings open. A woman in her early to mid-fifties walks out holding a tray of food. Jessica is following close behind her with a pizza box.

Jessica smiles as she plops the box down in front of me. "Here ya go. I didn't know what kind of pizza you like, so I ordered cheese. I hope that's okay."

I don't tell Jessica I only want one slice. "It's perfect. Thank you."

I open the lid and breathe in the wonderful aroma. New York style pizza is my favorite, but the thought of actually taking a bite makes me nauseous. I close the lid, worried I'll get sick. Thankfully, no one notices.

"Chloe, meet my mom Beth," Jessica says. "She is Willa's personal chef."

I look over at the woman who walked out of the kitchen with Jessica. She is Jessica's spitting image, except for the years between them. Beth has kind eyes like her daughter and dons the same feminine smile.

When I see what everyone else is having for lunch, I thank God I asked for pizza. A pale pink sliver of salmon rests upon a bed of seasoned green beans. The food looks like it belongs in a fancy restaurant. Too froufrou for me.

Frank peers down at his plate, then gives me his puppy dog eyes. I open the box and hand him a slice of pizza. He folds the slice in half and is about to take a big bite. He pauses when Beth sits down beside him.

"No offense Beth, but I don't think the salmon will be enough."

Beth laughs. "Next time I'll give you double servings."

Jessica takes the seat beside me and everyone digs in. My tablemates attempt the usual lunchtime conversation. The weather, TV shows and world news. But the conversation is stilted at best.

While the others try to maintain normalcy, I sit quietly and force myself to eat pizza. It's delicious and I should be starving, but I can't seem to get more than three quarters of a slice down.

"Do you want something else to eat?" Jessica offers.

I look up and see four pairs of eyes staring at me. I set the remainder of the slice down. "No. I'm fine."

Frank starts to say, "Chloe, you need…" but Willa puts her hand up to stop him.

"If she doesn't want to eat, she doesn't want to eat."

Frank huffs but says nothing.

I'm admiring Willa's ability to shut down my security guard when she turns to me. "If you're going upstate tomorrow Chloe, you need to leave by 10 a.m."

No one asks why I'll be going upstate. They all know it's for Chelsea's funeral.

"Okay."

Frank wipes his mouth with his napkin. "Are we going?"

I nod.

116

He pushes his chair back and stands. "I need to speak with the guys right away."

"The guys?"

"Yes, the Guard. A trip will take a lot of planning. We haven't set a plan in motion yet. We were waiting to see if you want to go."

"I'm going," I confirm.

I watch Frank walk off and get into the elevator. He's left me with three strangers.

"Jessica," Willa says, "why don't you give Chloe a tour of the building when we're finished eating?"

Jessica smiles. "I can handle that."

A tour? I don't want to go on a tour. I want to go back to my room. Actually, I want to go home.

"I'm tired, but thanks for the offer. Maybe another time."

Willa will hear none of it. "Walking around will do you some good. Let Jessica show you the place, then you can retreat to your suite."

I reluctantly agree. How can I argue with the Verhena?

"Don't worry," Jessica says as we embark on the tour, "it's overwhelming at first, but you'll figure out where everything is pretty quickly."

I trudge along behind Jessica. I have no idea what to expect from this tour, but I hope it's brief. Willa and Jessica mean well, but I'm not up for this.

Our first stop is the training facility. It is a huge gym with thick black mats covering hardwood floors. I'm thankful to see blue pads on the walls because slamming me into the gym walls at Leviston was one of Frank's favorite finishing moves.

I nod my head with approval as Jessica points out the state of the art workout equipment and free weights. "Nice. Very nice."

In truth, it's unlikely I'll use the treadmill or an elliptical, but I have to at least pretend to be interested. My attention wanes. I'm too worried about my parents to focus.

Jessica catches my attention though when she says, "In case you're wondering, we have a room that's fireproof."

Images of the dead werewolves in my apartment flash through my mind. "Great," I squeak out.

Next stop is the 8th floor – also known as Guard Headquarters.

The elevator doors open to a large office space. On the left side is a wall of television monitors. Five men sit in chairs watching them intently. With a quick glance, I can see the traffic moving on the city streets outside the building, as well as every entrance and exit to the building. Beth is walking around in the kitchen on one of the monitors and Willa is sitting on a black leather couch reading a book in another.

To the right is a row of desks. Men bustle around reviewing documents, sharing information and talking on telephones. One of them looks up and immediately stops what he's doing.

He pushes out his chair and stands in front of his desk. "Ms. Chloe, how can we help you?"

All of the men, including the men watching the monitors, turn to look at me. When they realize who I am, they all stand at attention.

I want to crawl back into the elevator. "Um…Jessica was just taking me on a tour. Don't let me interrupt your work." I turn to Jessica and hiss, "Let's get out of here!"

As the elevator doors close, I wave good-bye sheepishly to all of the men staring at me.

I put my head in my hands. "Wow. That was embarrassing."

"No it wasn't," Jessica assures me.

"Yes it was. They were expecting some kind of epic speech."

She shrugs her shoulders. "Oh well."

When we stop on the 12th floor, I notice the faint smell of chlorine. "Don't tell me…" I say out loud before the doors open.

And there it is. A pool. The lighting above is dimmed, making the water the center of attention. Beautiful, Spanish style tiling surrounds the pool and flows over the edge into the pool itself. Underwater lights shine through the crystal clear water. Steam rises from the Jacuzzi in the corner. Several chaise lounges and tables are set up throughout the room. Like my suite, one of the walls is nothing but floor to ceiling glass and showcases the city skyline.

"Do you like to swim?" Jessica asks.

"Yes. A lot actually."

"Want to go for a swim now?"

A few laps in the pool sounds wonderful, but there are things I have to take care of first. "Maybe later. I don't mean to be rude, but I'd really like to go back to my suite now."

"Okay. No problem." Jessica tries to sound nonchalant, but she looks disappointed.

"It's nothing personal Jessica, I have to call my parents. I'm worried sick about them."

Her eyes soften. "Absolutely. There's no need to explain. As soon as we get to your suite, we'll call Frank and ask him to bring you a cellphone."

As the elevator ascends, I feel the need to fill the silence. "How long have you worked here?"

"I haven't *worked* here long at all, but I've lived here most of my life."

"Really?"

The elevator doors open to my floor and Jessica leads the way to my room. "Uh huh. My mom came to work here when I was five. She was a single mom without any living arrangements, so Willa moved us into a two bedroom suite on the 14th floor."

"What about school?"

119

Jessica opens the door to my suite. "I went to public school. It's right around the corner."

Interesting. I wonder if it was cool or boring growing up here. I'm about to ask her if she went to Leviston, but she picks up my room phone and punches in three numbers.

"This is Jessica. I need to speak with Frank." There is a brief pause before she continues. "Frank, it's me. Chloe needs a cellphone." Another pause. "To call her parents."

She hangs up a few seconds later. "He's on his way."

"Thanks."

"I'll grab you a copy of the floor guide and the phone extension list."

When Jessica leaves, I stand in front of the windows and watch the city below me. I'd love to be down in the chaos shopping, meeting friends for dinner or catching a show. I'll probably never get to do everyday things like that ever again.

There's a quick rap on my open door. I turn to see Frank.

"Got a few things for you." He lays out a couple pieces of paper and a cellphone. "I ran into Jessica in the elevator and she gave me the floor guide and phone extension list for you."

I walk over and pick up the floor guide. It's a drawing of the building with each floor labeled.

B3 – Shelter

B2 – Quarantine

"Quarantine? What the heck is that for?"

"Holding cells," Frank says casually.

Of course. Because every proper home needs a jail. I continue reading the list.

B1 – Garage

1 – Lobby and reception

2 – Supplies and Surplus

120

3 – Laundry Facilities/Cold Storage

4 – Conference rooms

5 – Guard Housing

6 – Guard Housing

7 – Guard Housing

8 – Guard Headquarters

9 – Guard Office Space

10 – Kitchen/Dining/Sitting Room

11 – Lounge/Living Room/Entertainment Center

12 – Pool

13 – Guest Housing

14 – Staff Housing

15 – Staff Housing

16 – Library/Den

17 – Willa's Quarters

18 – Chloe's Quarters

19 – Storage

20 – Storage/Rooftop access

I'm surprised to see my name is already on the list.

"I get this whole floor to myself?"

"Yes."

"What in the world am I going to do with it?"

Frank shrugs his shoulders. "Whatever you want. Willa has an art studio, her office and a guest room on her floor."

"Where is your room?"

"I'm in a room on the fifth floor."

I put the guide down. "I want you on my floor."

Frank hesitates. "I don't think that will work."

"Why?"

"Because," Frank pauses, "I am a member of the Guard and I need to stay with them."

"But you're my friend too," I plead.

"I know." Frank sighs. "It wouldn't be right Chloe. My job is to protect you. Not to be your friend, as much as I might want to be."

Ouch.

Before I can protest any further, Frank hands me a cellphone. "Here's a new burner phone. There's sixty minutes on it. Will that be enough?"

I nod.

"Alright then, I'll give you some privacy."

"Thanks," I murmur.

I sit down on my bed. Chelsea is gone. It's not safe for me to be around my parents. It's too soon to ask Elliott to come here. And now Frank is bailing on me.

My hand shakes as I dial my home telephone number. Dad answers on the third ring.

He sounds exhausted. "Hello?"

"Dad, it's me."

"Chloe! Oh thank God! Are you okay?" I can hear the relief in his voice.

"I'm okay Dad."

"Are you safe?"

"Yes. About as safe as I can get."

He sighs. "Good. Good."

"How are you?" I'm trying not to get hysterical on the phone with him, but tears roll down my cheeks.

"Awful." My dad chokes up. "You're not supposed to lose a child."

I squeeze my eyes shut. I don't know what to say, so I say nothing. I just sit there and listen to my dad cry. The only other time I've seen my dad cry was at my grandmother's funeral.

"Chloe, sweetheart, please promise me you'll be careful," he says when he's calmed down.

"Dad, you don't need to worry about me."

"Yes I do. You're my daughter. I can't…. I can't lose you too."

This is unfair. My parents have not only lost a daughter, they have to worry about something happening to me. All while fearing for their own lives.

I should be the one they are burying, not Chelsea. If the wolves had killed me, my family would be safe. They would miss me, but they would move on. No more worries about wolves.

"How is Mom?" I ask.

"She's laying down. We had to give her valium."

My poor mom. I wish I could be there for her. "Do you have everything ready for tomorrow?"

It's a silly question to ask, but I want to be sure my sister gets the funeral she deserves.

"I think so. We went to the funeral home and made arrangements. They'll handle it from here."

"What about Rory?"

So help me if Rory and Chelsea are having joint funerals…

"His funeral is a few hours after Chelsea's. I don't think we'll go."

I'm about to tell Dad they shouldn't go to Rory's funeral when I hear my mom's voice in the background.

"Is that Chloe?" she asks.

"Yes, it's Chloe," Dad confirms.

123

I hear her say, "Give me that!" And suddenly she's on the phone. "Chloe?"

"I'm here."

"Listen to me. Don't even think about coming tomorrow. Do you hear me?" Her voice is hard.

"Mom…"

"I'm serious. Do not come tomorrow!"

"You don't want me to come?" I ask, my voice cracking. Does she blame me for Chelsea's death?

"No! Don't you dare put yourself at risk! I cannot, I will not, lose you. Do you hear me?"

I relax when I realize my mom is only worried about my safety. "Yes Mom. I hear you."

"Promise me!" she yells into the phone.

I hesitate. I don't want to lie to her.

"Chloe! Promise me!" She is frantic.

"Okay Mom. I promise. You will not see my face at the funeral tomorrow."

There, that's not really a lie. Is it?

She sighs, relieved. "Good. I love you."

"I love you too Mom."

My dad gets back on the line. "I love you Chloe."

"I love you Dad."

I hang up the phone and find myself staring at the ceiling again. I want to call Elliott, I want to hear his voice, but I don't want to put him in any danger.

Instead of calling Elliott, I find Jessica's number on the extension list and punch it into the keypad. While I don't feel like being social, I don't want to sit alone in my room either.

She answers after the second ring. "Hello?"

124

"Hey Jessica. It's me. Chloe."

She giggles. "I know it's you Chloe."

"Oh, okay."

"What can I do for you?"

"Do you want to go for a swim?" I ask.

"Sure."

"Cool. I'll meet you down there."

"Wait…" Jessica says before I hang up.

"Yeah?"

"I don't remember unpacking a bathing suit last night."

She's right. I didn't have a bathing suit with me at Leviston. "I don't need one," I say finally.

Jessica chuckles. "Your call. I'll see you in a few."

I grab a towel and my bathrobe before heading to the elevator. On my way down the hall, I stop and check out the other rooms on my floor. They are identical in size and shape. Giant, empty squares with bare white walls and tan carpeting. Each room has two standard windows, a ceiling fan and a closet. I ponder what I can do with these rooms as I wait for the elevator to take me to the 12th floor.

If things were different, one of those rooms would have been Chelsea's. Actually, I would have broken through the wall between two of the rooms and given her a suite like mine. We would have turned the other rooms into a living area with a TV, shelves of books, anything we wanted.

But that is never going to happen now.

Jessica beat me to the 12th floor. I find her poolside wearing a cute red bikini.

"Hey!" she says as I walk down the tiled steps to the pool area.

"Wow. This is so nice." I want to say it's so badass, but I don't want to offend Jessica.

125

"I know, right? Willa had it redone ten years ago and it's holding up really well."

I throw my towel and robe on a lounge chair. "Thanks for coming."

"Absolutely. Thanks for inviting me."

"I hope I wasn't interrupting something."

"Nope. I was just watching TV."

I'm not sure what Jessica's schedule is, or what she does, so I ask her.

"I'm glad you asked. My schedule is whatever you want it to be."

I raise an eyebrow. "Doesn't Willa decide that?"

"I'm your personal assistant Chloe. I'll work whatever schedule you want me to."

I'm sorry, what?

"My personal assistant?"

Jessica smiles. "Yes. Your personal assistant."

I must look skeptical because Jessica adds, "Trust me. As the Verhena, you're going to need a personal assistant."

I shrug. "If you say so."

I stand up and start to take off my shirt, then stop. I'm not a bashful person, but Jessica might be. "Will it bother you if I skinny dip?"

Jessica shakes her head. "Not at all. But I should warn you - there are cameras in here."

I scan the room. The cameras are hard to spot in the dim lighting, but I finally see one in the corner of the ceiling.

I walk over to it and stare into the lens. "Frank! Hey Frank!" I shout and wave my arms. "You have thirty seconds to turn that camera off, then I'm getting naked. You got me?"

I stand under the camera and wait until I see the red light turn off.

"All of the cameras better be off!" I yell as I walk away.

Jessica is laughing. "How much do you want to bet one of those cameras is still on?"

"They're going to get an eyeful then." I joke about it, but those freaking cameras better be off.

I take my shirt off with my back to Jessica. I hear a gasp as soon as my shirt is over my head.

Startled, I turn around, ready to spring into action. "What?! What is it?"

Jessica puts her hand up to calm me down. "I'm so sorry. It's just your tattoo. It surprised me."

I glance over my right shoulder. "Crazy, huh?"

Jessica gets a closer look. "I mean, I've seen Willa's, but yours is a little different."

"Really? In what way?"

Jessica's quiet for a minute. "Okay, this is going to sound mean. I think the difference is your tattoo isn't as droopy as hers."

I laugh out loud.

I turn around and Jessica's hand is on her mouth. "Oh God! Please don't tell Willa I said that!"

I'm still laughing. It feels good.

"Don't worry. I won't," I assure her.

I strip down and jump into the pool as quickly as I can, just in case the cameras are still on. The warm water doesn't shock my system as I plunge below the surface. I swim underwater until I reach the opposite wall. I come up for a breath of air, then slip under the water again and swim back toward Jessica.

"Let me see your brand," I say when my head is above water.

I'm guessing Jessica is a dove. She has a bit of spunkiness to her, but she seems too sweet to be a hawk.

Jessica's face goes blank for a second. "I don't have a brand."

"What?"

She shows me her back. Nope, no tattoo there.

"You're not a witch?" I ask shocked.

Jessica uses the ladder to climb down into the pool. "No. I'm a plain old human."

"How did your family get involved with Willa then?"

"It's complicated. My mom is a witch, but my dad isn't."

"Oh."

Jessica nods. "I had a fifty/fifty shot. Unfortunately, I wasn't lucky."

"I don't know," I say, "being a witch isn't that awesome."

She laughs. "Maybe not for you, but I think being a typical witch definitely has some advantages."

I can't argue with her.

We swim and make small talk for half an hour. Jessica is a nice person, laid back and funny. I'm sure she and I will get along fine.

Before leaving the pool area, I use the phone on the wall to call the extension Jessica gave me.

"Yes?" answers a male voice.

"This is Chloe. You can turn the pool cameras back on."

"Understood."

When we're in the elevator, I ask Jessica if I can get a TV for my room.

"Of course. I'll look into it while you're out tomorrow. Depending on timing, we may be able to install it before you get back."

128

The twisting in my stomach returns. "If I make it back."

"You will," Jessica says confidently. "Willa is fantastic at glamour spells. No one will ever know it's you."

I'm sure Jessica is right. Willa is the Verhena, her magic is legit.

But it's not Willa's magic I'm worried about. It's myself. Will I be able to maintain control of my emotions when I see my parents? Or worse, Chelsea's casket? Is there any way I can get through her funeral service without losing it?

When I return to my room, I call Frank.

"Hey Frank," I say when he answers.

"What's up Chloe?"

I twirl the phone cord around my finger. "I've been thinking about tomorrow."

"Okay…"

"It may be best if we just go to the gravesite. I don't know if I'll be able to make it through the service at the funeral home."

"Whatever you want to do, we'll make it happen."

"Thanks." I hang up the phone and stare at the ceiling once again.

Chapter Nine

Jessica wakes me the next morning. I slept like crap and I'm a hot mess.

I walk into the closet, but don't see anything funeral appropriate. I flop down on the chair in front of the vanity and consider not going at all. Wouldn't it be a lot easier that way? Then I can pretend none of this happened. I can tell myself Chelsea is at Leviston, crushing her Curing classes and becoming the amazing witch she was supposed to be.

I'm trying really hard to put on a brave face when all I want to do is curl up in the fetal position. I don't want to go to my sister's funeral. I don't want my sister to be dead. I don't want to see my parents torn apart. There's a part of me that doesn't want to be alive at all.

But I owe Chelsea more than that. I have to be strong. I can't let myself waste away.

Jessica walks into the closet. "Put on whatever you want. Don't worry about hair or makeup either."

"Does Willa's glamour include an outfit?"

Jessica smiles. "It's the works."

Well, getting ready just got a lot easier.

I put on a pair of cutoff denim shorts, a Rihanna t-shirt and a pair of black Chuck Taylors. It's not exactly February weather attire, but if Jessica's right, I won't be wearing this outfit outside.

Jessica and I join Willa, Beth and Frank for breakfast. I'm relieved to see bacon, scrambled eggs and toast. I haven't eaten since yesterday's pizza and my stomach is begging for food.

Despite being anxious about the day ahead of me, I eat my toast, most of my eggs, and a piece of bacon. I'm daydreaming about the funeral when Willa claps her hands together and snaps the fog in my brain.

She looks at me and Frank. "You guys ready?"

"I guess so," I respond at the same time Frank answers, "Yes."

"Stand up," Willa directs as she pushes her chair back. "Now, get your butts over here."

Frank and I do as told.

"I thought about it and I think it's best if I make you look like a couple in their early fifties. That is your parents' age, right Chloe?"

"Yes."

"Excellent. You will look like an average couple from your parents' jobs, neighborhood, bowling league, whatever, who are coming to pay their respects."

Frank nods. "Makes sense."

"Okay then. Stand still."

Willa's face turns into a wall of concentration. I'm not sure what to expect. Will I float into the air and transform like the Beast did at the end of *Beauty in the Beast*? Will electricity shoot out of Willa's fingers and zap me? Will it hurt?

A tingling sensation runs up my arms and legs. It reminds me of the pins and needles I feel when my foot is almost asleep, but not quite. The sensation stops as quickly as it started.

'There!" Willa exclaims with a smile. "All done."

I don't believe Willa has actually done anything until I turn to look at Frank. Well, what used to be Frank. He is now much shorter, has a full head of grey hair and is sporting a mustache. His Under Armour shirt and khakis have been traded in for black dress pants and a gray tweed blazer. Under his blazer is a button-down white shirt with a tie.

"You look hilarious!" I exclaim, then clap my hand over my mouth. I don't know whose voice that was, but it wasn't mine.

"You should see yourself," the new Frank responds in an unfamiliar voice.

I look down. I'm wearing a black dress, pantyhose, and black pumps with a kitten heel. I run over to the windows to see my full reflection. Big eyes, a medium-sized nose, and a lipstick painted smile are my new features. I have red, wavy hair that hits just below my shoulders. I look pretty good for a woman my mom's age.

"This is unreal," I say in my alien voice.

"Tell me about it," Jessica says from the breakfast table.

"Willa, can you turn me into Gisele Bundchen?" I ask excitedly.

The new Frank rolls his eyes. "Because that would be inconspicuous."

Willa laughs. "I save Gisele for myself."

I'm awestruck. "This is so cool."

"Alright," Frank grabs my arm, "let's go wifey."

My stomach rolls. Reality crashes back in. This glamour isn't for fun. It's for my sister's funeral. I don't know if I'm ready for this.

I say good-bye to the ladies and get into the elevator. Frank pushes B2 and the elevator starts to move.

I gaze at my reflection in the elevator doors. "This is too weird."

"I know," Frank agrees. "It's crazy."

The elevator opens to the underground garage and five members of the Guard are waiting for us. They stare at us for a moment, not sure who they are looking at.

"It's me," Frank confirms. "And this is the new Chloe."

The Guard members exchange glances, but roll with it.

"Chloe and I will leave through the auxiliary exit. Cars 1 and 2 leave first, then me and Chloe, and then Car 4. Got it?"

Everyone nods their heads.

"The auxiliary exit?" I ask as we walk toward the opposite side of the garage.

"We don't want to leave from the building's garage. If the rogue wolves know where this building is, they'll follow any car coming out of it."

We stop in front of a concrete wall. "Um, where are we going?"

"Patience my dear," Frank responds.

I stand there waiting for something to happen, but nothing does.

"Frank, I don't mean to be rude…"

I stop talking when the concrete wall in front of us begins moving backwards.

"What the hell?"

Old man Frank smiles. "O ye of little faith."

The wall pushes back about three feet, enough room for us to squeeze through to the other side. As soon as we've cleared the path, the wall starts moving back into place.

"Well that was different." I look around. We are in a parking garage identical to the one we just left. "What is this?"

Frank walks toward a white Toyota Camry. "It's the garage for the office building next to ours. We built an access into it years ago."

The Camry's lights flash as Frank hits the unlock button on his key fob. He takes the driver seat and I ride shotgun.

"How are the other cars going to know when we've left?"

Frank starts the car and shifts into drive. "There are two Guard cars in here with us. They have radios to the other members."

"Okay. So what's the plan?"

"Car 1 has just left the other garage. Hopefully it will draw the attention of anyone watching. Then Car 2 will exit this garage." Frank points to a red Ford ahead of us. Its driver looks like a business man. "Then we will exit, followed by Car 4."

134

"Are they following us to the funeral?"

Frank shakes his head. "No. As we drive through the city, those cars will turn off. Guard members are placed in cars along the route and will follow us until we reach the next set of cars."

I'm impressed. "You've thought of everything, huh?"

Frank shrugs. "We do what we can."

We cruise through New York City. I check the side mirror for any potential stalkers. My heart is racing, but everything seems to be okay. I don't notice the Guard members' cars coming and going and I know it's happening. Surely no one else would recognize their cars. Frank and I are silent, both ready and alert.

Once we're out of the city, I breathe a sigh of relief. After some time, Frank relaxes too. His new shoulders, not nearly as bulky as his real ones, are less tense and he lets one of his hands fall from the steering wheel.

It's odd to see Frank in the form of this older man. If I walked by him on the street, I would never put two and two together. Sitting in the car with him though, I notice certain facial expressions and gestures that I recognize as being unique to Frank. It lets me know Frank is really under the disguise.

I ask him if he's noticed the same about me.

"Honestly Chloe, I haven't paid much attention. I'm on the lookout for any potential danger."

I nod and go back to staring out the window.

"I want to talk to you about something though," he says.

"I'm a captive audience."

"What I said to you yesterday...about being your friend..."

"You mean about *not* being my friend," I correct him, looking straight ahead out the windshield.

Frank sighs. "What I meant to say came out wrong."

"How so?"

135

"I want to be your friend, but I have to remember that I'm also your bodyguard. I can't get too wrapped up in having fun with you."

"If you're my bodyguard, then why can't you stay on the same floor as me? It's boring as hell up there by myself."

Frank shifts awkwardly. "Those rooms are reserved for your personal guests."

"Yes, and you'll be my personal guest."

"I don't think you get what I'm saying." Frank looks at me meaningfully. "Your *personal* guests."

Ohhh.

"I see. So people will think we're doing it if you stay on my floor."

Frank rolls his eyes. "Yep. Chloe's still in there."

I smile. "I get it Frank. I really do. I'm just lonely."

Frank pats my shoulder. "I know you are, but it won't be like this forever."

He's right. As soon as the wolves are eliminated, there will be no need for extra security. Maybe I can even go home.

"Do we have a plan for taking care of the wolves?" I ask.

Frank shifts his weight again. "There is a plan in the works. I'm not a huge fan of it. You won't be either."

"When do I get the details of this plan?"

"We can discuss it on the way home."

"Not even a hint?" I press.

"Not right now Chloe. We have too much to worry about first. I promise on the way home we'll talk about it."

"Yeah right." I slump down in the seat. I'm being put off and I don't like it.

"Trust me, we'll discuss it. I don't have a choice."

"What do you mean?"

136

"Something is happening today while we're gone. The initial stage of the plan will be in full force by the time we get back."

What the hell is he talking about?

I cross my arms. I know Frank won't tell me anything until he's ready, so I don't bother trying to get more answers. Not yet anyway.

"Fine. On the way home then," I say firmly.

I ponder what could possibly be happening today while I'm gone, but give up when I can't come up with a single plausible option.

As I continue watching the world go by, I think of a question. "What did my parents tell their non-witch friends about Chelsea?"

"They told everyone that you, Rory and Chelsea were in a bad car accident. According to the story, you are badly injured, but recuperating at a hospital in Vermont."

Good enough cover story as any I suppose.

I think of another question. "Do the witches know about me? About what I am?"

Frank nods. "Yes. They know."

I'm sure that was a sight to see. The members of my coven were probably shocked as all get out. "Chloe?" I can see them asking. "Chloe from our coven? The girl who used to run around like a maniac? Are you sure?"

After a couple hours, we pass the welcome sign for my hometown. The sun is shining and it's an unusually warm day for February. Frank pulls into the entrance for the cemetery and drives around for a few minutes, then stops on one of the side roads. Down the row of tombstones is a green tent. The telltale sign of an open plot. The mechanism used to lower Chelsea's casket is ready and waiting.

I close my eyes and fight to maintain control.

You can't draw attention to yourself. You must go unnoticed, I repeat to myself over and over again.

137

Frank pulls out his cellphone and checks his messages. "They just left the funeral home. They'll be here in ten minutes."

He turns to look at me and notices I'm staring at the green tent. Motionless.

Frank reaches out his hand and grabs mine. "Are you okay?"

I nod, but say nothing.

"We can turn around. Right now."

"No," I mumble.

"I'm serious," he insists. "If you don't think you can handle it, I'll get us out of here."

"No," I say a bit stronger.

Frank nods his head and turns back to his window. We sit and wait for the procession. I practice breathing techniques while Frank scans our surroundings.

As promised, a black hearse pulls in ten minutes later followed by what seems like an endless stream of cars. Three of my cousins, Rory's brother, and two other male members of our coven lift a coffin out of the back of the hearse. They steady the coffin in their hands and walk toward the green tent.

My parents exit a black limousine. They look awful. My dad is wearing a black suit and a tie Chelsea and I gave him one year for Father's Day. He always told us it was his favorite because it has "I love Dad" written all over it in small white script.

He and my mom are both wearing dark sunglasses. My mom grips onto my dad's arm as they walk toward the gravesite. She is wearing a black dress suit and a wide brim black hat.

I want to run to them and hug them as tightly as I can. Instead, I remain glued to my seat.

"Are you ready?" Frank asks.

I open the car door in response. I inhale the winter air and tell myself I have to keep it together. At least until we get out of the cemetery.

We join the stream of people heading to the gravesite and I slip my arm into Frank's. Willa's plan worked perfectly. We blend in unnoticed with the other fifty-something couples.

We stand toward the back, but I can see my parents seated in the front row of chairs under the tent. They have chosen a dark cherry coffin. It's covered with pink roses, Chelsea's favorite.

A giant picture of Chelsea stands in front of the casket. It's one of my favorite pictures of her. It was taken when we had our senior pictures done in high school. She is laying on her stomach in the grass, propped up on her elbows. Her blue sweater makes her eyes shine and her smile is bright.

Samantha walks to the front of the casket and clears her throat. "It's time for us to say our final farewells. You all said beautiful things about Chelsea at the service and I echo every one of those sentiments. A wonderful girl taken from us too soon."

My mom cries softly into her tissue and my father pulls her against him as he fights to keep his composure.

Samantha continues. "Many of you have asked about Chloe."

I stiffen when I hear my name.

"She is recuperating, and she is now in stable condition. Her prognosis is good, although she is reeling from the loss of her sister."

Some in the crowd nod and look relieved. Others are whispering back and forth to each other, the witches gossiping about the truth.

My mom scans the crowd and I swear she stops on me for a second. I hold my breath until she turns away.

Samantha recites a traditionally Christian prayer, but throws in a few phrases the witches who are present will recognize. After she's done, a small line forms in front of my parents.

The bulk of the crowd begins walking back to their vehicles, but I move toward my mom and dad.

Frank pulls on my arm and gives me a warning look. His eyes are saying, "Don't be stupid."

"I want to give them my regards," I explain.

Frank isn't happy, but he relents. He doesn't want to cause a scene. I walk toward my parents and wait patiently in the line. Frank follows close behind me, ready to snatch me up if I do something stupid.

When I reach my parents, I kneel down in front of them. It kills me that I can't wrap them in my arms and tell them how much I love them. I search their eyes, hoping to see some recognition on their part. Frank nudges my shoe.

I glare at him for a moment, then turn back to my parents. "I'm so sorry for your loss," I choke out.

My mom leans down to give me a hug and softly whispers, "I want you to kill some wolves for me."

I almost fall over. She knows who I am.

I gather myself. "I will," I whisper back.

My dad leans down next. "We love you. Be careful."

I am stunned. Dad knew it was me too.

I want to hold on to them forever, but I need to keep moving. I stand and place my hand on the coffin. Some of the attendees have taken a pink rose off the casket. I take one for myself and quietly say, "Good-bye Chelsea."

Frank takes my hand. We stand solemnly beside the casket a moment longer before I say, "I'm ready to go."

Back in the car, I sit quietly until we are out of the cemetery.

When we hit the main road, I break the news to Frank. "My parents knew it was me."

Frank gapes. "They did?"

"Yes. I don't know how, but they did."

"What did they say?"

I smile. "My mom told me to kill some wolves for her."

"No shit."

140

"Yeah. And my dad told me he loves me and to be careful."

Frank loosens his tie. "Do you think anyone else recognized us?"

"I don't think so." I stop twirling the pink rose in my fingers and smell it. "I have to be strong now Frank."

"You are strong," he responds.

"No, really. I have a lot to take care of. A lot of people depend on me."

"There's a lot of people who will help you too."

I smile. "I know."

Frank pulls into McDonald's and gets in the drive-thru line. "Want anything?"

"Depends."

"On what?"

"Whether the food I eat will go against my own body fat percentage or my glamour's body fat percentage."

Frank considers this. "Good question. I'm thinking this body, not our own."

"Well then, I want a cheeseburger, french fries and a chocolate shake."

Frank laughs. "Going all out, huh?"

"Oh, and an apple pie," I add. A girl needs to take advantage of situations like this.

Twenty minutes later, I've finished off all the junk food I ordered. Frank crumples the wrapper of his fish sandwich and tosses it into the McDonald's bag.

"You ready to talk about the plan?" he asks.

As much as I want to hear all about this covert plan, there's something I have to do first.

"In a minute. Can I see your phone?"

141

"My phone? Why?"

"I need to call Elliott."

Frank frowns. "Now? I don't think that's a good idea."

"Yes, now."

Frank pulls his cellphone out of his back pocket and reluctantly hands it to me. I find Elliott's number and hit the "dial" button.

He answers on the second ring. "Frank? Frank? Is she okay?"

"It's me Elliott."

"Who is this?" Elliott asks.

"It's me. Chloe."

Has he forgotten the sound of my voice already?

"I know what Chloe sounds like. And you do not sound like Chloe."

Understanding finally pings in my mind. The glamour. I don't sound like myself.

"Elliott, it's hard to explain, but I swear it's me."

"Oh yeah? Tell me then, what song did I hum while giving Chloe her tattoo?"

I laugh. *Love Yourself.*

Elliott sighs with relief. "Oh my God. I've been so worried about you."

"I'm okay."

"I have to see you. I need to see for myself that you're okay."

A sad smile crosses my lips. "That's so sweet of you."

"You're my girl! I have to see you. When can I come?"

"You can't."

"What?"

I take a deep breath. "You can't come see me."

There's a pause. "Okay…so I can't come see you right now. Maybe in a week or so when everything has calmed down."

"That's just it. It may never calm down."

"Chloe, come on. Stop this. I need to see you." He's starting to sound desperate.

"Elliott, you need to forget about me."

"Forget about you? Are you crazy?"

I close my eyes. "I'm not crazy. I'm serious."

"Jesus Chloe. Are you breaking up with me?"

"I guess so."

"You guess so? You guess so?"

"I have to go."

"I know what you're doing."

I look out the car window, trying to avoid Frank's concerned old-man face. "If you know what I'm doing, then don't make it harder for me."

"You think you have to keep me safe. To protect me. You don't."

I sigh. "The thing is, I do. I do have to protect you. I can't let anything else happen to the people I care about."

"Let me come to you then. Let me be by your side," he pleads.

"You can't. You're a Reader. You have a responsibility to our people."

"Screw everyone else," Elliott snaps. Then softer he says, "I want to be with you."

"I want to be with you too," I admit, "but we can't. So please, move on. Live your life. Don't get caught up in this mess."

"Chloe, please," he begs.

I close my eyes and take a deep breath. I can't let my resolve crumble. "Don't call me again. I won't take your calls. And don't try to come see me."

"Well this is just great!" he yells into the phone.

"I need to go. I can't have any more distractions."

"A distraction? I'm a distraction?"

I can't keep talking to him or I'll give in. "Be safe. I love you."

I hang up the phone and give it back to Frank. I put my head against the window and start ugly crying. I don't care that Frank is here to see me break down. I have to let it all out.

Frank's phone rings immediately, but he silences it. "You did the right thing," he says after I've calmed down.

"Whatever." I lean the seat back and close my eyes.

I don't need Frank to patronize me right now. I may have done the right thing, but what was left of my heart has shattered.

"Chloe...Chloe...wake up."

I blink my eyes several times. Once they adjust, I realize we're back in the parking garage.

I rub my stiff neck and stretch my arms. "Man, I must have been out a while."

Frank nods, a frown on his new face.

"What's your problem?" I ask.

"We have to talk about the plan."

"Right now? Can't we go inside first?"

Frank grips the steering wheel. "The thing is, the plan is inside."

"What do you mean the plan is inside? Is it written down or something?"

"The plan is a person. People, actually."

144

"People? Who?"

Frank squeezes his eyes shut and pinches his nose. "Man, you're going to hate this."

I sit straight up. "What have you done?"

He sighs. "It wasn't my idea."

"Tell me," I insist. "Who is inside the building?"

"The leader of the werewolves." Frank cringes, knowing I'm about to explode.

"What?!"

"They got here this morning."

"There are werewolves in our building! Is that what you're telling me right now?!" My voice booms in the car.

Frank winces. "Yes."

"We're trying to kill those assholes and you've let them in the building?!"

"Calm down Chloe. Please, I can explain."

"You have two minutes to convince me I should stay or I swear to God I'm walking out of this garage by myself."

Frank launches into his explanation. "Willa has been allies with the leader of the wolves for years, like twenty years. He's been here before, and she visited his home two years ago. He agreed to help us track down the leader of the rogue group. He knows who the leader is and has a way to find him."

"He's a werewolf Frank! We can't trust anything he says. He could be making all of this up and then kill me in my sleep tonight."

"He won't."

"How do you know?"

Frank grimaces. "I read him."

"You read him?" I ask incredulously. "When?"

"This morning."

145

"This morning?! He was in the building with me this morning and you didn't tell me?!"

That's it. I'm out.

I open the car door and sprint toward the garage's exit. Frank swings his door open and chases after me. The damn heels I have on are slowing me down. Frank grabs me by the arms, but I zap him with a power surge. Frank lets go and I start running for the exit again.

"Chloe! Stop!" he yells from behind me.

"Screw you Frank! I thought we were tighter than this."

He catches up and stands in front of me. "Hear me out. Please."

I step to the right to get past him, but he anticipates my move and jumps right too. When I try to go left, he pulls me in tight for one of his signature bear hugs. Other members of the Guard stand around us, waiting to see what will happen.

"I didn't tell you this morning because I wanted to deal with the funeral first. Get that out of the way, and then worry about this."

I stop struggling. My only other option is to hurt Frank, and I don't want to. Even if I am mad as hell. Frank drops his arms and I step away.

Glaring at him, I ask, "You read him?"

"Yes. I wouldn't let Willa drop the wards on the block until I did."

I'm temporarily side tracked. "Willa has wards around the entire block?"

"Yes. A wolf can't get within a half mile of this place."

Good to know.

"What did you see when you read him?"

"He wants to help us. I would know if he is lying."

"Are you sure?"

"Yes."

146

"How can you be sure you can read werewolves?"

"Well, I wasn't at first," he hesitates, "but then I read one of them to be a liar."

My eyes narrow. "Explain yourself."

"Ivan, the pack leader, brought a traitor with him. One of the rogue wolves."

"What? Where is this rogue wolf now?"

Frank looks down at his feet. "In quarantine."

I explode. "You've gone mad! You let a rogue wolf in the building? And left him in our quarantine? You can't honestly expect me to go back in there."

"Just listen. I asked Ivan to bring the rogue wolf so I could be one hundred percent sure I can read wolves. He didn't tell me who it was. If I wasn't able to pick out the rogue wolf, I wasn't letting any of them in the building. But I *was* able to read the bad wolf. Which is how I know Ivan is telling the truth."

Frank always thinks of everything, but I'm pissed. I've been left in the dark and I hate it.

"How many are here?" I ask after a moment.

"Including the guy in quarantine? Four."

"Who are the other three?"

Frank relaxes. "Ivan and his two grandchildren."

"Who's the guy in quarantine?"

Frank shakes his head. "I don't know his name. All I know is he tried stealing documents from Ivan's office. When I read his skin, I saw he was lying about wanting to help us."

I stand in the garage, fuming. I'm not sure what to do at this point. I don't want to go inside the building, but I can't exactly walk out into the city by myself either.

"I don't like being painted into a corner Frank."

He puts his hands on my shoulders. "It won't happen again."

147

"Promise me."

He looks me square in the eyes. "I promise you."

I turn around and head toward the secret access to our garage. "Let's go meet some wolves."

Chapter Ten

When we step inside the elevator, a Guard member informs us Willa and her "guests" are in Conference Room 4. I don't even try to smile when Frank opens the door to the conference room.

The first person I see when I walk in is Willa. She is sitting at the head of a long conference room table. She stands when we walk in. "Ah, they're here."

Everyone in the room follows Willa's lead and stands.

I scan the room and assess the situation. The conference room is like any other boring conference room. The walls are painted a pale tan and a rectangular oak table sits in the center of the room. The table is surrounded by twelve black leather chairs – five on each side and one on each end.

Standing behind Willa are two Guard members in their typical uniform of khakis and polo shirts. They are standing tall and watching everyone in the room attentively.

The Guard member to Willa's right is a mountain of a man. Jessica told me Willa's personal security guard is a beast, but that was not an accurate enough description. The man looks like Bane.

I shift my attention to the group on Willa's left. Immediately beside her is an older gentleman with long, salt and pepper hair that sits below his shoulders. His well-trimmed goatee matches his hair. He is wearing a black suit and leans on an ebony cane with a silver wolf's head on top. His eyes are a brilliant green, bright as a gemstone.

I instantly hate him.

Next to him is a young woman who looks to be my age. She is tall and thin with long, brown hair that reaches the middle of her back. She's in a maroon sweater dress over black tights and knee

149

high black leather boots. Her eyes are the same brilliant green as her grandfather's.

I hate her too.

And finally, on the end is a tall, attractive man. His hair is shaved close to the skin, but I can tell it would be the same brown shade as his sister's if he let it grow out. He is wearing a grey-knit shirt, its sleeves pulled up to his forearms. A black and chrome watch with a huge sapphire face hangs on one of his wrists. His shirt is tucked into his jeans, which hit his black boots at just the right spot. Like the others, his green eyes shine a dazzling emerald.

He is Calvin Klein meets badass. I hate him the most.

Badass Calvin Klein appears skeptical. "This is Chloe?"

"Yes," Willa answers simply, then realizes the source of confusion. "Oh my goodness. Hold on a second."

The tingling sensation I felt earlier today creeps across my skin. When I look down, I'm in my Rihanna t-shirt, cutoff shorts and Chuck Taylors. My blonde hair in a messy bun. Had I known we were going to have company, I might have dressed a little better.

I turn to Frank. I smile when I see he's my bodyguard again. "It's good to have you back."

He returns my grin. "I was beginning to worry we'd be stuck like that forever."

I put my mean face on before re-focusing my attention on the wolves. The young woman's face is frozen in shock, her mouth open and her eyes wide. Ivan is smirking, while Calvin looks unimpressed.

"There! Much better!" Willa exclaims. She waves us over.

When I reach her, she puts her arm around my shoulders. She points to each of the wolves in turn. "Chloe, this is my dear friend Ivan, his granddaughter Whitney and his grandson James. Everyone, this is Chloe and her security guard Frank."

We all stand staring at each other.

150

Ivan extends his hand to me, but Frank takes a step forward, his jaw set tight. Seeing that I do not intend to return his handshake, Ivan drops his hand to his side.

Ivan exchanges a glance with Willa, then tries again. He smiles awkwardly and says, "It's a pleasure to meet you Chloe."

Before I can say the pleasure is all his, Whitney pipes up. "Can we see your tattoo?" she asks in a giddy voice.

Is she serious?

"No you may not," I say through gritted teeth.

Whitney mumbles, "Oh, sorry." She shrinks even more when she sees the angry look on her brother's face.

Willa clears her throat. "Let's sit, shall we?"

We all sit, except for Frank. He stands behind my chair and keeps a protective stance.

"Chloe, I understand your hesitation," Ivan says.

I tilt my head to the side. "I doubt it. You can't possibly understand how I feel about you. If you did, you wouldn't be here."

He frowns. "We were very sorry to hear about your sister. If I could turn back time and change it, I would."

"Why are you here?" I ask, trying to remain unmoved by what seems to be genuine sympathy.

"We're here to offer our assistance. We want the rogue wolves eliminated as badly as you do."

"Again, I doubt it. Seems to me if you had controlled your people properly, we wouldn't be in this situation."

James pounds his fist on the table. "How dare you! You don't know anything about it little girl."

Did he just call me little girl?

Ivan scolds his grandson. "James! Hush."

151

James keeps going. "You have no idea what you're up against. You should be begging us to help you. Someone of your abilities and immaturity cannot handle this on your own."

My chair leans back ever so slightly as Frank strengthens his grip on the top of it.

I've had enough of these wolves. "What do you know of my abilities and maturity level?"

"I know enough," James huffs.

Oh really?

"I like your watch," I say calmly.

"What?" he asks, confused by the sudden change in topic.

I smile. "Your watch. I like it."

"What are you talking..." James stops and looks down at his wrist. His watch is encased in ice.

I smirk.

"What the hell?" James taps the watch with his pointer finger. His attempts to break the ice are futile.

"I thought you'd like an iced-out watch," I explain with a cocky grin.

A laugh escapes Whitney's mouth. She bites down on her lower lip when James glares at her.

Willa extends her hand and pats my arm. "Enough Chloe."

I roll my eyes. "Fine."

Except I'm not done playing yet. For a second, James's watch catches fire. He throws his chair back and waves his arm in the air frantically. He stops when I put the fire out.

"There, all better," I say in a singsong voice.

He growls at me. "You bitch."

Frank starts to move, but I grab his arm.

I smile at James again. "You've got it all wrong. I'm a witch, with a 'w'''".

Poor Whitney is trying desperately to hold back a fit of laughter.

"James," Ivan snaps. "Apologize. Now."

James looks at Ivan in disbelief. "She set my watch on fire! She could have killed me!"

Such a drama queen.

"You were never in any real danger. If I wanted to kill you, I would have."

James chortles. "Oh please. You have no control over your abilities."

"Yes I do," I argue back.

"Really? Is that why you blew a wall out of an apartment?"

I slam my hands on the table and stand up. I point a finger at James and give him my best evil glare. "Don't you ever, ever talk about that day again! If you do, or if I hear my sister's name cross your lips, so help me God, you will be a pile of ash just like those other assholes I incinerated. You got me?"

James stands across the table fuming. Both of us locked in a death stare.

Finally, Willa steps in. "James. Chloe. Look at me."

We both slowly turn to look at Willa, neither wanting to be the first to give in.

Willa's face is distraught. "Please. Enough of this. We won't make any progress like this."

Ivan nods. "Willa is right. We need to be a united force. It's not going to be easy, but we don't have to make it harder."

James and I sit down, both crossing our arms over our chests. I give him the side eye until Ivan suggests he share his family story with me.

Willa approves. "Excellent idea Ivan."

"As you know, I am the leader of the werewolf pack. I have held the position since I was twenty-five years old. Unlike witches, our leadership passes down in a hierarchy. My father was the pack leader, as was his father, and so on and so on."

Ivan's eyes glaze over, lost in his own story. "I have two sons - Richard and Julian. Whitney and James are Julian's children."

Whitney smiles at me when Ivan says her name, but I ignore her.

"My eldest son Richard is standing in as pack leader while I am gone," Ivan explains. "Richard does not have any children. When he passes, the position of pack leader should go to his younger brother - Julian. But for reasons I will explain to you, Julian will never be our pack leader."

I look at Whitney and James. So these two are in line for pack leader. I know very little about werewolves, but I believe only a male can hold the position. Which means douche bag James will be in charge when Ivan and Richard step down or pass away.

Great.

"Julian was never happy being second fiddle," Ivan continues. "He could have held many high ranking positions in our pack, but he wanted to be pack leader. At one point, he even tried to kill Richard so he would be next in line."

Ivan pauses and rubs his temples. This is obviously a sore topic. If I didn't despise him, I'd feel sorry for him.

"Julian left our pack six years ago. He left my grandchildren behind without any word of where he was going. We tried finding him, but it was no use."

I glance over at Whitney and James. Whitney wears a small frown, her eyes focused on her grandfather. James is watching his grandfather as well, but his face shows nothing more than casual indifference.

Ivan sighs. "A year ago, when we found out the new Verhena was killed..."

I interrupt. "Her name was Barbara."

154

Ivan nods. "Yes, Barbara. When we heard about Barbara's murder, I reached out to Willa to let her know the act was not authorized by myself or anyone in my pack."

I turn to Willa and she confirms Ivan's statement. "We've been working together ever since Barbara's death to find Julian," she explains.

"What makes you think you'll be able to find him now?" I ask.

"There's been a bit of a development." Ivan looks at James. "Julian has reached out to James."

James's face is holding its emotionless gaze. I look down meaningfully at his scorched watch and smirk. He grits his teeth when he notices my expression, then quickly returns to his stone face.

I shift my attention back to Ivan. "So what's the plan?"

"James is keeping in contact with his father. We don't know where Julian is, but we're hoping we'll get to a point when Julian trusts James enough to reveal his location."

"Won't that all fall apart when Julian realizes James is here? When he sees you're helping Willa?"

Ivan shakes his head. "Julian already knows James is here with me."

"What?" I ask in disbelief. I turn to James, "You told your dad you're here? Why?"

"I told my father I'm here on a reconnaissance mission. He believes I tricked my grandfather into bringing me here so I can spy on the new Verhena."

I put my hands up. "Wait, wait. Your father knows I'm here?"

"Yes."

I glare at Ivan and Willa. "Are you crazy? I thought my location was supposed to be top secret!"

Neither say anything.

I look over my shoulder at Frank. "Did you know about this?"

His face reveals it all. He knew.

I turn back to the others. "Let me get this straight. We've spent months trying to keep my location a secret and now it's okay for my biggest enemy to know where I am?"

Ivan tries to explain. "Chloe, when your identity was put online, you were outed."

I huff. "That may be true, but did you have to tell him exactly where I am?"

James interjects. "My dad knew you were here. We didn't have to tell him anything."

"How?" I ask.

James responds again. "It doesn't take a rocket scientist to figure out the Guard would bring you here. It's the safest place for you. You should have been here the entire time."

Frank's grip tightens on my chair again.

I close my eyes and take a deep breath. Julian knows where I am. I hope Willa's wards will keep him out, but as I learned the hard way, wards are not fail safe.

I open my eyes when I've gathered my thoughts. "Okay. Your dad knows I'm here. He also knows that you two are here." I point to James and Whitney.

"Yes," James answers.

"And he thinks you are here to double-cross me?"

James nods. "He thinks I'll give him inside information about you, Willa, the Guard, the entire operation."

"But you're actually double-crossing him?"

"Exactly," Whitney answers this time.

I shoot her a look and she wilts. This girl needs to work on her backbone.

I ask the question again in a different way. "You expect me to believe you are going to double-cross your own father to help me?"

James doesn't hesitate. "I expect you to believe I'm double-crossing my father to help my people."

James is making it clear he isn't doing any of this for my benefit.

"Chloe," Ivan says, "we are here because our people don't want a war with you. My son has found a group of lunatics and rebels to follow his lead. Our pack is terrified of what a war with the witches could mean. We are strong and smart, but we can't compete with magic. Especially the type of magic you and Willa possess. A war with you would mean the end of my people."

"Then why does your son insist on pursuing one?"

"He's unstable. He always has been. The only positive thing he has ever done is leave me with two wonderful grandchildren." Ivan reaches out and grabs Whitney's hand. "He doesn't understand what he's doing. He thinks if he defeats the witches, he will usurp my older son and take the pack leader position."

I sit quietly for a minute and consider everything they've said. They could be a tremendous help to me, if for no other reason than finding out Julian's location. I can't find any glaring holes in their story, but more importantly, Willa and Frank trust them.

"You're sure it is Julian who is behind all of this?" I ask.

Ivan nods. "Yes."

"How? How are you sure?"

"Two ways," James answers. "First, he gave me details about Barbara's death he wouldn't know unless he was involved. He also bragged about killing your sister."

I cringe at this.

James continues unfazed. "Also, we've seen the surveillance video of your apartment prior to the power going down and footage from the other cameras at Leviston. My dad is in the backseat of the getaway vehicle."

157

I'm momentarily frozen by the thought of footage from our apartment. What exactly is on it? Did the wolves shut the power down before or after they entered the apartment? Are my sister's last moments caught on tape?

I shiver, then refocus on the conversation.

"One of the men in your apartment was a cousin of ours who went missing at the same time as our dad," Whitney says. Realizing I'm the one who killed her cousin, she quickly adds, "We didn't like him anyway."

I shake off the mental image of charred bodies and turn to James. He is the one I need to worry about.

"You're sure your readings are right Frank?" I ask without looking away from James.

Frank doesn't hesitate. "Yes."

My eyes burn into James. "How do I know I can trust you?"

He returns my stare, green eyes glowing. "You don't."

We lay out the initial steps of our plan for the remainder of the meeting. James is going to return to his home in the west and bring back five of his best men. Frank will read each one of them before they are allowed to enter the building. I also insist Frank read James again when he returns.

"Just to be on the safe side," I explain.

James is annoyed by this, but agrees.

In the meantime, Whitney and Ivan will work with me and Frank to prepare for potential combat with werewolves. James will stay in contact with his father and maintain their relationship. He will give Julian false updates about my progress. All with the goal of Julian revealing his location. Once he does, we attack.

This all sounds good, in theory. But Ivan admits his son is a wild card and the game can change at any moment.

I glance at the clock on the wall and see that it's 9 p.m. I'm absolutely exhausted.

Willa must sense my tiredness. "It's been a long day for all of us. Why don't we call it a night?"

"Agreed," Ivan says. "We have the basic idea of where we need to start. Anyone have anything they want to add?"

We all shake our heads no.

"Alright then, I'm out of here," I say. Frank pulls my chair out and I stand up. I stretch my arms to the sky and yawn.

James stands next. "I'm off to the airport."

"Now?" Whitney asks.

"Yes, now. The sooner I get out of here, the sooner I can get back."

"Okay." Whitney seems disappointed to be left behind. Not that I blame her. She is in enemy territory.

We all exit the conference room and head for the elevator.

I can't help but snicker when I hear Whitney say, "Man, I smell burnt hair."

The next morning, I head down to breakfast in my pajamas. I don't see the point in putting clothes on when I'll be changing into my training gear immediately after we eat.

My usual dining companions are already seated, but I'm annoyed when I see Ivan and Whitney are at the table with them. I wondered how chummy we will be with the wolves while they are here, and I guess I have my answer.

I say a general "hi" to the group and they all return the greeting. Everyone is chowing down on pancakes, but I won't be indulging with them. Beth brings me my usual bowl of strawberry oatmeal, a Greek yogurt and a banana.

I thank her and dig into my oatmeal.

159

"Good morning Chloe. Did you get a good night's sleep?"

I look up and see Whitney with a big smile on her face.

Ugh. I can't stand morning people.

I shrug my shoulders. "I guess so."

Jessica turns to me. "Your TV is being installed today."

"Sweet!"

"And while you are at training, I'm going to visit a few stores to see if I can find furniture for your office."

"My office?" I ask in between spoonfuls of oatmeal.

"Yes, your office. I'll bring back photographs of different furniture configurations and you can let me know what you like best."

"Okay." I'm totally confused. I'm trying to kill werewolves. What do I need an office for?

Jessica continues, "And, if you don't care, I'll order you the same desktop computer and tablet I got Willa not too long ago. They were a great price and they work wonderfully."

"They are fantastic Chloe. I think you'll like them," Willa affirms.

I set down my spoon and grab the banana. "Sounds good to me."

The conversation switches to news stories, celebrity gossip and weather patterns. While everyone is chatting, I ponder my future office. I don't think I need one, but it will be nice to have internet access. Plus, I have four empty rooms on my floor. Might as well fill one of them with office equipment.

I stand up from the table. "I'm heading upstairs to change and then I'll be down for training."

"Oh, you don't plan on training in that?" Frank asks.

I glance down at my cotton t-shirt and pink plaid pajama pants. "I guess this will work. I mean, I can kick your ass in just about anything."

160

Frank rolls his eyes, but doesn't return the jab.

I change quickly and hit the gym fifteen minutes later. I walk to the center of the mats to stretch. I close my eyes and begin a Pilates routine I have memorized.

I'm about halfway through the routine when I hear someone walking toward me. I open my eyes and do all I can to not sigh loudly.

It's Whitney. She's wearing skin-tight black yoga pants with a hot pink tank top. Her hair is pulled up into a high ponytail. She has on jewelry and full makeup. She looks like a member of the Real Housewives of New York City gym.

"Hey Chloe!" she says, her ponytail swaying side to side behind her.

I keep stretching. "Hey," I respond with much less enthusiasm.

"Is it okay if I stretch out with you?"

"Yeah. Sure." What am I supposed to say? No?

As I move through my flow, Whitney copies my movements. I don't know if I should laugh or be pissed. She's trying very hard to play nice with me, but I can't be bothered.

After a few minutes, Frank saves me. "Alright Chloe. Let's go."

Whitney is right on my tail as I walk over to Frank.

"What's on the agenda for today?" I ask, anxious to get started.

"Ivan and Whitney are walking us through werewolf fighting techniques." Frank waves Ivan over, who's been standing against the wall.

Ivan slowly makes his way over to us, leaning heavily on his cane. The softness of the gym mats doesn't help his stability. Nice to see we've brought in some real heavy weights. I'd find this hilarious if my life wasn't at stake.

Ivan reads my thoughts. "I may look rough young lady, but I created our wolf training and fighting protocol. So I know a thing or two. And this one," he points to Whitney, "trained side by side with her brother when they were young."

I give Whitney another onceover. She is in great shape, but she doesn't look like much of a fighter. Although to be fair, I probably don't either.

With Ivan's instructions, Whitney goes through combat techniques with me and Frank. Like fighters shadowboxing in the ring, we are not landing full blows or doing takedowns, just moving through the steps. When we've got some of the moves down, Frank shoos Ivan and Whitney off the mat.

"You ready?" he asks.

I nod my head. "Bring it."

Whitney gasps as Frank and I charge toward each other. I summon my power spells and make myself ten times stronger. We practice the moves Whitney and Ivan showed us and incorporate some of the moves Frank has already taught me. I'm spent and exhausted after twenty minutes of going full force.

I start to walk off the mat, but Frank stops me. "Where are you going?"

I turn around to see him standing with his hands on his hips. "Aren't we done?"

"Not quite."

I drop my head, but make my way back to him.

"This time," he instructs, "I want you to use nothing but magic to stop me."

Sounds easy enough. Until he says, "But you can't freeze me in place or use fire."

Dammit. Those are my go to tricks!

I quickly rack my brain, trying to think of other techniques I can use.

"Time's up!" Frank yells.

162

He charges toward me and I temporarily freeze.

Whitney screams, "Move Chloe!" and breaks me out of my stupor.

Remembering what Dean Lucas taught me, I run toward the closest wall. I leap out of the way just before Frank grabs me. I plant my feet and hands on the wall. I scramble up and climb high enough to be out of Frank's reach.

Frank stares up at me from ten feet below. "That was good."

Whitney cheers as I climb down. "You looked like Spiderman!"

I smile, proud of myself.

"Okay, something else this time," Frank says.

I frown. "I don't know if I have anything else."

Frank gives me a knowing look. "Which is exactly why we need to work on diversifying your skills. You are obviously great at freezing someone in place and shooting fire, but you need more tools. The climbing thing is good, but only if you have access to something to climb on, right?"

No response is really required, but I still say, "Yeah."

"For the next few days, we're going to work on learning more magical combat techniques. I can teach you some new power moves and other members of the Guard will teach you new skills too. Willa is also going to spend a lot of time with you showing you all she knows."

"Sounds good."

Frank claps me on the back. "Okay. Go grab a bottle of water and then follow me. I want to show you the fireproof room."

Our group, because of course Whitney and Ivan have to come with us, heads to the back corner of the gym. Frank takes us to a small room that is completely walled off from the rest of the training facility. There is a glass cutout in one wall allowing you to see inside the room.

"This room is completely fireproof. You can practice your fire skills as much as you want in there," Frank explains. "Wanna give it a try?"

Everyone looks at me expectantly.

I don't want to practice in front of the group. It's weird. Plus, my fire skills have only been truly impressive once - when I killed the werewolves.

"Not right now," I answer. Hiding my anxiety, I add, "Ivan yelled at me the last time I used fire."

Ivan and Whitney both smile and the subject is dropped.

I say good-bye to everyone and return to my room. I'm not sure what to do with myself after I'm done with my shower. Jessica is still out shopping; Frank is with the Guard; and Willa has retreated to her suite. Whitney told me I can catch up with her this afternoon, but no way in hell I'm doing that.

She seems nice enough, but I'm not interested in making friends with Whitney. I'm not interested in making friends with anyone. I've been like this my whole life. I always had Chelsea. Who needed friends when I had her?

I turn on the new TV mounted on the wall across from my bed, but nothing is on. I find myself thinking of Elliott. Is he branding someone today? Or hanging out at home in Vermont? Does he miss me like I miss him? Has he called Frank's phone and asked to speak with me?

I'm about to give in and ask Frank for a burner phone when Jessica knocks on my bedroom door. I'm grateful for the distraction. We go through the pictures she took on her cellphone and pick out office furniture. We discuss paint colors, office supplies and art for the walls. We manage to kill the bulk of the afternoon.

I never thought time could move this slowly.

The next four days are as monotonous as the first save for my training sessions.

164

Ivan and Whitney continue to supervise our combat training and add in things here and there. I also meet with a different Guard member each day and they show me a new skill. Some of the Guard members show me fighting techniques, while others show me healing and protection spells.

I don't tell Frank, but I'm a bit concerned about my fire magic. I thought this was my strongest skill, but when I go into the fireproof room, I feel like I've regressed terribly. I'd be great at starting a campfire, but I don't know how I ever blew the wall out of a building.

I took a stroll around the library yesterday and saw a few interesting titles about the history of wolves. I considered reviewing them, but went back to my room and took a nap instead. Funny how exciting sleep sounds when you're bored out of your mind.

Willa is trying very hard to make me happy. She and I are different people though. And it's not because of age. She is a pacifist by nature, dove-like. I'm not like that at all. Willa wants to talk to me about keeping the peace and making others happy. All I want to talk about is how we are going to take down the wolves.

Ivan and Whitney have proven to be fine housemates, but I don't spend time with them outside of meals and training. I get the sense Whitney is as restless as I am, but at least she gets to go outside the building if she wants to. I'm stuck in here.

Jessica is the only person I feel any kind of connection with. She is fun and does what she can to make me feel at home. But this is also her job. Sometimes I feel like she gets paid to be my friend. Plus, Jessica can go out. Again, not homebound like me.

I've continued my skinny dipping sessions. Every night around 10:30 I go down to the pool and swim laps for twenty minutes. As soon as I walk in, the camera lights go off. I don't have to ask anymore, the Guard already knows me so well.

I push hard in the pool tonight. I'm frustrated about everything. My fire training; being stuck in this building; and the urge to reach out to Elliott. The worst part is how bad I miss Chelsea. I cry every night. I manage to hold it in all day, but when I lay down to sleep, I think of her.

When I'm done with my laps, I rest on the side of the pool. I cross my arms on the tile ledge and rest my head on them like a pillow. I let my legs float out behind me and slowly catch my breath.

Suddenly, a flash of light catches my eye. At first I think it's a camera flash. After a second I realize it's lightning. The end of February is an unusual time for a thunderstorm, but it has been unseasonably warm.

I lift my body out of the pool and walk toward the glass wall. I've been assured the windows are tinted and no one can see in, so I don't bother to grab a towel or my robe.

I stand in front of the glass and watch the lightning crack across the sky, its blue light illuminating the room. Raindrops hit the glass and slide down in snake-like patterns. Below me, people on the sidewalk are jogging to avoid the rain. Some struggling with umbrellas, others hiding under overhangs and canopies.

Black clouds move across the midnight blue sky. The moon hidden somewhere behind them. Thunder rolls on the other side of the thick glass.

I extend my right hand and press my palm against the glass. I wish I was outside. I wish I could run in the rain with the people below me.

Standing here in this moment, high up in the sky with the storm clouds, I can't help but be moved by the power of Mother Nature. A force even witches cannot control.

I don't know how long I stand like this waiting for the storm to pass. At one point, chills run up my spine and I feel like someone is with me. I turn to look, but no one is there.

When I can no longer see the lightning strikes in the distance, I put on my robe and head for the elevator.

I call the Guard. "The pool is all clear."

"Understood." I'm about to hang up, but the male voice says, "Ms. Chloe?" This is the first time one of the Guard members has said anything more than "Understood" when I call.

I press the phone against my ear. "Yes?"

"Frank wants me to let you know James and his men have arrived. They all passed his test."

Great. More werewolves to deal with.

"Okay. Thank you."

"Goodnight Ms. Chloe."

"Goodnight."

The next morning, I'm relieved to see James is not at the breakfast table. I can tolerate Ivan and Whitney; I don't think I can put up with him.

Despite his absence, James's name comes up rather quickly.

"James and his men are joining us for training today," Frank tells me as I pull the lid off my yogurt.

"Can't wait," I mutter.

"My brother is an excellent fighter. Much better than me. He can teach you a lot," Whitney says in his defense.

Willa looks at me expectantly, like she's waiting for me to agree with Whitney. When I don't, she does it herself. "I'm sure he will be incredibly helpful."

Frank and I exchange a silent glance, both wary of what James has planned for us.

As promised, James and five men are in the training center when I arrive. All six turn to look at me. I glare as each of them gives me a onceover.

"Yeah, I'm little," I want to shout, "but I will kick your ass!"

I stay quiet. Let them underestimate me. I've come to learn it will be an advantage later.

167

Frank walks over and joins me as I approach the group. All of the men are wearing black tank tops with black Adidas training pants and white shell toe shoes. They look like they're about to bust out some breakdancing moves. I have to admit though, they are all well-built and attractive. Where were all of these hot guys when I was just a normal witch?

James doesn't bother to say "hi" or ask me how I'm doing. Which is fine with me. I don't want to chit chat with him either. Instead, he goes right into introducing all of the wolves to me. I'm awful at remembering names, but I'll do my best to remember Ben, Mark, Tim, Andy and Mike.

"Whitney and my grandfather told me a little about your training over the last few days. Sounds like it hasn't been anything intense," James says to Frank.

"We haven't done full-on combat with Whitney or Ivan. Whitney wasn't comfortable with all out exchanges and Ivan isn't healthy enough for it," Frank explains.

James nods. "I get it. I do. But we've got to ramp things up or she'll never be ready."

Frank is about to respond, but I interrupt their conversation. "Hello! You realize I'm here, right?"

They both turn to look at me.

"Sorry Chloe." Frank steps back to allow me to join their circle.

James clenches his jaw, then continues talking to Frank. "All I'm saying is pretend combat won't do any good."

"If you think I'm going to let you or your buddies attack her, you're crazy!"

I put my hand up. "Enough of this. What are you proposing?" I ask James.

"I say we let my boys turn into their Were forms and really practice combat."

I nearly come out of my skin when Frank roars, "Absolutely not!"

168

James puffs his chest and walks closer to Frank. "You can't keep her in a castle forever. She needs to know what she's up against."

They are nose to nose now. Men. So ridiculous. I step between them and push them apart. They both recede easily enough.

"This is the stupidest thing I've ever seen." I glare at the both of them. "We're supposed to be working together, right?"

The wolves against the wall talk quietly back and forth. Like me, they're probably thinking this is a tremendous waste of time.

I pull Frank by the arm. "Come with me."

We walk a few feet away and convene quietly.

"No way they're going to transition in here," Frank hisses.

I'm not ready to see that either. I've never seen a werewolf in its Were form. Even the men who killed Chelsea were still in their human form.

"How about this?" I suggest. "We'll agree to let them work with us as a full pack. To show us what the pack combat technique looks like. We'll do that for a few days and if we feel like we can trust them, we'll let them transition."

Frank considers this. "Fine."

"This was all your idea, remember?"

Frank frowns. "Not *all* my idea."

"We need their information. We need to work with them," I reason.

Frank nods and walks away. He and James talk while I stretch out. The other wolves join me when they see me warming up.

One of them, Ben I think, extends his hand. For the first time, I return a wolf hand shake. His hand is warm and strong.

"Thanks for letting us in," he says with a smile.

"What can I say? I'm a glutton for punishment."

169

Ben is about to say something else, but his smile drops when James approaches.

"We're not here to gossip," James snarls.

Ben scoots away after muttering, "Sorry."

I stick my tongue out at James when he turns his back to us and a few of the wolves laugh. James whips around to see what we're laughing at, but we all resume our warmups.

It's not the most mature thing I've ever done, but I want the wolves to see I'm not taking shit from James. He is not my boss. This is my house.

Chapter Eleven

Training the next few days is exhausting. At any given time I have three to five wolves coming at me. Fending off all of them is a challenge. I have to use a lot of magic and by the end of our combat training sessions, I'm completely spent.

My healers are a huge asset. They can fix any injury in seconds. I had a nasty fall yesterday that may have broken my pinky finger. I gritted my teeth and refused to cry as I waited for the healer. I cannot let these men see me break down.

My magic training is going fairly well. I've learned how to put a protective bubble around myself, to shoot electricity from my hands, and enhanced my ability to move objects without touching them. It's all coming at me fast, but I'm doing the best I can.

One thing I've had zero luck with is Willa's glamour spell.

"It will come," she keeps telling me.

I'm not so sure.

After magic training, it's dinner time. Then I hang out with Jessica in the "Entertainment Center", i.e. a room with a huge TV, games and a ton of movies. Jessica invited Whitney to join us one night after dinner and Whitney has come every night since.

I am not thrilled about Jessica asking Whitney to join us. I fight with the wolves all day long. I don't want to hang out with one in my free time. I let it go when Jessica tells me how lonely Whitney is.

I think what annoys me about Whitney is her neediness. She's so desperate for attention and it bothers me. She is over the top nice and that's not my personality at all. Chelsea would have loved Whitney. Me, not so much.

Being in the pool is my favorite part of the day. I find the water relaxing, like a getaway. I'm not thinking about combat training or being the Verhena while I'm swimming. I'm too focused on my breathing as my hands and feet glide through the water to worry about anything else.

On the fifth day of training with the wolves, I walk into the gym to find Frank and James arguing with each other. Again.

I glance at the other wolves and roll my eyes. They all give me "yeah, we know" looks.

"What are you two fighting about today?" I ask loudly to get their attention.

Frank and James turn to look at me. They're both scowling.

James talks first. "It's time to up the training. It's time for you to see a werewolf in action. Frank doesn't agree with me."

Frank crosses his arms. "It's unnecessary. I do not trust any of you to fight with her in Were form."

I grit my teeth. "What you really mean is you don't trust *me* to fight a werewolf."

Frank drops his arms. "That's not what I'm saying."

"Yes it is," I press.

"No, it's not," he argues back.

"And you," I turn to James, who has a smirk on his face. "How do I know these wolves have enough self-control to stop attacking if they get an advantage? You're asking me to put my life in the hands of strangers."

"Exactly," Franks says from behind me.

"Is that your only concern?" James asks.

Umm, that's a pretty big concern in my book.

"Yes," I answer.

James shrugs. "In that case, I'll do it."

He takes off his tank top and throws it aside. I pause momentarily to take in the hotness that is James. Of course he has six pack abs. Of course his body looks chiseled out of stone.

I hate him. I hate him so much.

"Wait, you're going to do it?" Frank asks, sounding as surprised as I am.

This is the first and only time James has volunteered to fight with me. He usually stands around barking instructions at everyone and yelling at me.

"Yes," James answers simply as he takes off his shoes.

When he starts taking down his pants, Frank puts his hands up. "Whoa! What are you doing?"

"I don't want to rip my pants. We only brought two hundred pairs of these." James grins and the wolves laugh.

Wait a second, did James just crack a joke? He is chocked full of surprises today.

James steps out of his Adidas pants and stands in front of us in nothing but black boxer briefs.

"Won't those rip too?" Frank asks.

Before James can answer, I interject. "He wishes."

James shoots me a look before responding. "These will stretch. They'll be fine."

A part of me is truly disappointed to hear that.

"Are you ready?" James asks me.

I'm not sure I am, but I straighten my back and take a deep breath. "Yes."

Everyone stands back against the wall as James slowly moves toward me. His graceful movements remind me of a tiger stalking its prey.

Suddenly, his skin ripples. I stare in horror as James begins to pulsate and expand. All over his body, hair begins to sprout from

173

his skin. I'm struck with the memory of a movie or music video I saw as a kid. I used to run from the room screaming when it came on. I'd really like to do that now too.

James's face twists and contorts. A long snout with massive white teeth sits where James's mouth and perfect smile used to be. The only part of him I recognize are his brilliant green eyes. James is no longer James.

A deep growl rumbles in the werewolf's chest as it grows in width and height. I wait for the beast to fall down onto all fours, but it doesn't. It stands upright and is at least seven feet tall. It's a terrifying sight.

I see the werewolf run at me, but I'm paralyzed. I can't seem to get my thoughts straight. The werewolf hits me full force on the shoulders and slams me onto the ground. My head bounces off the mat and I struggle to maintain consciousness.

The beast sniffs my throat and I hear a guttural laugh from deep within its chest. "And just like that…you're dead." I hear James in there, but the voice is a deeper, crueler version.

I should be scared to death, but the taunting pisses me off. My haze is lifted when I remember it is James, and not some terrifying beast, on top of me.

I hear Frank yelling, "Get off of her!"

I only have a few seconds before Frank jumps in to help me. I have to act fast. I summon my strength and power spells. I put my hands on James's chest and push as hard as I can. I'm not sure if it's working at first, but then his body flies across the room and slams into the wall.

James shakes his head for a second, but is relatively unfazed. He growls and comes at me again.

Yes, that's right my dear. Run right into my trap.

When James is five feet away from me, I put up my hand and freeze him in place. Everyone in the gym is silent, stunned by the sudden change of events.

174

I approach James's frozen figure and reach up to gently touch his face. His mouth immediately snaps and his eyes move from side to side. He tries to move the rest of his body, but he can't.

I smile. "And just like that…you're dead."

I turn my back on James and walk over to Frank. "I train with him from now on."

"Are you crazy?" Frank asks in disbelief. "I'm pretty sure he wants to kill you."

"Which is exactly why I need to train with him."

Frank sighs. "I never knew you were a masochist."

"If I want to be the best, I have to train with the best."

One of the wolves walks over. "Um, excuse me. Chloe?" he asks sheepishly.

I give him a big smile. "Yes?"

"Are you, um, going to let him go?" The wolf points over to the still frozen James.

"Oh yeah, sure." I wave my hand again and James falls to the ground. He begins to shift back into his human form.

"Well, I could stay and gloat, but I think I'll go take my nap now," I announce.

I make a bee line for the exit and hope James isn't following me.

I wake up from my nap with a killer headache. No doubt it's compliments of James slamming my head against the floor.

The thought of James's Were form sends shivers down my spine. I never imagined he could look like that. Our coven showed us photos of werewolves, but I've never seen one in person.

As much as I hate to admit it, James was right. I needed to see it. And I need to continue seeing and fighting him in his Were form so I'm not distracted in any way if a werewolf does attack me. I'm

175

proud of myself for rebounding as quickly as I did, but I also know if the attack was happening for real, I'd be dead.

I head down to the 8th floor and visit the Guard. All of the Guard members stand at attention as soon as I step onto the floor.

"Please, please," I say, "stop doing that. You don't need to stand when I walk in." Judging from the looks on their faces, they are going to keep doing it anyway.

"How can we help you Ms. Chloe?" the Guard member standing closest to me asks.

"I'm looking for Frank. And a healer."

"I'll page Frank. Sherman can help you with your medical needs."

A tall man with long, silky black hair approaches. "Come with me Ms. Chloe."

Sherman is Native American and when I ask, he tells me he is of Iroquois descent. He takes me to a conference room and shuts the door.

"How can I help you Ms. Chloe?"

"I have a bad headache. I think you can help me faster than a Tylenol."

Sherman smiles. "Absolutely. May I touch your forehead?"

"Yes."

Sherman approaches and puts his right hand on my forehead. I feel a warming sensation and almost instantaneous relief. A few seconds later he steps back.

"Better?"

"Much! Thank you."

Sherman's forehead creases. "Next time, don't wait so long to come and see me. You had a mild concussion."

Before I can ask how he can tell I had a concussion, Frank comes into the room.

Sherman gives Frank the lowdown. "Ms. Chloe is feeling much better now. I advised her that she suffered a mild concussion." Sherman turns to me. "Good day Ms. Chloe."

I smile. "Thanks Sherman."

Sherman leaves the room and shuts the door behind him.

"A mild concussion? Freaking werewolves," Frank says before taking a seat across the table. "Shouldn't you be at magic training?"

I roll my eyes. "Your concern for my welfare is heartwarming. Truly."

Frank grins. "I wish you would have left James frozen a little longer."

I laugh. "Were you planning on using him for target practice?"

"Nope. I would have turned off the lights and left him there."

"I'll consider that next time." I stand up. "I'm off to magic practice. At least I'll have a good excuse today if my magic sucks."

Frank clears his throat. "I have something I need to tell you first."

I don't like the look on his face. "What is it?"

"I've gone back and forth about whether I should tell you this." Frank pauses and shifts his weight.

Oh God. This isn't good.

"I promised I won't keep you in the dark if I have information I think you'll want to know."

"Okay..."

"And I think you'll want to know this."

I'm scared. "Is there something wrong with my parents?"

Frank shakes his head. "No, nothing like that. Your parents are perfectly fine."

I relax, then tense up again. "Is it Elliott? Is he alright?"

Frank hesitates. "Not exactly."

177

I will lose it if something has happened to Elliott. I have been on the verge of inviting him here at least ten times a day. If something happened to him that I could have prevented, I'll never forgive myself.

"What is it Frank? What is wrong with Elliott?" I'm frantic now.

"There's nothing *wrong* with him, per se."

"Jesus Christ! What is it?! Tell me already!"

He frowns. "Elliott got married."

I'm sorry, what? Is this mild concussion messing with my brain?

"Married?" I ask to make sure I heard Frank correctly.

"Yes, married."

I lean against the closest chair, completely shocked. Elliott got married?

"To who?"

Frank sighs. "To his ex-girlfriend. My family is upset about it. None of us like her."

"The ex-girlfriend who didn't like that he traveled so much?"

"That would be the one."

The full weight of what Frank is saying finally hits me. I feel like I've been punched in the stomach.

My Elliott? Married?

I start crying. "This is all my fault! I shouldn't have pushed him away!"

Frank stands and walks over to me. "Don't you dare say that! You did the right thing."

"Oh yeah? Then how come I'm alone now?"

Frank pulls me to his chest. "Because my little brother sucks. Because he wasn't strong enough to handle this."

"Don't. Don't give me the 'he isn't good enough for you' speech."

"But he isn't. Trust me, this is classic Elliott. Anytime something gets complicated, he bails out. If it wasn't now, it would be sometime down the road."

Frank gets me a tissue.

"Thanks," I mumble. "He said he saw something between us. A future for us."

"We are Readers Chloe, not fortune tellers."

Frank spends the next few minutes trying to console me, which I appreciate. He isn't successful though. He leaves me alone so I can get a hold of myself. No way I'm walking onto the Guard floor like this.

"Oh Elliott," I say out loud and cry again. I think of our phone conversations...the time we were able to spend with each other...the love making in my room at Leviston...

Was any of it real?

Was I just another notch in the belt?

Did he want to be with me because I'm the next Verhena?

My anger builds inside me and I need a release. I leave the conference room and make my way to the elevator. Before I can get there, Whitney is suddenly in my face.

"Hey Chloe! I thought you might be here."

I grunt in response and push the button for the elevator.

"What you did in training today was so awesome!"

I give her the side eye, but say nothing. Where is the damn elevator? I push the button again for good measure.

Whitney is rambling on about something when the elevator doors open. I jump inside, but she gets in with me. She doesn't miss a beat and keeps talking as I hit the button for the gym.

"We should hang out sometime. I could get us carry out from this really good Mexican place down the street. Their burritos are delicious! The nachos aren't as crunchy as I like…"

The elevator doors open to the gym and I try to make an escape. Whitney follows me and continues listing all of the restaurants within a ten mile radius that she recommends. I can't take it anymore.

I turn around and glare at her. "Do you ever shut the hell up?!"

She takes a step back. "I'm sorry, I…"

I interrupt her. "I just want to be left alone, okay? So get out of my face!"

I leave Whitney practically in tears. I walk as quickly as I can to the fireproof room. I slam the door behind me and focus on the target painted on the back wall. I gather all of my rage and send fire shooting from my fingertips. A giant ball of fire erupts and explodes. I use a protection spell to form a bubble around myself so I'm not burned by the flames. I scream as loud as I can and continue shooting fire across the room.

Flames engulf the room and I stand inside my bubble marveling at the fiery reds and oranges all around me. I did this. I created this massive fire and I am strong enough to protect myself from it. After a few deep breaths, I release cold energy and put the fire out. I feel much better now, a lot less like I might combust.

As the smoke and fire clear, I see a figure watching from the small window. Probably Frank making sure I'm okay. Or Whitney, waiting to tell me about a great barbeque place she found.

When I step outside the room, I discover I am wrong on both counts. It is James. He is still shirtless, but his Adidas pants are back on.

"That was pretty impressive," he says. Despite the compliment, his face is blank.

"Thanks." I try to walk past him, but he stops me.

"You need to figure out how to control your energy so you can summon it at any time. Not just when you're angry."

James is always ready to give me advice on something, which evidently includes magic.

"I'll take that into consideration. What are you doing here anyway? Still training?"

James steps to the side so I can walk by. "You shouldn't talk to my sister like that, she wants to be your friend."

I wince. "You heard, huh?"

"Yes, I did. I was in the corner doing push-ups. You must have been too busy yelling at Whitney to notice."

"It wasn't my proudest moment, okay? I just found out my ex got married and your sister was in the wrong place at the wrong time."

James raises an eyebrow. "Married?"

"Yes! Married! And we've only been broken up for like two weeks!" I go on a rambling tirade. "Sure I told him he shouldn't call me or see me because of what's going on right now, but that was only to protect him! Married! Can you believe it?"

James looks at me with his stone face.

I turn away. "I don't know why I'm telling you any of this."

James walks with me. "Who is he? A boy you met at Leviston?"

"No. Yes. Sorta."

James raises the eyebrow again.

"I met him before Leviston. He is the Reader who gave me my tattoo."

"Elliott?" James asks surprised.

"Yes. Do you know him?"

"Not personally. I know *of* him. I know he's Frank's younger brother."

"Yeah, that's him."

"And he's married now?"

I frown. "Yes. Married." It still doesn't seem right to say.

"Sounds to me like you dodged a bullet. You should be happy."

Is he serious?

"You're right. I'll go throw a party."

"Any man who doesn't fight for you isn't worth your tears."

I don't have a smartass comeback to this. "That's what Frank said too."

"You see? His own brother tells you he's not worth your time. That alone should be all you need to know." James walks over to grab his shirt and shoes. "Apologize to my sister. If you take the time to get to know her, you'll find you two have more in common than you think."

"I will," I promise.

"Good. Because if you talk to her like that again, I'll kill you."

As I watch James leave, I'm not sure if he's joking.

Magic training with Willa doesn't go so hot. No pun intended.

I expended all of my energy in the fireproof room during my little 'roid rage incident. There's nothing left in the tank. Frank is impressed when I tell him about the fire ball and protective bubble, but is annoyed when I fail to recreate it.

It's been a long day, but I have to take care of the Whitney situation. I make my way to the 13th floor. It looks exactly like my floor - two doors on each side of the hall and a door at the end. I'm guessing Ivan is in the luxury suite. So which room is Whitney's?

I knock on the first door to my right. No answer.

I knock on the first door to my left. No answer.

0 for 2.

182

I try the second door on the right and Ivan opens the door after a few seconds.

"Chloe!" he says surprised. "Nice to see you."

"Hi Ivan. I'm sorry to disturb you. I'm looking for Whitney."

Ivan smiles. "How nice. She's in the room at the end of the hall."

"Gave her the big room, huh?"

"I figured she would appreciate it a lot more than I do."

Ivan and I say our good-byes and I knock on Whitney's door.

"Come in," she yells from inside.

I push open the door slowly. "Whitney?" I find her sitting on the bed, braiding her own hair. She stops when she sees me.

"Chloe?" Her initial expression is confusion, then her face hardens. "Come to yell at me some more?"

I shake my head. "I came to apologize. I was upset about something, and I took it out on you."

Whitney picks at her fingers. "No, it's my fault. I was a blabbering idiot."

I sit down in a desk chair identical to mine. The desk looks the same too. "Really Whitney, it was all me."

Tears well in her eyes. "I haven't been around another female in forever. I'm stuck in a house with James and my grandfather 24/7. When we came here, I thought maybe we could be friends. It's stupid."

"No it's not. I was being a royal bitch. You have been nothing but nice to me since you got here. And I keep pushing you away."

Whitney wipes a tear off her cheek. "You are ridiculously busy. I shouldn't be bothering you. I'm just so bored."

I can relate. "It is boring here, isn't it?"

"I thought being stuck in my house back home was bad, but this is awful. I can't see my boyfriend. The few friends I have are back

183

home. No one here talks to me. The only social interaction I get is over meals and when we get together with Jessica for movie night."

Now I feel awful. Whitney is worse off than I am. Doesn't help that I've treated her like crap the entire time.

I need to explain what happened. "I found out tonight that my boyfriend, or should I say ex-boyfriend, got married."

Whitney's jaw drops. "What?"

I nod my head. "Frank just told me about it when you ran into me at the Guard center. I needed to let off some steam, and I wanted to get away from everyone."

Whitney frowns. "But I wouldn't let you."

"It's no excuse. I'm sorry."

"What a jerk!"

Ouch. Jeez, I said was sorry.

I start to stand up. "I guess I'll go."

Whitney laughs. "Not you! The ex-boyfriend."

I laugh too, relieved.

"How long ago did you break up?" Whitney asks.

"Same day you guys got here."

"That's like two weeks ago!"

"I know! He works fast."

Now that I think about it, everything with us went fast. One minute I hardly know the guy, the next he's telling me there's a future for us.

Whitney rolls her eyes. "Men."

"Exactly!" I agree.

We sit in silence for a second. "Whitney, can I ask you a question?"

She shrugs. "Sure."

184

"Where's your mom?"

A flash of pain crosses Whitney's face. "She's dead."

Wow, I was not expecting that. It takes me a second to recover from the shock. "I'm so sorry Whitney. That's terrible."

"She killed herself."

I'm stupefied. I can think of absolutely nothing to say. Why, oh why, did I ask such a personal question?

Whitney is the first to talk again. "She was never mentally stable, even when James and I were kids. She was like my dad in some ways. Always rebelling. Living life dangerously. I don't know what we would have done without my grandparents."

I try to imagine what my life would have been like if my parents were not there for me and Chelsea. I can't picture it.

"When my dad left, it crushed her. He didn't even say good-bye. She cried and cried. She thought even though he was a dark person, there was a soft spot for her somewhere in his heart. Obviously, there wasn't. A week after my dad left, James found her lying in bed motionless. An empty bottle of pills by her side. She was gone."

"Damn. That must have been hard on you." And James too, I add mentally.

"Can I admit something to you without sounding like a terrible person?" Whitney asks sheepishly.

"Sure."

"My life was easier after she was gone. I didn't have to worry about what crazy thing she would do next. I didn't have to help her out of whatever mess she'd gotten herself into."

Whitney looks up to gauge my reaction. I keep my face sympathetic, so she continues.

"Don't get me wrong. She was my mom and I loved her, but her life had spiraled out of control. I feel lucky she didn't take anyone's life with her."

185

In a million years, I never would have guessed Whitney had such a rough childhood. She is so happy all of the time. A lot of people in her position would use that history as justification to be unhappy and angry.

I judged Whitney too soon and too harshly. Whitney is a lot stronger than I thought.

We talk for a few more minutes before I stand up and stretch.

"It's been a long day and I'm exhausted. Maybe after training tomorrow we can watch a movie."

Whitney smiles. "Sounds great."

I leave Whitney's room thankful I took the time to mend fences with her. I hate to say it, but James was right.

The next morning proves chaotic. When I go downstairs for breakfast, James is occupying a seat at the table.

Great…

I say "hi" but everyone is wrapped up in whatever James and Frank are talking about.

"What's going on?" I ask as I take my seat.

"James is meeting with one of his father's men today," Frank answers.

"Seriously?"

James nods. "My father called this morning and told me to meet one of his men at a coffee shop a few blocks from here."

Knowing the enemy is close makes my stomach churn.

Frank fills me in on the details. "A member of the Guard went down to the coffee shop this morning and placed a hidden camera on the surface of a coffee brewer. We'll be able to see the meeting and swoop in if James needs any help."

"I won't need any help," James says.

I resist the urge to roll my eyes.

186

"I'm helping with the wire," Willa chimes in.

"How so?"

"I'll put a concealing charm on it. No one will ever know it's there."

I look at James. "Will they check you for a wire?"

"I don't know," he answers without any hint of nervousness.

Everyone is hyped up about the meeting over breakfast. Everyone but James. He is cool as a cucumber.

A half hour later, we are all standing in the Guard operations center watching the monitors as James walks down the block. He is eventually out of our camera range and we have to wait until he enters the coffee shop to see him again.

We've already spotted the man we believe is the rogue wolf. He looks to be in his mid-forties. He is wearing a black blazer over a white t-shirt and ripped up jeans. His black hair is slicked back with an entire bottle of hair gel. He sits at a small table in the corner rapping his knuckles on the wooden surface.

We watch intently as James opens the door to the coffee shop and strides in confidently. Women turn to watch him as he passes. One woman even elbows the woman next to her to check him out.

James approaches the man in the corner and they both raise their chins to acknowledge each other.

James takes a seat at the table. "Rawley, you look well."

"As do you James."

"What's up?" James asks.

Rawley smiles. "Your dad wanted me to check in with you. See how things are going."

"Better than we expected. She's completely clueless," James sneers.

I narrow my eyes. Am I the "she" he is referring to?

"She can't be totally inept. She killed three of our men."

That's right, I want to yell at the screen.

"Total fluke. She can't make it happen again unless she's angry."

"You've seen this for yourself?" Rawley asks.

"Yes," James confirms. "I've trained with her for over a week. She's got nothing."

I step back from the screens, everyone else is totally wrapped up in the drama. I would be too if James wasn't talking crap about me.

"Any other skills?"

James shrugs. "She can climb a wall like a freaking gecko."

Rawley laughs. "Anything else?"

"She is pretty good at strength enhancing spells. She can also freeze you in place. That's how she charred your men."

Rawley nods. "I figured as much."

"She is completely unprepared though. They are treating her like she's made of glass. She'll never know what hit her."

Rawley clasps his hands together. "This all sounds promising."

"I think so," James agrees.

"Your dad wants you to stay undercover a while longer. He's putting together a plan, but we will not be successful if you fail on your end."

"I will not fail," James says with the same confidence he had this morning.

"Good. Keep close to her. Learn all you can about the Guard. But don't take any shots at her. Your dad wants her for himself."

"Understood." The word rings in my ears. This is a Guard phrase. Not a werewolf phrase.

"We'll meet again in two weeks."

"Two weeks?" James and I ask simultaneously.

People turn to look at me, but their eyes quickly return to the screens.

"Yes. We want to gather as much intel about her as possible."

"Fair enough," James says smoothly.

"What we'd really like to see is the two of you in a relationship together."

Never going to happen, I think to myself.

James smiles. "You want me to bang this chick? Seems like an extra perk for me."

Gross!

Rawley laughs. "I'd give my right nut to trade spots with you, that's for sure."

I nearly gag.

"What's the point in me hooking up with her? Where does it get us?"

Rawley leans in. "I'm not supposed to tell you this yet, but the goal is for her to trust you enough to leave the building with you."

James taps his fingers on the table and considers this. "Should be easy enough. She's not the brightest crayon in the box."

Rawley smiles. "Good. Make your father proud."

James stands and extends his hand to Rawley. "I intend to."

James exits the coffee shop intact. No one jumps out at him. No one tries to attack him. He is in the clear.

James eventually appears in our television screens again as he approaches the building. I watch as he goes through security in the lobby and is checked for any weapons. All who are present in the Guard control room are elated. Everything has gone according to plan.

So why am I pissed off? I know James said what he did to throw the wolves off, but it hit a little too close to home for me.

"I'm out," I say as I turn away from the monitors.

"Why don't you stay?" Frank asks. "I'm meeting with James when he gets back for a briefing."

"Nah. You can give me the details later."

"You sure?"

"Yep." While I realize James's observations are important, I don't need to re-live all the nasty things that were said about me.

Before I can leave, Frank says, "Let's skip training today. You need a rest day."

While I'm thankful for the break, I have nothing to do and I'm sulking. Jessica and Whitney listen to me bitch and moan.

"He only said those things to throw them off," Jessica says after I'm done ranting.

"Maybe, but I think he believes a lot of what he said."

Whitney shakes her head. "No way. He's seen what you are capable of. He knows you can do great things. And he didn't even tell Rawley about your super speed or magnetism."

Jessica chimes in again. "He's here to help you. He has to say mean things about you to the wolves so they don't figure out you're allies."

"I know, I know. Still hurts to hear it."

"We haven't talked about the biggest part of the conversation," Jessica points out.

"Yeah, what's that?"

"James has to convince the wolves you are a couple."

Jessica is right, I did forget about that part.

"How's he going to do that?" Whitney wonders out loud.

Jessica laughs. "No idea, but I'm going to enjoy watching him try."

Chapter Twelve

Training the next day is a bit different than normal. James is the only wolf in the gym when I get there.

"Where is everyone?" I ask.

"Just me today," James responds.

"And me." Frank comes up behind me.

"And Frank," James concedes.

"Um, okay."

"We want to see how long you can hold your protection spell," James explains.

"That's it?" This seems too good to be true.

And it is.

Most witches can only hold a protection spell for thirty seconds or so. Obviously, the longer I can hold the protection spell, the better.

James and Frank explain that while I hold the spell, James will stand outside the bubble in Were form, ready to pounce as soon as the spell wears off. Which means I need to be prepared for combat.

"Sound good to you?" Frank asks.

Not really. Sounds like I'm about to get my butt kicked.

Showing no weakness, I nod my head. "Yes. Let's do it."

I'm curious myself how long I can hold the spell. A protective bubble could be my greatest weapon if used correctly. I've heard about witches who can also throw protection spells onto others. I'll have to work on that next.

I stand in the middle of the mat and close my eyes. I repeat the spell in my mind before I open my eyes again. I cannot see the

191

bubble around me, but I can feel it. Frank walks toward me and is stopped two feet away.

"Can you push it further out?" he asks. I thought his voice would be garbled by the bubble, but it isn't. I can hear him clear as a bell.

I visualize pushing the bubble out away from me, and watch as it slowly pushes against Frank. I move him about five feet before I stop.

Frank gives me a thumbs up. "Perfect!"

"Are you timing this?" I ask him.

"Yes ma'am. I started as soon as you opened your eyes."

I nod my head and look for James. He is behind me transitioning into his Were form. I quickly turn back around. I avoid watching James transform as much as possible. Too unsettling.

A few seconds later, James is in Were form and circling my protective bubble with a menacing look on his face. Perhaps we should have tried this without James stalking me first...

I know in my heart James is in there, but the werewolf is so terrifying. I can't help but envision him ripping me to shreds the first chance he gets.

A bead of sweat falls from my forehead and splashes onto the mat. I won't be able to hold the spell much longer.

I survey my surroundings and try to come up with a game plan for my escape. I panic when nothing immediately comes to mind. Luckily, I get an idea right before my bubble is about to burst. James stalks me as I move toward the wall. My bubble is getting smaller and smaller as my power weakens.

The protective barrier falls and James lunges at me. Just in the nick of time, I jump onto the wall and start climbing. James jumps as high as he can and almost gets my shoe. I climb beyond his reach and glance down at him with a grin.

I'm momentarily elated, but James has not stopped the training exercise. Instead of walking away, he stands underneath me, growling and snarling. My arms and legs are weak and I don't know how much longer I will be able to hold on. I need to come up with something fast, or I'm going to fall right into his arms.

I look around the gym, hoping inspiration will hit. I see the rack of dumbbells in the corner and a light bulb goes off. I release one of my hands and reach out to the metal dumbbells across the room. A twenty pound dumbbell shakes, then lifts off the rack. I pull the dumbbell as hard as I can with my magnetic energy and it sails through the air.

James turns to see what I'm doing, but he's too late. The dumbbell slams into his chest and sends him reeling backwards. He hits the floor with a loud thud.

"Woo hoo!" I exclaim.

My celebration is short lived. James isn't moving. In fact, he doesn't appear to be breathing either.

Holy crap!

Frank yells for healers. The concern in his voice heightens my fear.

I jump down from the wall and run over to James. As soon as I am within reach, James suddenly comes to life and grabs my leg. I scream and try to pull myself out of his grip, but he is too strong. He lunges upwards and plants his hands on my shoulders. Instead of slamming me onto the ground, James cradles my head in his arms and rolls us across the mat.

He has bested me. Again.

When we come to a stop, I am on top of James, both of us panting from our efforts. I look into the werewolf's eyes, hoping to find James in there.

Werewolf James rolls us over and stands up. His skin trembles and shakes. I lay back on the mat, catching my breath. I don't know if I'm angry or relieved James is okay. Maybe a little of both.

A completely human James stands over me. "Let this be today's lesson. Never approach a werewolf unless you are one hundred percent sure he is dead."

"Duly noted," I get out in between breaths.

Frank comes over and extends a hand to help me up. He grunts as I make him do the bulk of the work.

He claps my back. "Nice!"

"Yeah, right."

"You kept the protective bubble going for almost three minutes! That is unheard of!"

"Really? I did?" I ask, my mood brightening.

Frank smiles. "You did. It was awesome!"

"How about the dumbbell thing? Was it okay?"

Frank is pumped. "Yes! Totally unexpected!"

I am beaming.

"Did those healers ever show up?" a voice asks from behind us.

Frank and I turn to see James slumped against the wall holding his chest. He has a large bruise forming where the dumbbell hit. I feel bad for what I did to James. Then I remember him pretending to be dead and feel a little less guilty.

"I can help you!" a cheery voice calls.

It's Willa. I'd forgotten all about doing glamour training with Willa today. I don't know if I'll have much energy, but I don't have a choice.

James winces as he sits up. "I'd really appreciate it."

Willa bends down next to James and puts her hand on his chest. The bruise fades under her fingertips and James's breathing becomes less labored. Once he is healed, James and Frank make their exit. I can hear them discussing the fight today and how I can improve on their way out.

Given my energy level, I'm surprised when I have a breakthrough in my session with Willa. For the first time, I successfully complete a glamour spell. Mind you it only changed my shoes, but it was something.

"I watched your combat practice today," Willa tells me as we're wrapping up. "Very impressive."

I snort. "Until the part where my throat would have been ripped out."

"That was my favorite part."

I raise an eyebrow.

Willa smiles. "Never be hard on yourself for showing compassion."

I go upstairs for a much needed nap. I sleep like a rock and feel great when I head down for dinner. James is sitting at the table with us again. He is quiet and only speaks when spoken to, which is fine with me.

I'm enjoying my steak when Willa asks if I will join her in her office after dinner. "Of course," I tell her.

I spend the rest of dinner wondering what Willa wants to talk about. This will be my first trip to Willa's office. I feel like I did when I was in ninth grade and had to go to the principal's office. My biology teacher did not appreciate it when I swapped the wildlife DVD we were supposed to be watching with *The Hangover*.

Willa and I ride together to the 17th floor. I am surprised when the elevator doors open. I expected her walls to be painted white, but they are a pale blue. Wildlife photographs, animals in striking poses, hang in the hallway. I pass a panther crouched down and ready to pounce; an elephant spraying water onto his back; a lion running through the grass; a panda bear munching on some bamboo; and a red fox curled up in a tiny ball while he sleeps.

Willa's office shocks me even more. It is wild. The walls are covered in black and white zebra-print wallpaper. Hot pink carpet covers the floors and her desk is white marble. While the patterns and colors in the office are a bit crazy, it is chic and professional at the same time. I would never guess an eighty-year-old occupies this space.

"Please sit," Willa says, pointing to a white leather couch. She takes a seat behind her desk and clasps her hands together. "There's something I need to discuss with you."

I'm nervous as can be. "Okay."

Willa looks out the window, then back at me. "Being the Verhena is a great responsibility. A job I didn't fully appreciate when I first came here. Even now I am in awe of the position, and I occupy it. Do you understand what I'm saying?"

I'm not sure I do, but I nod my head.

"You are a smart girl Chloe. A strong girl. You have been through so much these last few weeks. You have lived a lot of life in a very short amount of time."

I nod again to let her know I'm listening.

"But I'm concerned for you. Your quest for vengeance is blinding you."

"My quest for vengeance?" I ask confused.

"Yes." Willa pauses. "How can I explain this?" Willa taps her fingers on her desk as she ponders what to say. "Ah, yes. Today in training we worked on glamour, right?"

"Yes."

"When you were successful, your first thought was how you could use the glamour against the wolves."

I think back to the training and what I said. I believe it was, "Yes! I can fool the wolves into thinking I'm someone else!"

"Willa, I'm training to fight wolves. Of course that's going to be the first thing I think about."

"I understand, but I get the sense it's the *only* thing you're thinking about."

I start to protest, but close my mouth. What else am I supposed to be thinking about?

Willa continues when I don't say anything. "I encourage you to go to the library. There are excellent books down there about leadership. Inside and outside of witchcraft. There are also journals from the prior Verhenas. I think you will find them incredibly useful."

Ah, yes. The journals I had with me at Leviston that I never bothered to crack open.

To appease Willa, I tell her I'll hit the books.

"This is a confusing time for you Chloe. There's a lot going on. It was hard for me when I first came here, and I didn't have half the trouble you're dealing with."

I stand up and thank Willa for her suggestions.

"There's one other thing." She walks out from behind her desk.

"Alright," I say sheepishly.

"I don't know how to say this…" Willa plays with her beaded necklace.

"It's okay Willa. You can say anything to me."

She frowns. "I'm worried you aren't dealing with the loss of your sister."

I suck in a breath. What does she know about my grief?

I steady myself, not wanting to snap at her. "I don't want to talk about it."

Willa's brow furrows. "I know. That's what worries me."

I stare at my feet and fight back tears. "When this is over, when I've defeated the rogue wolves, I'll face it." I look up and meet her eyes. "I promise."

Willa nods her head. "I understand. We all handle grief in our own way."

When I don't say anything, Willa clears her throat. "Well then, I've said all I need to say. Please come to me with any questions or concerns you may have. I would love to talk with you about my

197

experience as the Verhena and the things I've learned along the way."

"Thank you Willa."

Willa gives me a big hug and then sends me on my way.

I leave Willa's office in a daze. My conversation with her was like being doused with cold water. She isn't happy with me, and it sucks. I thought I was doing so well. Really progressing.

I take the steps down to the library. I've only stopped in the library once before, but I have a feeling it will be my new home.

The library is the least touched floor in the building from an architectural standpoint. It speaks of antiquity and heritage. The walls are nine feet high with dark cherry shelves floor to ceiling. Each shelf is filled with rows of books.

A long table occupies the center of the room with benches on both sides and a chair at each end. A gas burning fireplace and two large chairs are tucked into the back corner. The fireplace is glowing and projecting a halo of light onto the shelves above it.

Built into one of the walls is a small desk with a laptop computer. Willa told me the Guard created a program that catalogs the library's contents. I should start there, but what do I type in the search field? Werewolves? Witch leaders?

I sigh and walk toward the fireplace. Between the two chairs is a brass tray with a glass top. Sitting on the glass is a large decanter and two drinking glasses. The decanter is filled with a golden colored liquid resembling cream soda. I take the lid off the decanter and smell the contents.

Whoa! My face twists awkwardly as the stench fills my nose.

"It's bourbon," a male voice says.

I nearly drop the decanter. I didn't even notice James sitting in one of the chairs. "Jesus James! You about gave me a heart attack."

"Not a drinker, huh?"

I set the decanter down. "No, not really. You?"

He shakes his head. "No, although I have sampled the bourbon."

After a moment's pause, I ask, "Isn't there some other dark corner you should be lurking in?"

James smirks. "I come here every night. This is the first time I've seen you here. In my book, that means you're interrupting me. Not vice versa."

I take a seat in the other chair. The heat from the fireplace has warmed the soft, maroon leather. It's nice and cozy.

"You come here every night?" I ask.

"Yes."

"Why?"

James puts a bookmark in the book he's reading and shuts it. "There is a wealth of knowledge in here. Willa has books about wolf history I've never even heard of before. I'm taking advantage of every second I have here."

"Hmmm," I say as I gaze at the fire.

"What brings you here?" he asks.

I frown. "Willa yelled at me."

"Willa *yelled* at you?" James sounds skeptical.

I turn to him. "Alright, I'm exaggerating." I look back at the fire and sigh. "She made it clear I disappoint her."

"Is that what she said?"

"Not exactly, but in so many words."

"What exactly did she say?" James presses.

"That my thirst for revenge is clouding my judgment. That I need to worry about more than werewolves."

James considers this. "She may have a point."

Really? I don't need another lecture. Especially from James. I sit back in the seat and stare at the flames.

James lets me sit quietly for a minute before he asks, "Have you thought about what you're going to do after we defeat the rogue wolves?"

"No," I answer honestly.

"Maybe Willa wants you to start thinking about what kind of leader you will be. Your legacy with your people."

Tears well in my eyes. "I'm not...I'm not like you James."

He snorts. "There's an understatement."

I lean forward so he can see my face clearly. "I'm serious. I wasn't born into this. I didn't grow up my entire life knowing this was my destiny." I'm using my hands to make my point. Something I do when I'm upset.

"This was thrust upon me less than a year ago. My whole life is different now. My sister is dead. I'm living a life I never wanted. I'm self-centered and immature. The last person in the world who should have this position." I wipe tears from my face and fall back into the chair.

James passes me a tissue. "You're right."

Is he rubbing salt in the wound? I look at him for a second, then down at my hands.

"You're right," he repeats. "You're new to this."

I smile a little, relieved James wasn't taking a jab at me.

"The bad news is you didn't see this coming. The good news is you have a lot of resources around you."

I nod. "I know, I know. I need to hit the books."

"Sure you've got all of this," James gestures toward the books, "but you also have Willa, and my grandfather. Two people who have been successful leaders for a very long time. Use them. Get as much advice from them as you can."

James is right. Again.

"Have you met with Willa?"

"Yes, I have. I've met with her a few times."

"To get tips on leadership?"

"That's one reason."

"And the other?"

James purses his lips, but answers my question. "If something happens to my grandfather, Willa and I will deal with each other a lot. I need to know what kind of person she is. And she needs to know what kind of person I am."

I hadn't thought about that. James is the future leader of his pack. He's preparing for it, unlike me. The thought of James and I being the leaders of our people doesn't seem real. But it is real.

What will I do if Willa has a heart attack tomorrow and is unable to lead? I don't have the slightest clue what she does in a day. She's involved in our plan to take down the rogue wolves, but it by no means consumes the bulk of her time.

I admit my epiphany to James. "Willa is right. My quest for vengeance has clouded my judgment."

"Understandable."

I reveal another truth. "To be honest, it was the only thing keeping me going."

After chewing on my confession for a minute, he says, "Your people need you Chloe. The rogue wolves are definitely a threat, but the witches will need more from you."

I ask James a question I've been asking myself a lot lately. "Would you want this for yourself? If you had a choice?"

James is surprised by my question. "I don't know. I've never thought about it."

"Ha," I say with zero humor. "I think about it all the time. Every night I wonder what my life would be like if I'd gotten a simple black hawk tattooed on my right shoulder."

James pauses before speaking. "I've never envisioned what my life would be like outside of this."

"You never wanted to be an astronaut or firefighter?" I ask with a smile.

"No. I never allowed myself to dream of things like that. I knew I could never be those people. Why be disappointed?"

Damn. I think back to my younger years when Chelsea and I used to pretend to be doctors, secretaries, princesses, cowgirls, and an endless string of different people. How sad James didn't play those games.

"People always tell you power has privileges," I say. "What they don't tell you, is it can also be a prison."

James meets my gaze, the glow from the fireplace dancing in his emerald eyes. For the first time, I feel like he and I have an understanding.

As quickly as the moment begins, it's over. "Well, I need to get back to it," he says, patting the top of his book.

"Sure." I stand up. "If you and I are going to be great leaders, we'll have to play nice, won't we?"

He gives me a small smile. "I wouldn't go that far."

I walk around the library hoping something will grab my attention. After watching me wander around aimlessly, James recommends a book about leadership from his stack. When I turn my nose up at it, he laughs and promises to give me the Cliff Notes version.

He also shows me the stack of books he has on the table discussing werewolf history. I turn those down too.

"Willa already thinks I spend too much time thinking about wolves," I explain.

"Here." He hands me a thin, leather bound book. "Maybe you should start with this."

"What is it?" I ask, not seeing a title on the cover.

"It's Willa's first journal from when she was the Verhena-to-be."

"You read Willa's journal?" I ask with disbelief. Doesn't he know it's wrong to read a woman's diary?

"She told me where to find it. I think there's a reason she wanted me to read it."

I open the cover to find yellowed pages filled with black ink. I run my hands down the page and try to picture Willa at my age. Was she scared too? Or was she better prepared than I am?

I tuck the book against my chest. "Thanks for your help."

"No problem." James sits at the table and opens a large book. A clear signal he's ready to get lost in his research again.

I leave him to it.

I hate it here.

Rose won't let my family come to see me. I'm not allowed to have any friends visit either.

I hardly had the chance to say good-bye to my family before the Guard snatched me and brought me to this place.

I'm supposed to be happy because I will be the Verhena. I'm supposed to be thrilled that I will lead our people. I feel none of those things.

When I told Rose I don't want this, she told me I'm ungrateful and should relish the chance to be the leader of the Witches.

"It's an honor," she tells me.

It's really a curse.

Willa's words hit home. A part of me is relieved she was in the exact same mindset I am now.

I stay up late reading Willa's diary and realize how lucky I am. Willa didn't have the support group I have. Rose was a tyrant and awful to Willa. Rose would taunt her and call her "insufficient." Members of the Guard were not friendly like they are to me. Willa felt like she was nothing more than a burden.

When I close the diary, I see it is 1:30 in the morning. I was so caught up in Willa's words, I missed my nightly swim. I lay in bed, half watching a repeat of *Frasier* and counting my blessings.

Willa is a great mentor.

Frank is an awesome security guard.

Jessica and Whitney have the potential to be good friends.

I am able to speak with my parents as much as I want.

I am safe, relatively speaking. It sucks being stuck in this building, but it's full of all the modern amenities a girl could want.

I told Frank the day of Chelsea's funeral I was going to be strong. But I have to be more than that.

"It starts today," I say out loud. "I can do this."

As if responding to my statement, a television commercial pronounces, "Yes you can!"

The man shouting on TV is talking about getting a new car without a down payment, but it feels like his excitement is directed at me.

I put my new mindset into action immediately. Instead of hanging around doing nothing after my training sessions, I spend time in the library learning all I can about witch history and the former Verhenas. Not all of them kept journals like Willa, but they all had biographies written about them.

One thing they all had in common was an absolute sense of terror and panic when they received their white hawk tattoo. All but one never envisioned this for herself. The one who did, Emma, was comical. She knew from day one she had this whole Verhena thing locked down. I wonder several times as I read about her if she had a bit of a sixth sense. There were times when Emma took action to control a situation before the situation even began.

I was curious to learn about the Verhena who was in charge when we were at war with the wolves. Her name was Ellie, short for Elizabeth, and the poor woman was shocked and saddened by the war with the wolves.

So many lives lost to this silly war, on both sides. I cannot bear to hear the stories about witches who have lost loved ones. We are winning this war, and I have no doubt that we could completely eliminate the werewolf population one by one. But I do not want to lose anymore witches. I don't see the point in killing the wolves just because we can. If I continue to let this go, their blood will be on my hands. I wrote to the new pack leader, Isaiah, and hope to meet with him soon.

It was Ellie who negotiated peace with the werewolves and spearheaded the massive project of creating the ward between the two territories.

There were many witches who wanted the war to continue, even some of Ellie's closest advisors. She would hear none of it. Ellie believed every being, witch or not, deserved a happy and peaceful existence.

Willa is thrilled with my newfound excitement about becoming the Verhena. We discuss various policy issues and the types of problems she deals with on a daily basis. I was surprised at the amount of conflict between covens and fully appreciate for the first time how great my coven back home really was.

My combat training is going well too. I'm working on increasing the longevity and durability of my spells. I hold my protection spells for as long as possible and work on increasing the intensity of my magnetism and strength spells.

Even my glamour spells are showing improvement. While I'm not great at changing myself into someone else, I am able to shut off

Willa's glamour spells. So if she turns me into a seventy-year-old man, I can undo her spell.

I'm also seeing a lot more of James. He is usually in the library at the same time I am. We talk about the material we are reading and he helps me when I have questions. Tonight, we discuss werewolf and witch urban myths.

"True or False," I ask, "werewolves howl at the moon?"

James is unimpressed by my question. "Have you heard any howling since we've been here?"

"No."

"Well then, there you go," he answers without further explanation.

"Does the moon have any control over your transformations?"

"No, not at all."

I'm confused. "Why do all the movies and books about werewolves make such a big deal about the full moon? Where did that come from?"

James sets his pen down. He was taking notes from yet another massive book about wolf history. "Centuries ago there was a serial killer, often called the Moonlight Killer, who only killed on a night with a full moon. The townspeople swore the man was over seven feet tall, but had the face and body of a wolf. He would rip out the throats of his victims."

I shiver.

"Most think that's how the connection between werewolves and the moon started."

James gets back to his notes, but I think of another question. "What about silver?"

"What about it?" James asks without glancing up from his book.

"Is it true being touched by silver can burn your skin?"

"No."

"What about silver bullets? Are they the only bullet that can kill you?"

James chortles. "I wish." He looks at me again. "In some ways, we are as vulnerable as an average human. We just have additional abilities to help us survive."

"Hmmm…" I want to ask where the urban myth about silver came from, but I've interrupted him enough for the night. I start reviewing the book in front of me, a book about leadership written by a former Prime Minister.

"What about broomsticks?" James asks out of nowhere. "Where did that come from?"

I smile. "When I was little, my grandmother used to tell me a story about a witch named Polly. Polly really wanted to fly, but couldn't come up with a spell for it."

James interrupts. "I assume no witch can fly, or you'd be doing it in training."

I nod. "I wish we could, but we can't."

James waves his hand. "Proceed."

"Anyways, Polly was good at moving inanimate objects. She could hold them in the air for a long period of time and could move them great distances. So she decided the best way to fly would be to sit on an inanimate object and move it."

James considers this. "Why the broom?"

"Sweeping was one of Polly's daily chores. Plus, she could control it easily because it was lightweight."

"Makes sense."

I continue the story. "One night, Polly decided to take her broom further than the boundary line of her family's farm. Unfortunately, it was still early enough in the evening for people in the local village to see Polly flying through the sky. While no one in the village knew who was on the broom, the story about the flying woman spread quickly. Polly's coven punished her by shaving her hair off and throwing her broom into a fire."

207

"That seems harsh."

I laugh. "Grandma would tell me about Polly whenever I used magic in public. She would threaten to shave off my hair and throw my toys into a fire."

James chuckles, then returns to his book. I hope he will ask me about another witch urban myth, but he doesn't.

Chapter Thirteen

"You're overdoing it Chloe. You're wearing yourself out," Willa tells me during magic training.

I can't win.

"I'm fine. This is the best I've felt since I got here."

"You promise?" she asks, her brow furrowed.

I smile. "Yes, I'm good. I promise."

"Well, I've decided you need some fun."

"Fun?" Does that exist here?

"Yes. Fun. Which is why I've arranged a sleepover for you, Jessica and Whitney tonight," Willa says. I can tell by the look on her face she's proud of herself. "After dinner, the three of you can retreat to the 11th floor. I have some surprises for you."

I give her a hug. "You're so thoughtful. Thank you."

"You're welcome. You deserve a break."

Jessica, Whitney and I are giggly at dinner, excited about our slumber party. Frank and James exchange glances, but don't spoil our fun.

As we're leaving the dinner table, Frank pulls me to the side. "I have a favor to ask you."

I'm curious. "Okay. What is it?"

"My parents and sister are in town this week. Is it okay if I take the rest of the day off?"

"Of course! You don't need to ask me for a day off."

"I'm your personal bodyguard. I absolutely have to ask you before I take a day off."

I shrug. "Take off whenever you want. There are plenty of Guard members here to cover for you."

Frank ignores my carte blanche vacation day policy. "If you and the girls are having a slumber party tonight, it might be a good time for me to slip out and meet up with my family."

I nod. "You should. And let me know if you want some more time off."

"Will do."

I start to walk away, but Frank calls out to me again. "Oh...and Chloe..."

I turn around. "Yeah?"

"If you need anything, call Sue."

"Sue? Who the heck is Sue?"

"Willa's personal security guard."

"Bane? Bane's real name is Sue?"

Frank smiles. "Yes. I think he likes Bane better though."

I head for the 11th floor, whistling Johnny Cash as I go.

Willa went all out for us. We find sleeping bags with matching pillows, a popcorn machine, and a snow cone maker. I love snow cones! We take turns using the flavored syrup to dye our frozen treats bright colors.

When we're done with our dessert, we slip into our pjs, grab some popcorn and watch *Jerry McGuire*, one of my favorite movies.

When Tom Cruise delivers his famous lines to Renee Zellweger, Whitney sighs. "That's how I feel about Brandon."

Jessica and I look over at her.

"Who's Brandon?" Jessica asks.

"My boyfriend back home." Whitney looks at her cellphone. "He hasn't texted me today and I miss him."

"I didn't know you have a boyfriend," Jessica says. "How come I've never heard about him?"

"Because James hates him. I don't talk about him if James is around."

"Why does James hate him?"

"When we were kids, Brandon used to talk a lot of crap about our parents. He wasn't a very nice guy back then. James hasn't forgiven him for it."

I turn off the television and tuck my legs underneath me. "So what's Brandon like?"

Whitney gets dreamy eyed. "He's gorgeous! Tall with dark hair. Fit. He's obsessed with motosports, so he's out riding dirt bikes a lot."

"He sounds exciting!" Jessica interjects.

Whitney nods enthusiastically. "Oh, he is." She pauses and then adds, "We're mates."

Mates?

Jessica and I exchange glances and then break out into giggles.

"What?" Whitney asks confused.

"Whitney, you slut!" I exclaim. Jessica and I burst into another laughing fit.

"No!" Whitney puts her forehead in her hand. "It's not what you think!"

"Yeah? What is it then?" Jessica asks, still laughing.

"Mating for werewolves doesn't mean sex. Well, I guess mates have sex, but 'mating' doesn't mean having sex."

Jessica and I calm down. Whitney's face is flush with embarrassment.

I help her out. "We're sorry Whitney. Please, explain it to us."

"When you say you're someone's mate, it means you are his life partner."

"Like getting married?" Jessica asks.

"Sorta, but more than that. It's an acknowledgement that you are spiritually connected, one is a part of the other. You don't want to exist without each other."

My turn for a question. "How does it work? How did you let Brandon know you wanted to be his mate?"

Whitney blushes again. "It's a long held tradition with our pack. You…you bare your neck to him."

Jessica holds her hand over her throat. "Your neck? Isn't that a vampire thing?"

Whitney rolls her eyes. "No! If a woman bares her neck to a man, it means she wants to be his mate. If he licks her from her collarbone to her jaw line," Whitney runs her finger along her neck to show us, "it means he wants to be her mate too."

"And you and Brandon are mates?" I ask.

Whitney nods her head. "Yes."

Jessica is as interested in this werewolf tradition as I am. "Do mates stay together forever?"

Whitney frowns. "Most do. There are occasions when mates split up. It's sad because it's usually one sided. I've seen people devastated because their mate left them."

I think of the story Whitney told me about her mom's reaction to Julian leaving. Were they mates?

Jessica interrupts my train of thought. "Any traditional mating rituals for witches Chloe?"

I shake my head. "None that I'm aware of. I've been to witch weddings, and there are a few phrases we add in, but nothing like what the werewolves do."

"What about you Jessica? Do you have a special someone?" Whitney asks.

"Nope," Jessica responds. "Not at the moment."

"Anyone you're interested in?"

Jessica's face turns pink.

"Oh my God!" I throw a piece of popcorn at her. "Jessica has a crush!"

Jessica tries to play it off, but we see right through her.

"Who is it? Tell us! Tell us!" Whitney begs.

I giggle. "Come on Jess, spill it!"

Jessica sighs. "Okay, okay. But you have to promise you won't tell a living soul!"

Whitney and I nod our heads vigorously in agreement.

"It's Frank."

Whitney and I both exclaim "Frank?!" at the same time.

Jessica shrugs. "He's a nice guy. And he's really hot."

I rub my chin. "I need to put my matchmaking skills to work."

Jessica shoots me a look. "Don't you dare! You promised!"

I stick out my pinkie and Jessica does the same. As we entwine our fingers, I say, "I won't tell Frank. Promise."

Jessica relaxes.

Whitney changes topics. "Do you guys like Ariana Grande?"

"Yes," Jessica and I both answer.

"I have her new CD. I bought it today at a store down the street."

I raise my eyebrow. "They still sell CDs?"

"Yep. I like buying the actual CD better than downloading the album. I have a collection back home."

Whitney puts in the CD and we continue talking about boyfriends, exes and dating horror stories. A song comes on with a great dance beat and I can't help but get up and strut around the room. Soon Jessica and Whitney are up with me and we are dancing to the music.

I haven't had this much fun in a long time. I feel like my old self again, the girl who loved to laugh and dance. I owe Willa big time.

Three songs in to our dance party, Whitney launches a pillow past my head.

"Hey!" I protest.

Whitney is glaring, but it's not at me. I turn and see James standing in the doorway. He takes a few steps into the room and Whitney throws another pillow at him. James deflects the pillow easily and it thumps to the floor beside him.

"No boys allowed!" Whitney yells at him.

"Are you ladies aware that there's a room full of men watching you on television right now?"

Whitney freezes. "What?"

I cross my arms over my chest. "If you're referring to the Guard, Frank would never let that happen."

"Frank isn't here though, is he?" James sneers.

Dang it. I forgot I gave Frank the night off.

"No," I admit.

James gets a superior look on his face. The one I see in training when he's got an advantage over me. He turns and walks out of the room without another word.

"Has your brother always been this lame?" I ask Whitney when he's gone.

She frowns. "Pretty much."

James's interruption deflates the energy of our party.

Not wanting to bail completely on the slumber party idea, we all trek up to Whitney's room and lay our sleeping bags on the floor. There are no cameras in bedrooms, so we're free to talk about whatever we want without worrying about a bunch of Guard members listening in. We talk late into the night and one by one we fall asleep.

I don't know if it's the snow cone, the popcorn, or what, but I am smack dab in the middle of an awful dream. I'm in my pajamas standing in an open field. There's a full moon in the sky and a chill in the air. As if the darkness isn't bad enough, fog rolls in all around me. I can't see past my extended hand as I make my way through the mist. I try using magic, but none of my spells work.

I call out to Frank, but I don't get a response.

I shout for Willa. Nothing.

I try both Whitney and Jessica, but neither responds.

I yell out desperately for James.

Suddenly, a werewolf jumps through the fog. Its mouth open wide and razor sharp teeth gleaming. It is coming for my throat. I scream as loud as I can.

I wake to the sound of my own screams. Whitney and Jessica are both scrambling out of their sleeping bags, terrified looks on their faces. Whitney's bedroom door slams open and James rushes into the room. He immediately drops to my side and puts his hands on my shoulders.

"Chloe! Chloe! Are you alright?"

My face is in my hands and I'm sobbing. "The werewolf…"

James flinches and pulls back from me.

I look up at him. "No, not you. A different werewolf. It was…it was trying to kill me."

"God Chloe!" Jessica says, her hand covering her heart. "You scared the crap out of me!"

"I'm sorry."

Ivan scrambles into the room as quickly as he can on his cane. "Is everything okay?" he asks, winded from his efforts.

"Yes," I assure him. "Bad dream. I'm sorry to wake you."

Ivan lets out a deep breath. "Okay. Good." He nods at us, then turns around and leaves Whitney's room.

"You good now?" James asks me.

I nod. "Yeah. I'm fine."

James searches my eyes for a moment, then stands and heads for the door. Before closing it behind him, he says, "Good night ladies."

"Good night," we all respond.

I lay my head on the pillow, afraid to go back to sleep. I play a game in my mind my mom taught me when I was little. You pick a category and name a thing in that category using the letters of the alphabet. Tonight I select fruits and vegetables. Apple, banana, celery... I make it to nectarine before I fall asleep.

"How are you doing?" James asks me the next night in the library.

He's going through yet another book about werewolf history and I'm reading a book called *Harnessing the Leader Within*. It's a real page turner.

"Pretty good. Sorry I woke you up last night."

"No problem. But that's not what I meant. How are you feeling in general? You seem more content."

I think about this for a second. Am I content?

"You know, I do feel good. I think branching out and learning more about being the Verhena has helped me find balance. I'm not angry all the time like I used to be."

James jots something down on his notepad. "Did you and your ex make up?"

"Who? Elliott?" I haven't thought about Elliott in a long time.

"Yes, Elliott."

"He's married James. That pretty much put the kibosh on our relationship."

"Do you miss him?" James asks without looking up.

216

Why this line of questioning? Why the interest in me and Elliott?

James glances at me. "You can tell me if you don't want to talk about it."

"No, it's fine. Really. I was just thinking about your question."

James looks back down at his book. I envy his ability to read and carry on a conversation at the same time. My brain doesn't work that way.

"I don't. Miss him I mean. I did for the first day or two, but I realized we were never what I thought we were."

James flips a page of his book. "Meaning?"

"I got into it so quickly, I never stopped to think about how real it was. He was there for me the second I found out I was the Verhena. He showed interest and I liked him. It snowballed from there. Maybe things would be different if I was a normal girl and he was a normal boy. But we're not. End of story."

I realize as I'm saying all of this out loud that I really don't miss Elliott. He was a great distraction from all of the crap happening in my life. But there wasn't anything deeper to it than that.

James smiles. "Well, I'm just glad you aren't trying to burn down the building anymore."

We're quiet for a minute, then I ask, "What about you?"

"No, I don't miss Elliott either," James says without skipping a beat.

I laugh. "I mean your mate. Do you miss her?"

He raises an eyebrow. "My mate?"

"Whitney told me she has a mate, and you're older than her, so I assumed…" I trail off. Judging by the look on his face, I'm way wrong.

"I don't have a mate," James says, his eyes dull.

Uh-oh. I hope I'm not dredging up some sordid history.

217

I try to lighten the mood. "Can't find someone good enough for you, huh?"

"I haven't looked," he responds.

"You've never had a girlfriend? Anyone you thought stood a chance?"

James smiles a little. "I guess I deserve this after the Elliott questions." He puts his pen down. "Yes, I've had girlfriends. No, none of them were serious. I have no problem getting a girlfriend. The issue is keeping one."

I crinkle my nose. "Maybe if you weren't such an asshole all the time."

He laughs out loud. "You're probably on to something there." His face turns serious again. "None of the girls wanted to take on the responsibility of being my mate."

"The responsibility? You make it sound like a job."

"In a way it is. I'm never going to be in a 'normal' relationship." He uses his fingers to make air quotes around the word normal. "My mate will have to deal with the reality of being the wife of a pack leader. As you said the other day, it can feel like a prison."

"No, I get it. I do. It will be the same for my partner." I frown. "If I ever date again."

James returns to his book and we are quiet for a while. My concentration is broken when he stands to stretch.

"What are you reading?" I ask him.

"The life and times of my great-grandfather. It's funny to think that someday my great-grandson will read about me." He sits back down. "How about you?"

"One of the books your grandfather recommended. This chapter talks about determining and eliminating your biggest character flaw."

"What's your biggest character flaw?"

"That's easy. I'm self-centered. You?"

218

"I'm impulsive."

I laugh. "You? Impulsive?"

"What's so funny about that?" he asks.

"You don't have an impulsive bone in your body."

"Not anymore. I determined my biggest character flaw, and I eliminated it."

I roll my eyes. "Sorry, I forgot you're perfect. Just out of curiosity, how did you eliminate this flaw?"

"I learned how to exercise self-control. In all things."

"Gee, sounds fun."

He gives me a sly smile. "It can be."

I blush. I look down at my watch. 10:28 p.m.

"Well, I gotta go." I stand up and grab my book. "Time for my swim."

"Ah yes, your nightly swim," James says, acting like he wasn't flirting with me a second ago. "It's the only predictable thing about you."

I make haste for the exit. I can't get to the pool quick enough. I need to cool down.

An hour later, I step out of the shower just in time to hear my phone ringing. I make a mad dash for it.

"Hello?"

"Chloe, it's Frank."

"What's up?"

"We need to have a meeting. Can you come down to the Guard operations center?"

"I'm on my way."

219

I put my wet hair in a bun and throw on a pair of jeans and a hoodie. A group has convened in a conference room by the time I get down to the Guard's floor.

"What's going on?" I ask when I walk in.

"I got another call from my dad," James answers. "I'm supposed to meet with Rawley tomorrow at a coffee shop eight blocks from here."

"We're debating whether we should plant a camera in the coffee shop tonight," Frank adds.

"Why wouldn't we?"

"Julian's men may have the place staked out. They're getting closer and closer to their end game. Which means they could be taking extra precautions. We don't want to raise any red flags," Frank explains.

I turn to Willa. "You can conceal a wire again, right?"

"Absolutely," she says with conviction.

"I vote we send him in with just the wire. We don't need visual. Why take the risk? It's not worth the reward."

James nods. "I agree."

We talk logistics for a few more minutes, then disperse. I head back to my room and climb in bed after changing into pajamas. Worrying about tomorrow's meeting with Rawley keeps me up. I can't imagine how worried James must be. Then again, ice runs through his veins. He's probably sound asleep.

I think about our conversation in the library. He was flirting with me, right? Or was I imagining it?

I replay it in my mind. Yep, he was flirting with me.

Then again, it's James. Just because he's being nice to me doesn't mean he's flirting with me.

I slam a pillow over my head and clamp it down over my ears. No, no, no! I will not act like a middle school girl and overanalyze conversations. It's James. He hates me and vice versa.

So why am I so worried about him?

My stomach is in knots during breakfast. I swirl my oatmeal around the bowl, hardly eating any of it. Everyone at the table has the same disposition. Except for James, who is pounding his blueberry muffin and scrambled eggs.

How can he be calm at a time like this? Does anything rattle this man?

Whitney asks a few questions about the upcoming meeting with Rawley. She wasn't at our brainstorming session last night. I'm not sure why.

"I don't like this," she says after James explains everything to her. "Do you really have to meet with him? There has to be another way."

"This is the quickest way to find out where Dad is."

"Quickest isn't always best," Whitney pleads.

"That's what she said," Jessica whispers to me.

I nearly spit out my water.

"It will be fine Whit. Nothing bad is going to happen," James says in a soothing voice. I'm warmed by his obvious concern for his sister.

Whitney frowns but doesn't press the issue any further.

James pushes his chair back. "It's time for me to go."

"Promise me you'll be careful," Whitney says as he's leaving.

James leans over and kisses the top of her head. "Always am."

We're huddled together in front of the monitors watching James leave the building and walk down the block. Once he's out of our cameras' range, all we have is the sounds picked up by his mic. My heart races as I listen to the chatter of people walking by and the city traffic.

After what seems like forever, a bell jingles through our speakers. I'm guessing it's the bell hanging over the door of the coffee shop.

James confirms my suspicion when he says, "Rawley. Good to see you again."

"Same to you," Rawley's husky voice answers.

"Has it been two weeks already?"

Rawley laughs. "Time flies."

"I guess so."

"How are things going with the new Verhena?"

"Good. Really good actually," James responds.

"Fuck her yet?"

I curl my hands together and make fists.

"C'mon Rawley. You know my track record. Was there ever a doubt?"

Whitney turns to look at me.

"He's lying," I whisper.

She nods. "I figured as much."

Frank shushes us.

I miss Rawley's next question, but I hear James say, "She's decent."

Decent?! Decent?! Would it have killed him to say I'm a tiger in the sack? He'll pay for this in training tomorrow.

"Enough about the bedroom," Rawley says. "Tell me about her skills."

"She's getting a little better, but the progress is slow. If you're going to act, you should do it now. While she's still in the beginning stages. I've seen what Willa can do. You don't want to deal with that."

"Exactly what your father thinks too."

222

"Great minds," James says.

"Indeed." There is a pause in the conversation, but Rawley finally continues. "Before your dad moves forward with his plan, he needs to see you out with her."

"What do you mean?"

"He wants to see you two together. As a couple. He needs to see that she trusts you."

James whistles. "Getting her out of the building will be tough."

"Sure it will. But if she trusts you, she'll do it."

We hear a faint thumping sound, Rawley or James strumming their fingers on the table.

"She's been bitching about wanting to go dancing. Would that work?" James asks.

"Sure. Take her out to a club. A public place where others will see you together."

"Give me a few days. I'll work on her tomorrow and convince her we should go out. Once she goes to the Guard, it will take a day or two for them to work out a plan."

Rawley laughs. "Speedy crew, huh?"

"Fast as a sloth."

A few Guard members flex their jaws, but no one says a word.

"Today is Tuesday. Have her out Friday night."

"I can make it happen by Friday."

"I'm sure you can."

"Here's my question - how will I know we've been seen by the right people?"

"You're a smart boy James. Figure it out."

The two exchange good-byes, and soon James is out on the city streets. Once he's back within camera range, we head to a conference room for a briefing session.

223

Frank opens his mouth to start talking, but I put my hand up. "Let's wait until we're all here. This is too important for anyone to miss even the smallest detail."

"You're right," Frank agrees.

The conference room is silent as we wait for James, none of us wanting to engage in small talk. I run through James and Rawley's conversation in my mind. Julian is certainly testing his son's loyalty by asking him to get me out of the building. How can we pull this off without making it obvious I'm in on it?

James walks into the conference room ten minutes later. He lifts his shirt so Willa can remove the wire. I myself cannot see it until she touches it.

"That went well," James says before taking a seat.

I nod. "I think it did too. Rawley doesn't seem to doubt what you're telling him."

"He doesn't completely trust you though either," Frank notes.

"True, but if we can make Friday happen, I think we're golden."

"Any suggestions on where we can go Friday night?" I ask the group.

Whitney lights up. "I know the perfect spot! I just read about it on Marley White's Facebook page."

"Who is Marley White?"

Whitney takes out her cellphone and taps the screen like a madwoman. "She is this amazing werewolf blogger. She travels around the country and reviews new dance clubs and restaurants. She's going to a new club here in New York City this weekend. She's been talking about it all week. It's perfect timing!"

Whitney hands me her phone.

"She crosses the barrier line?" I ask. "Pretty risky."

Whitney nods. "It's why she's so popular. The wolves back home love seeing the places she visits east of the dividing line."

I scroll through Marley White's Facebook page. She has a ton of followers and she posts a lot of pictures of the venues she's reviewing.

"Whitney is right guys. This is perfect."

I hand the phone to James so he can look at it. Frank leans over and they review the blog together.

"If Marley sees you at the club James, she is going to write about it. She may even post pictures. It will be all over social media." Whitney's face is beaming.

"Do you know Marley?" I ask James.

He shakes his head. "I do not."

"But she will know you!" Whitney exclaims. "Every werewolf knows you. You're a future pack leader. Just like every witch knows Chloe."

"I think this could work," Frank says.

"Me too," James agrees.

Frank stands and pushes in his chair. "Okay then. We know where we're going and we know we're going Friday night. I'll get the travel arrangements and security details worked out."

Willa speaks up for the first time. "I don't trust Rawley. We need to do all we can to protect Chloe. This could be a trap."

Frank nods. "As soon as our group leaves this building we will be followed by Julian's men. We have to set up perimeters around the club and along the route."

"We can use my guys too," James adds. "Have them in the club before we get there. They can check the place out and make sure we're not walking into an ambush."

I push my chair back. "Well, I'll leave the security details to you guys. Whitney and I have some important work of our own to do."

"We do?" Whitney asks.

225

"I haven't been out dancing in forever. I need a new outfit."

Whitney jumps up. "Yes! Let's go."

I turn to the guys and use my big girl voice when I say, "We'll meet Friday morning to confirm the final details of the plan. Willa and I will make any changes we feel are necessary."

Willa gives me a wink as I leave. Those leadership books are paying off.

Chapter Fourteen

Whitney, Jessica and I "ooh" and "aah" over several outfits we see online. Nothing is jumping out at me though.

"I tell you what," Whitney says, "I'll go shopping for you. I'll find you the hottest outfit. I promise."

At this point, I don't have any other options. I'm excited about going out, but I'm terrified at the same time. If Marley White is at the club, it's possible other werewolves will be there too. What if one of those wolves is a member of the rogue group? What if he comes after me?

I push the thought out of my head during my meeting with Willa on Thursday. We're discussing her current policies and where we'd like to see them go in the future.

"When Whitney was talking about social media the other day, it clicked with me how far behind I am. Maybe it's time we have more of a social media presence," Willa suggests.

"We can make it happen, but we need to be careful. It would be nice to have a webpage for witches to interact, but the log-in credentials and overall security will have to be carefully thought out. We don't want the average person somehow stumbling across it."

"Agreed," Willa says. "Work with the Guard. I'm sure you can come up with an easy solution."

I jot down some notes on my pad of paper. "Anything else for today?"

"Yes. It's a bit of a morbid topic though."

"Okay..."

She hands me a file folder.

"What's this?" I ask.

"A copy of my Will and a description of my preferred funeral arrangements."

My jaw drops. Her Will? Funeral arrangements?

"Willa, this is crazy."

She shrugs. "I'm old. I need to be prepared for these things."

I sigh. "Fine, I'll take this, but I'm not looking at it."

Willa smiles. "Alright. But just so you know, I'm leaving everything to you. My belongings, my money, everything. I don't want you to ever worry about finances."

I tear up. "I don't know what to say." I lean over Willa's desk to give her a hug. "Thank you."

"Absolutely. You're doing a great job Chloe."

Willa's praise means the world to me.

"You have to promise me you're not going to leave me any time soon," I say as I pull away.

Willa laughs. "I'll do what I can."

Friday morning I wake up full of energy. Tonight is the night! I get to break out of this place.

Frank and James confirm the security plan over breakfast. I listen intently for any potential hiccups, but Frank has every minute detail covered.

When Willa and I give our stamp of approval to the plan, Whitney claps her hands. "I'm so excited! I found you the best outfit Chloe! You're going to look so freaking hot!"

James rolls his eyes. "This isn't a girls night out. This is business."

Whitney brushes him off. "Get over yourself. We're going out and we're going to have fun."

I can't help but laugh, Whitney's energy is infectious. For the first time in forever, I'm going to do what normal girls my age do.

228

But first, I have to get through training with my skin-reading bodyguard and a hot werewolf.

Training goes well because I'm hyped up. James and two of his wolves circle me as I stand in my protective bubble. I'm now able to hold my protection spell for five minutes. I can also throw a bubble over someone else and protect them for thirty seconds.

Unfortunately, I haven't figured out how to hold the protective shell over myself and someone else at the same time. As it stands, the other person has to be right next to me for it to work.

When my bubble pops today, I use my super speed to zoom in-between the werewolves as they lunge. I want to try one of the glamour spells Willa and I have been working on. The problem is, I don't think I'll be able to hit all three werewolves with it at the same time.

The werewolves come at me quickly. I freeze James and one of his companions. The third werewolf lunges for me and I shoot the glamour spell at him. In a flash, instead of a growling werewolf, I'm looking at a small kitten. The orange and yellow striped cat meows loudly and chases its tail for a few seconds. Confused, it sits down, its green eyes staring up at me.

My glamour spell worked!

"Take care of the others!" Frank barks at me.

Oh yeah, right. I almost forgot about the other two wolves trying to kill me. I release the second werewolf and leave James frozen in place. When the second werewolf comes for me, I send electric energy out of my fingertips. The werewolf's body stiffens and jerks awkwardly as if he's been hit by a taser gun. He falls to the mat and transforms back into his human form.

And then there's James. What to do with him today?

Beating James has gotten a little old. I now know what Ivan meant when he said werewolves don't stand a chance against a powerful witch. The element of surprise is the only way James can get the best of me. And unfortunately for him, that's hard to achieve in our training sessions.

I stand in front of James's frozen body. I wonder what it feels like in there. Does he think any fluid thoughts, or is he literally stuck in time?

"Chloe! Focus!" Frank shouts.

I turn to Frank. "Not really sure what to do at this point. I mean, that one is a kitty cat; that one is taking a nap; and James is frozen. If this was the real world, I'd roast them all and be done with it."

"Fair enough," Frank concedes, "but you know as soon as you release James, he's coming after you."

"Not necessarily."

"What makes you think he won't?"

I shrug. "He can't come after me if I'm not here."

Frank smiles. "You're going to leave him frozen, aren't you?"

"Yep. Let me know how long the spell lasts."

Before I leave, I change my feline friend back into a werewolf. He shakes his head, then morphs back to his human form.

"That was the weirdest experience of my life," he says to me stupefied.

I grin. "You're welcome."

I wave good-bye to James's frozen figure and leave the training center.

Half an hour later, my room phone rings.

"Ms. Chloe, I'm calling to inform you that a werewolf is approaching your room."

My heart races. "Who is it?"

"James."

I relax. "You scared the crap out of me!"

"My apologies Ms. Chloe. I'm just following Directive Number Five."

230

"Directive Number Five?" I ask. Never heard of it. In fact, I've never heard of any of the directives.

"Yes Ms. Chloe. Per Frank's orders, I am to alert you when a werewolf is on your floor."

Have I never had a werewolf up here before? Now that I think about it, Whitney's never been in my room. We've always hung out somewhere else.

A loud banging ricochets off my door.

"I think said werewolf has arrived."

"Do you need assistance?" the Guard member asks.

"No, but thank you." I hang up the phone.

Fresh out of the shower, I'm in my robe and my hair is twisted up in a towel on the top of my head. This isn't the best way to open the door, but I don't think James will patiently wait while I get dressed.

"Come in!" I yell.

James walks into my room. His chest heaves and his hands are clenched into fists by his sides. Veins are popping out of his neck.

Crap.

Per my usual, I make light of the situation. "Hey! You're unfrozen!"

His eyes bulge. "How dare you leave me down there like that!"

Do I still have time to call for reinforcements?

I want to hide in my closet, but I stay and face the music. "It was a training exercise, I wanted to see how long I could keep you in place." My explanation sounds hollow even to me.

"Do you realize you've taken a half an hour of my life I'll never get back?!"

And now I feel even worse. "I'm sorry," I stammer. "I, I didn't look at it that way."

231

"Next time you want to conduct experiments, ask permission first."

I step toward James, but he backs away. "James, please. It was a stupid and inconsiderate thing for me to do. I didn't think it through."

"I know you hate me, but that was cruel."

I tilt my head to the side. "I don't hate you. I don't hate you at all. In fact, I thought we were becoming friends."

The anger in his eyes dims. "You have an odd way of treating your friends."

"I'm very sorry. Please accept my apology. I won't do it again. I promise."

He takes a deep breath and releases it slowly. "Alright then. I've said my peace and I accept your apology. Sorry for interrupting your shower."

I'm suddenly very aware that I'm in a robe and he's in boxer briefs. My heart flutters. I need to get him out of here.

"I was already done, but it is time for my nap."

James walks toward the door. "Get some rest. It could be a crazy night."

Jessica comes to my room around 9:00 p.m. to help with my hair and makeup.

"Please come with us tonight Jess. You'll have fun."

"Nah," she says as she pulls my hair up into a high ponytail. "Dancing isn't really my thing."

"Frank will be there," I tease.

"Frank will be working."

"True," I admit. "You guys wouldn't be able to hang out."

Jessica smiles sadly. "Frank wouldn't be interested in me anyway."

232

I turn and look at her. "Are you kidding? You're amazing. He'd be an idiot not to fall for you."

"I'm not a witch Chloe. He doesn't even notice me."

"Don't be ridiculous. Frank isn't the average male witch. He isn't concerned about your witch status."

Jessica slides a bobby pin in my hair underneath my ponytail. "If you say so."

When Jessica is done with my hair, I call down to Whitney.

She nearly shouts into the phone when she answers. "Hello!"

I hold the phone away from my ear for a second. "Whitney, when are you coming up? I need my clothes."

"I'm almost ready. I'll be there in ten minutes."

Next, I call the Guard.

"How can I help you Ms. Chloe?"

"Whitney is coming to my room. No need to worry about Directive Number Five."

"Understood," the male voice says, then hangs up.

Jessica raises an eyebrow. "Directive Number Five?"

I shake my head. "Don't ask."

I take one more look at myself in the mirror. The outfit Whitney picked out for me is awesome. A white silk shirt with long sleeves sits just above the beltline of skintight white leather pants. The shirt covers the front half of my body, but leaves my upper back exposed. My hawk tattoo is on full display and I love it.

The outfit is completed by beautiful, white suede high-heeled boots that come up to my knees. Whitney even bought me a slim-fit leather jacket the color of caramel to wear while I'm outside. I don't mean to brag, but I feel like a badass.

"You look amazing!" Jessica exclaims.

233

"Thank you! I feel amazing!" Whitney stands next to me in the mirror and I laugh. "We are complete opposites!"

Whitney is wearing a tight black dress. Her black stilettos have five inch heels and tiny metal spikes sticking out of them. Her dark hair is down and her green eyes shine.

We all climb into the elevator and descend to the Guard operations center where we're supposed to meet up with the guys.

Jessica lets us off. "You ladies have a good time."

Whitney is back to nearly shouting again. "We will!"

We wave at Jessica as the elevator doors close. Whitney and I lock arms and make our way to the conference room.

"We're ready!" Whitney announces when we walk in.

Frank, James, Willa, Ivan and Bane are huddled over a map confirming our route. They all look up and stare at us. I think I see Bane's jaw drop, but I can't be sure.

Willa breaks the silence. "Chloe! Whitney! You girls look fantastic!"

Whitney and I pose for her.

"If only I were sixty years younger!" she exclaims.

"I haven't shown you the best part." I turn around and let my jacket slip down to my elbows.

Willa gasps. "Oh Chloe…your hawk… it's gorgeous!"

"There's a lot more gold now, right?"

"Yes."

"A lot more," Frank adds.

I pull my jacket up. "You guys ready?"

Frank nods. "Yes. Our escorts are waiting outside."

Willa pulls me in for a tight hug. "Be careful."

"Don't worry Willa," Frank promises, "I'll bring her home safe."

Five black Escalades are running and ready to go when we step outside. Frank opens the back door to the third vehicle in line and I climb in. I'm surprised to find the two rows of backseats face each other. Whitney and I sit across from James and Frank as we ride to the club.

I look out the window and watch the city go by. It's my first time out of the building since Chelsea's funeral. Feels a little bizarre to be in the hustle and bustle I usually watch from my bedroom windows.

"This is going to be so much fun!" Whitney exclaims, her excitement reaching its boiling point.

James and Frank don't seem to share her enthusiasm. Mine is waning the closer we get to the club.

I crack my window open and take in the cool, fresh air. "Think the club will be busy?" I ask Whitney.

"It's already packed!"

She shows me Marley White's Instagram feed. Marley's photos show a long line waiting to get into the club and the packed dance floor inside.

I'm half-listening to Whitney as she goes on and on about how great the club looks, her guesses at what type of music will be playing, and the drinks she wants to get. I'm too busy watching out for stalkers to really appreciate what she's saying.

"We're good Chloe," Frank assures me, seeing my anxiety.

"There are so many hot guys there," Whitney says as she puts her phone back in her small black purse. "You going to dance with any of them?"

I don't want to dance with any guys, but before I can tell Whitney this, James says, "She will not."

"Excuse me?" I say with attitude. "I think that's my decision, not yours."

"A werewolf would never let his woman dance with another man. If you do, it will discredit our story."

235

I huff. "I didn't know you are the jealous type."

"All werewolves are the jealous type," Whitney informs me as we pull up to the club.

Everyone in line turns and stares at our Escalades as they come to a stop.

I see the look of anticipation on their faces. "They think we're celebrities."

"To werewolves and witches, you are," Whitney responds.

Frank presses his finger against his earbud, then says, "We're clear to exit."

Whitney pushes the door open, but James steps out first. He scans the sidewalk, then waves us on. Whitney steps out, then me, and then Frank.

Frank looks the part of a professional bodyguard in an all-black suit. He has an ear piece in one ear and a walkie talkie clipped to his suit pocket. He's on high alert as we walk through the crowd.

James isn't nearly as formal, but then again, he's not playing the part of my bodyguard. He's playing the part of my boyfriend.

He's wearing jeans, a grey t-shirt, and a brown leather jacket. He looks fantastic. It won't be hard for me to pretend I'm attracted to him. As he turns to make sure we're close behind him, I notice his shirt has a giant outline of a hawk on the front. Is this an homage to my tattoo?

James slips the bouncer a hundred dollar bill and the bouncer unhooks the red velvet rope to let us in. The music is pumping when we enter the building. We walk down a long, dark hallway that suddenly opens up to a giant dance floor.

The club is a refurbished warehouse. The lights are low and the music is loud. Neon lights shoot across the ceiling – yellow, pink, green, blue and orange. The Weeknd is singing about being a starboy as the bass thumps.

We weave our way through the crowd. James finds an open space near the bar.

He yells over the music, "There's an empty spot over there." He points to an area across the room. "We should head that way. Walk past as many people as we can. Hopefully someone will recognize us."

We all nod, the music too loud for a conversation.

We make our way across the floor, Whitney and I dancing a little as we go. The energy in the club is high and people are having fun. By the time we make it across the room I'm ready to dance.

James finds an open table and sits down.

"What are you doing?" I shout over the music.

"What does it look like I'm doing?" he yells back.

"I came here to dance!"

I take off my coat and throw it on the chair next to James. Whitney follows suit and throws hers on top of mine. I scan the club and see people dancing on an elevated platform fifteen feet away.

"Up there!" I yell to Whitney. "We'll definitely be seen up there!"

She grabs my hand and we make a bee line to the platform. When we get to it, Frank boosts me and Whitney up. The platform is a giant circle ten feet in diameter. We stay close to the edge so Frank can keep an eye on us from down below. Plus, more people will see us this way.

A Flo Rida song comes on and I start moving to it. I lose myself in the music and for a few minutes, I'm the girl I was six months ago. No worries, just the beat flowing through my body. Ice Cube comes on next. Whitney and I sing the song to each other as we dance.

I'm having a great time, but I stay mindful of the potential danger. I scan the crowd periodically for any red flags. Frank stays next to the platform, the heels of my boots level with his waist.

I see a few Guard members positioned around the club, their black suits making them easy to pick out. James's men are somewhere in the crowd as well, but they're harder to spot in the sea of unfamiliar faces.

I look over at our table, but James is gone. Probably sulking in a corner somewhere.

I turn back to Whitney and she shows me how to twerk. I'm laughing too hard to even attempt it when Ariana Grande suddenly coos over the speaker.

Whitney and I both squeal, "Ariana!"

I'm singing along to one of my favorite Ariana songs when I feel someone press his body against my bare back. A strong hand pulls me in and holds tight around my stomach. I glance over my shoulder and see James.

"We have to be seen together, and I don't think you want to hang out with me at the table," James whispers in my ear.

Goosebumps run up my arms. His body is warm and strong, protective but not domineering. I put my hand over his, keeping it in place.

We move together to the music and I close my eyes. Chelsea had a theory about the correlation between a man's dance skills and his skills in the bedroom. If she were here, I'd tell her James is a good dancer, and we'd both giggle about it.

James leans down and kisses the back of my neck. Heat shoots through my entire body. I don't care who's watching us. I'm not putting on a show. I like the feel of his body against mine, and I want him to know it. I turn around to face him and he steps back, concerned he may have gone too far.

I pull him toward me and whisper in his ear, "Don't stop. I want this."

He lowers his lips to mine, eyes gleaming in the flashing lights. His arms hold me close as I separate my lips and let his tongue explore mine. All the pent up attraction. All the flirtation. All crashing together. If we weren't in the middle of a club, I'd rip his clothes off and have my way with him. I'm tempted to do it anyway, regardless of the crowd.

238

In the midst of being completely wrapped up in James, I wonder what took us so long. He's smart, he's caring, he'll be a great leader, and I'm ridiculously attracted to him.

I pull away and look him in the eyes. "I want you. More than anything."

He smirks and whispers in my ear, "You don't know how long I've waited to hear that."

He kisses my neck again and a small moan escapes my lips. I remember what Whitney told me about werewolves and their mates. How a female bares her neck to the male to let him know she wants him.

I arch my back and tilt my head back as far as I can. I don't open my eyes to see if James understands what I'm doing, I know he will.

James groans and leans over. He runs his tongue from the base of my neck up to my jaw line. My body is quivering from the sensation. It is like warm ice running down my skin. His tongue stops just under my ear.

My eyes meet his. The intensity burns. He stands me up straight and our mouths meet again. Every part of me fully engrossed in the way his body feels against mine.

James lifts his head. "Umm...Chloe?"

I'm disappointed he's pulled away. I don't want the moment to end.

"Yeah?" I manage to say, trying to get myself together. After a second I realize the music has stopped. "What the..."

I look around and realize everything has stopped. The entire club is stuck in place. People holding drinks halfway to their mouths; Whitney's hair frozen midair as she whips her head around; others stuck in awkward dance movements.

"I've frozen all of them," I say with disbelief.

James scans the crowd, impressed. "Everybody but us."

I turn to him. "I better fix this, huh?"

239

"You probably should."

I focus on breaking the spell and the club comes to life. No one seems to notice what happened. I'm about to get back to where James and I left off, but I'm hit with a wave of dizziness. My body slumps into James.

"Hey, are you alright?" he asks concerned.

I put my hand on my forehead. "I feel tired all of the sudden."

James sweeps me up into his arms and yells to his sister, "Time to go Whit!"

Whitney starts to pout, but then she sees me in James's arms. "What's wrong? What happened?"

"Chloe needs to leave."

Frank reaches out his arms and James reluctantly hands me down to him.

"Can you walk?" Frank asks me.

I nod. "Yeah, I think so."

I hang my arm over Frank's shoulder and we walk toward the exit. Thankfully, the Guard has cleared a path for us to get out quickly. The cars are waiting at the curb and we climb into our Escalade.

As soon as I get in my seat, I lean my head against the window and close my eyes. My head is throbbing and blood pulses through the veins over my temples. Even though I didn't realize I was doing it, the magic I used in the club drained all of my energy.

Whitney climbs in and takes the seat next to me. James sits directly across from me, and Frank takes the last empty seat.

"Are you okay?" James asks.

I nod. "I just need to rest."

"You should see Sherman when we get home," Frank says.

"It's late, he's probably asleep."

James doesn't care about Sherman's beauty rest. "We'll wake him."

Frank hits the button on his walkie talkie. "Someone call headquarters. Make sure we have a healer ready upon arrival."

"Oh my God you guys! It worked!" Whitney exclaims.

Her loud voice makes me cringe.

"Sorry," Whitney says in a whisper. "But it worked! Look!"

Whitney hands me her cellphone.

I look at the screen and scroll down. "It did. It worked," I confirm.

"Are you sure?" Frank asks.

I turn the screen so Frank and James can see. "It's Marley White's Twitter page. James and I are all over it."

I scroll through the entries and read them aloud:

11:25 p.m. *Future pack leader James is in the house! And so is his little sis Whitney! Love her outfit!*

The post is accompanied by a picture of James as he walks through the club.

11:27 p.m. *Holy shit guys! The future Verhena is here too!*

This post is a picture of me, my back and hawk tattoo front and center.

11:50 p.m. *OMG!!! James and the Verhena are here together! And it's serious!!!*

The picture with the last post sends a flash of heat through me. It's me baring my neck to James. He is bent over me, about to slide his tongue up my neck. She must have taken this seconds before I froze the club.

I hand the phone back to Whitney without saying anything. The whole point of tonight was to be seen, but I feel like my privacy has been invaded. My most intimate moment is now plastered all over the internet.

241

Whitney scrolls through the posts again. "We have to send Marley flowers or something. She did exactly what we needed her to do."

No one says anything in response.

Not one to enjoy silence, Whitney continues talking. "Great job you guys!" she says looking at me and James, then back at the pictures. "You totally look like a couple. And you Chloe, baring your neck like that, genius!"

James narrows his eyes from across the aisle, then stares out the window.

I should correct Whitney and tell her it wasn't an act, but I need to talk to James in private. I don't want to announce how I feel about him in front of Whitney and Frank.

I lean my head back against the seat and close my eyes until we get home. When we pull up to the curb, all I can think about is getting to the Guard's operations center so I can stop the pounding in my head.

We file out of the car and into the building. James doesn't come anywhere near me. He won't even look me in the eye. Maybe everything in the club was an act for him. Maybe he doesn't care about me at all. I'm so upset by the thought of this, I tear up.

As soon as the elevator doors open, I rush out. Sherman is waiting for me and we go to a conference room. He shuts the door behind us and puts his hand to my forehead.

"You've run yourself very low."

"I know. I used a lot of magic tonight."

"Take deep breaths and I'll do the rest."

I follow Sherman's instructions and the pounding in my head dulls. It gets weaker and weaker until it's gone.

I give Sherman a hug. "Thank you so much. I feel a lot better now."

He pats my back. "That's what I'm here for."

I walk out into the common area of the Guard's operations center, but Whitney and James are gone.

"Where is everyone?" I ask Frank.

"They went up to bed."

"Oh," I say disappointed.

I guess my talk with James will have to wait until tomorrow.

"What happened tonight?" Frank asks.

"I didn't mean to, but I froze the entire club. It drained my energy."

His mouth drops open. "The entire club? For how long?"

I shake my head. "I don't know. I didn't realize I was doing it."

Frank smirks. "Too busy swapping spit with wolf boy, huh?

I slap his arm. "Don't be gross!"

"It's about time you guys hooked up."

"What are you talking about?"

He rolls his eyes. "C'mon Chloe. I may be a highly trained assassin, but I know sexual tension when I see it."

"Frank, have you been reading *Fifty Shades of Grey* again?"

He laughs. "Go upstairs. Get some rest."

I step into the elevator and turn to see Frank making kissy faces at me. I flip him off as the doors close.

Chapter Fifteen

I'm back in the club with James. Our bodies entwined, both feverish with desire. James is about to whisper something when a shrill ringing noise plays over the speakers. It's so loud, I cover my ears.

"What is that?!" I scream over the music.

Then I wake up. The loud ringing noise in my dream is my bedside phone. I roll over and look at the clock. 5:30 a.m.

What the hell?

"Hello?" I croak.

"Ms. Chloe, a werewolf is approaching your room."

I sit up, my heart pounding. "Who is it?"

"James."

I sigh. "Can you please stop calling me when he's coming to see me? You scare the hell out of me."

"Ms. Chloe, per Directive Number Five," the voice starts.

I cut him off. "Yeah, yeah, yeah."

"Do you need assistance?" the voice asks.

"No, I'm fine. But thank you."

"Understood."

I hang up the phone and yawn. What could James possibly want this early in the morning? A deep part of me, a part I'm trying to suppress, is hoping he's coming to finish what we started in the club.

My bedroom door opens without a knock.

"Chloe?" James whispers into the room.

"I'm here. I'm awake."

He shuts the door quietly. I can't see him very well, so I turn on my bedside lamp. He's still in the same clothes he wore to the club.

"What's going on? Did something happen?" I throw back my covers and jump out of bed, ready to spring into action.

"Why did you do it?" he asks, his voice hoarse.

I stop short. "What?"

He steps closer. "Why did you bare your neck to me?"

I stammer. "I, I don't know."

"Was it to put on a show? To make us more believable?"

"James, what Whitney said in the car..."

"Yes, what my sister said in the car was very illuminating. And you didn't dispute it, did you?"

I'm completely flustered. He's upset and I don't know how to handle it.

I stumble over my words. "I didn't say anything in the car because I was sick. Plus, I felt like it was a conversation we should have in private. Just the two of us."

"Tell me, do you understand what that ritual means to my pack?"

"I think so. Whitney told me about it."

"Then why did you do it?"

I throw my hands up, frustrated. "We were in the club, and we were dancing. And it felt so good to kiss you. I got caught up in the moment."

"Caught up in the moment?" he barks. "Caught up in the moment?" His eyes are wide and wild. "I should have known better. You are a silly, impulsive woman who acts without thinking."

"What are you talking about? You're not letting me explain."

"Oh, you've said plenty." James turns to walk out.

"Where are you going?" I implore him. "Let's talk about this."

"I'm done talking."

246

He leaves me standing in my room, my arms hanging by my sides.

What just happened?

I replay the conversation in my mind. A silly, impulsive woman? Screw him! I flop down on my bed and crawl under the covers. I pull them all the way up to my chin. I lay there trying to figure out where this went off the rails.

I should have said something in the car, or at least gone to see him as soon as we got home. Instead, I let it fester and his anger grew. The lunatic had already convinced himself I was putting on a show. Anything I said, he twisted to fit that belief.

Why does he automatically assume I don't really care? Does he think I'm the type of person who would play mind games? I thought he and I were getting to know each other pretty well. Between the training sessions, and our chats in the library, I thought he and I were on the same page last night at the club.

The only thing giving me a glimmer of hope is the thought that if he's this upset, he must have feelings for me. Right?

I want to go see James right away and explain everything, but it's probably best if I let him calm down. If I go now, the same scene may play out again.

I try to fall back to sleep, but there's no way that's going to happen. At 6:30 I give up on sleep and take a shower. Then I go down to the kitchen for a bowl of cereal and bring it back to my room.

I stare blankly at the TV, my mind somewhere else. By 8:30, I decide enough time has passed. I take the steps down to James's floor, practicing what I want to say one last time. I open the door to the 13th floor and tiptoe down the hall.

James's room is on the left-hand side, the door closest to Whitney's room. As I approach the door, I hear two male voices. The door is open just enough for me to hear their conversation. I can tell right away it's James and Ivan.

"You need to apologize to her," Ivan says.

"No I don't," James protests. "She is in the wrong here."

"You're being ridiculous. Don't throw all of this away because your feelings are hurt."

"It's more than my feelings. What she did was disrespectful."

"Do you know what a union with her could mean for us?" Ivan asks in an angry tone.

"Yes, you've told me a million times."

"You could be the savior of the pack. You have the power to ensure our people will be safe for generations to come. With the witches on our side, we will be protected. We will thrive again."

"I know, I know," James says.

"You were making such progress with her. You have to patch this up."

I feel sick, like tiny daggers are stabbing me in the chest. I think back to the first time I met James. He made it clear he was willing to do whatever it takes to protect his pack. I never thought it would include messing with my heart.

I should walk away. No, I should run away. But I don't. Instead, fueled by my anger, I slam the door open with my hand.

"*That's* what this has been about?"

Ivan's mouth drops open in shock and James jumps up from his bed.

"Chloe?" James asks surprised. "What are you doing here?"

"I came here to apologize, you dick!"

"It's not what you think."

"Ha! That's what everyone says when they're busted."

Ivan starts to speak, but I put my hand up to silence him. His mouth closes and his shoulders slump.

I glare at James. "This is why you've been so nice to me? This is why you've been spending more time with me? So you can win me over? All for the benefit of your pack? So we can be a supernatural power couple?"

I'm full-on enraged now. I feel my fingers tingling with heat, fire desperate to shoot from them.

A dark laugh escapes my lips. "You know what the crazy thing is James? It was working. I was falling for you. I let you have my neck because I wanted to. I wanted it more than anything." My voice cracks. "Congrats to you, your game worked. Until now."

I turn to leave. I have to get out of here before I break down.

"Chloe, wait! Please!"

James reaches out for me, but I freeze both him and Ivan. Ivan is leaning on his cane, eyes cast down. James is lunging for me. I take a long look at his face and remember how it felt to kiss those lips. It was all fake, all a ruse.

I run for the elevator, tears spilling from my eyes. On a good day, I've got thirty minutes before James is back in motion. But I'm tired from last night and I have no idea how my emotions will affect the power of the spell.

I hit the button for the elevator over and over again, like pushing it a hundred times will make it move faster. I keep checking over my shoulder to make sure James and Ivan aren't coming after me.

I'm angry, embarrassed and brokenhearted. I'm not sure which emotion to deal with first.

The elevator finally makes its way to the 13th floor and I jump inside. I hit the "door close" button several times, watching for James and Ivan as the doors shut. I look at the number pad on the elevator control panel. There is not a single number I want to pick, no place in this building I want to be. I want to get the hell out of here. Now.

I press the "1" button for the lobby and main entrance. I don't have a plan. I'll walk out the front door and go from there.

I'm crying hysterically into my hands as the elevator makes its descent. Who can I trust? I trusted the werewolves, but they were here to play me.

Is Whitney in on this too?

What about Willa? Did she know? She'd love a werewolf/witch union.

My mind is reeling when the elevator doors open. I have to move quickly if I want to make it out of the building. The Guard is probably already watching me and wondering what I'm up to.

I run through the lobby, my eyes focused on the exit. I can see the sidewalk and people walking by on the other side of the glass. I'm so close.

"Ms. Chloe!" a Guard member yells from the reception desk. "Stop!"

I ignore him and run faster. I push the door open and I'm hit with the cool spring air. I don't have a jacket, but I don't care. I need out.

I'm through the door and running down the sidewalk. People look at me as I run by, but this is New York City, people run on the sidewalks every day.

Just as I'm starting to feel good about my escape, I turn the corner at the end of the block and run into Bane and Willa. Literally.

I slam into Bane's hard body and the impact sends me flying backward. I land on my butt and hit my funny bone in my left arm.

"Oww!" I holler in pain.

"Chloe?" Willa asks surprised. "Sweetie, are you okay?"

Bane helps me up.

"Yeah, I'm fine," I say, rubbing my elbow.

Willa takes a good look at me. "What is going on? Why are you crying? What are you doing out here?"

I narrow my eyes. "What are *you* doing out here?"

"I'm strengthening the wards. I do every morning."

"Oh," I say with less hate.

"Your turn, what are you doing out here?"

I open my mouth, but I don't know what to say. Instead, I start crying. "Willa, I have to get out of here. I can't be in the same building as the werewolves anymore."

Willa pulls me in for a hug. "There, there Chloe. It's okay." She strokes my hair and lets me cry on her shoulder.

After a few minutes, I pull away from her. She hands me a tissue from her pocket.

"I'll make you a deal. If you go back into the building with me, we'll talk about whatever is bothering you. Then we'll figure out a way to get you out of here for a few days."

I wipe the tears from my eyes and sniffle. "Really?"

Willa nods her head. "Really."

"Okay," I choke out.

Willa puts her arm around me and we head back to the building together. A group of Guard members is huddled in the lobby when we walk back in.

"It's alright," Willa tells them. "I've got her."

We get on the elevator and take it to the Guard's operations center.

"We'll go into one of the conference rooms. The werewolves won't be able to get to you here," Willa explains.

We take seats at the table in the conference room. By this time I've stopped crying and calmed down a little.

"Now, you want to tell me what's going on?" Willa asks warmly from across the table.

I tell her the story. Every gory detail. How James has been extra nice to me lately, what happened in the club, James coming to my room early in the morning, and the conversation I overheard.

251

Concern furrows Willa's brow. "This is upsetting. I've known Ivan for years. I would never guess he'd play a game like this."

I shrug. "I heard what I heard Willa."

"Hmm…" Willa looks as upset as I feel. "I'll have to talk with Ivan about this."

"I figured you would."

Suddenly, the conference room door swings open. The sound of it crashing against the wall makes me jump.

"Are you crazy?!" an enraged Frank screams as he comes in the room. "You could have been killed out there!"

I shrink in my seat. "I'm sorry."

"You're sorry?! You're sorry?!" Frank's face is bright red, his flexed arms about to bust out of his shirt. "I spend my days trying to protect you and train you so you can protect yourself! Then your dumbass runs out of the building and comes within twenty feet of being outside the wards! Twenty feet Chloe!"

"Enough," Willa says softly. "She is safe now."

I get up and walk over to Frank. He's taking deep breaths, his chest heaving in and out. I grab him in a big hug. At first he resists, then he relents and hugs me back.

"You scared me to death," he says, resting his chin on my head.

"I'm sorry Frank. I just wanted out of here. I didn't think about the consequences."

"Or who you might hurt," Willa adds.

I shake my head. "No, I didn't think of that either."

Willa stands. "Chloe, tell Frank what you told me. While you two chat, I'll pay Ivan a visit. We need the whole story."

I cringe. "Um, about that…"

"Yes?"

"Ivan might still be frozen."

Willa sighs. "Undo it Chloe."

"I don't know if I can from here."

"Try," she presses.

I close my eyes and envision James and Ivan the way I left them. I visualize releasing the spell.

"Okay, I did it."

"Good. I'll track down Sue. We'll find out what Ivan has to say about all of this."

"Definitely bring Bane, I mean Sue, just in case."

Willa leaves me and Frank in the conference room.

"What's going on?" Frank asks.

I tell him about my fight with James this morning and the conversation between James and Ivan.

"Makes sense," Frank says when I'm done. "Shacking up with you would protect his pack."

I nod. "It does, but I hate the part where he pretended to like me."

"How do you know he was pretending? He seems pretty into you. Why, I have no idea."

I sigh. "A man who really loves me is too much to ask for I guess."

Frank rolls his eyes. "Stop being a drama queen. We need to get to the bottom of this. Now that they're unfrozen, James and Ivan will want to talk to you ASAP."

As if on cue, shouting erupts from the floor of the Guard center.

"Where is she?!" James shouts.

Frank scrambles out of his chair. "Get down!" he hisses. He turns off the light and huddles next to the door.

"I'm not authorized to give you that information," a member of the Guard answers.

"I need to see her. Now!"

"Not possible," the Guard member responds blandly.

"Where is Frank?" James demands next.

"Frank is with Ms. Chloe."

"Is it true she left the building?"

"Affirmative."

"Damn it!"

"James, you need to calm down." It's Ivan. "Let's go back to your room. You need to rest. We can clear things up when Chloe gets back."

"Get off of me!" I cringe at the tone James uses toward Ivan. "This is all your fault! You had to go on one of your rants about how great it would be for the two of us to be together. Now she thinks the only reason I want to be with her is for the pack!"

"James? What is going on?" Now Willa is involved.

"Willa," James's tone softens. "Please, please let me see Chloe."

"I'm sorry James, but Chloe doesn't want to see you."

"Is she safe? Will you tell me that? I heard she ran out of the building."

"She is safe," Willa confirms. "You don't have to worry about that."

"Okay, good." James calms down.

"You look exhausted James. You should rest," Willa says.

"I can't. I'm too worked up."

"Tell you what, let's go up to my office and chat."

James gives in. "Fine."

When we're sure James and Ivan are gone, Frank stands and turns the light back on.

"What do you think?" he asks.

"James is pissed."

Frank snorts. "That's an understatement. I told you he'd want to see you."

I pick at my fingers. "Of course he does. He has to cover his ass."

"He sounds genuine to me."

"I don't know which way is up." I lay my head on the table. "The last twelve hours have been a shit show."

"Do you still want to leave?"

"I think so."

He frowns. "I'll see what I can do, but I won't lie, that's going to be difficult. We have emergency evacuation plans, but this isn't an emergency. I don't want to use all of those resources."

"Understood," I whisper.

Frank comes over and sits beside me. "This will all be worked out."

"What if James has been faking it the whole time?"

Frank thinks before responding. "I believe James and his family want to help us with the rogue wolves. Agreed?"

I nod my head.

"Maybe they did talk about how a union between the two of you would be beneficial to them. It makes sense, right?"

"Sure it does."

"So the real issue is whether James genuinely cares about you, or if he's been playing you?"

I frown. "Yes, that's the issue."

Frank runs his hand through his hair. "I don't think we should sever all ties with them. Not now. We need their help to get Julian. We'd have to go back to square one if we kick them out."

I play out the scenario in my mind. If we make the werewolves leave, we will have no connection to Julian. Finding him would be a lot more difficult, and we're so close.

"They have to stay," I conclude. "We need to keep working with them."

"Willa will talk to Ivan. She'll find out what's going on."

"What if they lie?"

Frank shrugs. "It's possible. But so what?"

"So what? So what?" I slam my hand on the table. "They come in here with a grand scheme to hook me up with James and it's no big deal?"

"So what," Frank repeats. "Don't play along with it. Game over. You work with James toward a common goal – catching his father – and that's the end of it."

I put my face in my hands. "I'm such an idiot."

Frank rubs my back. "You're not an idiot. You fell for the guy. No big deal."

"It is a big deal! I act tough, but I'm still a woman. I still want the guy I like to like me back. No one wants to hear it's nothing more than a scheme."

"You don't know for sure it's been a scheme. You're putting the cart way ahead of the horse. Talk to him."

I shake my head. "I don't want to. I can't."

"Let the dust settle, then talk to him." Frank stands. "I'll see what I can do about getting you out of here." He slides a television remote to me. "In the meantime, find something funny to watch."

Frank leaves me alone in the conference room. I turn my chair toward the big screen TV on the opposite wall. Not finding better options, I settle on a game show. The thoughts running through my mind eventually settle. I'm about to nod off when Frank comes back in the room.

"I'm still looking into it, but I think you're stuck here," Frank tells me.

I groan. "That's what I thought you'd say."

Willa knocks on the conference room door. "Okay if I come in?"

Frank steps out of Willa's way. "Of course."

Willa sits down and clasps her hands together on the table. "I had a long talk with Ivan and James."

"And?" I ask.

"Ivan admits he has been pushing James to form a union with you."

My face drops.

"But," Willa quickly interjects, "James insists that wasn't his motivation. He says he really cares for you."

"Do you believe him?"

Willa nods. "I do. And I don't think there was any ill intent on Ivan's end either. He saw a connection between the two of you and was excited by the prospect of you being a couple. He feels badly for what's happened."

I sit quietly for a couple minutes. Frank and Willa let me stir my thoughts around. "I need some time. Some peace and quiet."

Willa smiles. "I bought you some time."

"What do you mean?"

"I may have told Sue to let the word 'Florida' slip out during a not-so-private conversation in front of Ivan and James."

"Florida? What does Florida have to do with anything?

Frank laughs out loud. "That's awesome!"

Willa blushes. "It was cruel, but I didn't know what else to do."

Frank is still laughing.

"You two want to let me in on the joke?"

Frank calms down and explains. "Willa has a secured living quarters in Florida. We go down there every year for a few weeks. We haven't gone this year because of everything that's going on. When Bane mentioned Florida, it was to make James think that's where you are."

"Oh, he does," Willa says. "He's already left the building."

This makes Frank crack up again.

I gasp. "Willa! You can't let him go all the way to Florida!"

She shrugs. "He'll come back. I'll call him when he gets down there and let him know you're here. No harm done."

I smack my forehead. "You are cruel. I didn't know you had it in you."

Frank is in awe. "It was genius Willa! Pure genius!"

"I couldn't get you out of the building, so I got James out for a while."

"He really left?"

Willa nods her head. "Our vehicle tracker says he's at JFK. He could be on a plane by now."

Guilt washes over me as I think of James getting on a plane and flying all the way to Florida. Willa was trying to help, but it just makes me feel worse.

"What about Ivan and Whitney? Are they still here?"

"Yes. Whitney is rather upset."

Poor Whitney. She has no idea the firestorm she started last night with one stray comment.

I sigh. "I'll talk to her later."

Willa stands. "Well, I'm going upstairs for a nap. All this chaos has worn me out."

"Thank you for everything Willa. I appreciate it."

"No problem kid," Willa winks, then she's out the door.

I strum my fingers on the table. "This is a mess."

"Young love," Frank says in a dreamy voice.

"Shut up!" I punch Frank in the arm and he pretends it hurts.

"What are you going to do now?" he asks when he's done pouting.

"I don't know. I guess go up to my room and try to get some sleep."

"That's a good idea. Get some rest. You'll feel better with a clear head."

We stand and push in our chairs.

"Chloe..." Frank hesitates.

"Yeah?"

"For what it's worth, I've seen the way he looks at you. He can't fake that."

I smile. "Thanks."

I turn to walk away, but stop myself. "You're a great friend. An excellent bodyguard, sure. But you mean a lot to me. I wouldn't be able to handle any of this without you."

Frank's cheeks redden. "Come on now, you're making me blush."

I smile bigger. "I just wanted you to know."

I walk out of the room before either of us feel inclined to crack a joke. It might kill the moment.

Chapter Sixteen

I should go see Whitney, but I don't feel like it.

Jessica comes to visit me for a little while to see how I'm doing.

"I don't know what to think Jess," I say after I fill her in on the details.

"It's a tough one," she agrees. "What does your gut tell you?"

"That he cares about me. But it might be telling me that because it's what I want to believe."

"You have to talk to him. Look him in the eyes. Whatever your instincts tell you in that moment, it's right."

Jessica leaves me to my misery. No need for her to sit around and suffer with me.

Willa calls around 6:00 p.m. to let me know she spoke with James and he's on his way back to New York.

"How did he sound?" I ask.

"Tired."

"I'm sure he is. Any idea when he'll be back?"

"I bought him a ticket for a flight leaving Miami at 8:30 p.m. It's supposed to land at 11:15 p.m. I suspect he'll come right home."

"Okay. Thanks."

"Do you want me to have someone call you when he gets here?"

"Yes, that would be good."

"Will do."

We hang up and I consider my options.

I don't want to train.

I don't want to swim.

I don't want to watch TV.

I don't want to read a book.

I don't want to see Whitney.

I don't want to bother Frank.

I can't think of a single thing I want to do except see James.

Then an idea pops in my head. If I hurry, I can see the sunset.

I've never been on the roof, but I know Willa has a garden up there. I hit the "20" button when I get in the elevator. The doors open to a completely empty and open area. This is unused space set aside for storage. The only light in the room is coming from the windows. The echo of my footsteps on the concrete floor is a bit creepy.

I'm about to turn around when I see a door in a dark corner. Above it is a sign that reads "Rooftop Access." I push the door open and find a stairwell. As I ascend the steps, I feel like an actress in a horror movie. Maybe this wasn't such a good idea after all.

When I get to the top of the stairs, there's another door with a giant "Exit" sign over it. Praying this is the last and final door to the outside, I push it open. To my tremendous relief, I've made it to the roof.

The sun is about to slip under the western horizon, sending its pink light across the sky. I move toward the edge of the roof and do a 360 degree turn. The crisp air feels good in my lungs. The Manhattan skyline is in the distance and the city is about to switch on the lights.

"Ms. Chloe?" a voice says behind me.

I nearly jump out of my skin. I turn around prepared to fry the hell out of someone. Thankfully, it's a Guard member.

He smiles. "I didn't mean to scare you."

"You all say that, but I swear you have some kind of contest going on down there to see who can make me pee my pants first."

262

He laughs. "As fun as that sounds, I promise it's not our objective."

"Sure," I say sarcastically.

I've never seen this Guard member before. Like me, he has blonde hair and blue eyes. His hair is spiked with gel and he has an ear piece in his left ear. He's decked out in black cargo pants and a bulky black jacket.

"Is there something I can help you with Ms. Chloe?"

I shake my head. "No. I'm up here for the sunset."

He smiles. "One of the perks of being up here - I get to see the sunset every day. Plus, I don't have to sit around with a bunch of guys talking about combat techniques."

I laugh. "I'd rather be out here too. Except when it snows."

He points to a small building. "When the weather is really bad, I stay in the hut. It's heated in the winter and it has A/C in the summer."

"Is there a TV in the hut?"

"Just surveillance televisions. I'm on duty you know." He looks around. "Which I should probably be getting back to."

"What's your name?" I ask before he can walk away.

"Marcus."

I extend my hand. "Nice to meet you Marcus."

He returns my handshake. "It's very nice to meet you too Ms. Chloe, but I'm getting yelled at in my ear bud. I have to go back on patrol."

"Is it Frank?"

"How'd you know?"

I laugh. "It's always Frank."

"There are some chairs by the greenhouse if you want to sit and enjoy the sunset. I'll see you later."

Marcus turns and walks back toward his hut.

I head in the direction of the greenhouse and find the chairs sitting beside it. I turn one toward the sunset and take a seat.

I can see my breath in the air as I sit and watch the sun go down. When the sun has descended and the stars come out, the twinkling lights from the city start shining too.

I'm cold, but then I remember I can solve that problem. I form a small bubble around myself and it slowly warms up. It's my own portable space heater!

When I'm done watching the sky, I take a tour through Willa's greenhouse. I know nothing about plants, but it is a sight to see. Beautiful flowers surrounded by lush green vegetation. Intricately detailed stained-glass butterflies are stuck here and there in the soil. White lights are strung across the top of the building and light up the night. I'm in awe of the time and attention Willa must give her greenhouse. This is obviously her passion.

Next, I walk around the perimeter of the roof and look at the sights above and below. People laughing, taxicabs honking, the smell of the pizza shop down the street, and the cool, crisp air all come together to form the perfect urban puzzle.

Why haven't I been up here before?

I pass Marcus as he's making his rounds and he puts up his hand to say, "hi." He doesn't stop to talk, likely because he'll get yelled at again if he does.

How many Guard members don't I know? I've never seen Marcus before, yet every day he's here protecting me. I promise myself that when this werewolf business is over, I will meet and thank each and every Guard member in the building.

I eventually trek back inside. When I walk in my room, Whitney is sitting on the bed. I consider bolting, but it's too late for me to back out. She's already seen me.

"Hey," I say, taking off my hat and gloves.

"Hey." She looks so sad. "I hope I'm not bothering you."

I hang up my coat and take a seat in the desk chair. "You're not bothering me."

"It feels like you're hiding from me."

"I'm hiding from everyone Whitney. Don't take it personally."

"I want you to know," she tears up, "if there's some great conspiracy going on, I didn't know about it. I swear."

I sigh. "I never thought you did. Okay, for a second there I thought you might be involved, but only when I was angry."

Whitney wipes a tear away with her fingertip. "I have no idea what's going on. Everyone leaves me in the dark. When I woke up this morning, James was acting like a lunatic. Throwing things in his room, yelling at my grandfather. He was out of control."

"Did they tell you what happened?"

"Eventually."

I'm curious to hear what Ivan told Whitney, so I ask.

"My grandfather told me James is super pissed at him. He said you overheard a conversation between the two of them. They were talking about my grandfather wanting you to marry James."

"Is that why your grandfather is here?"

Whitney shakes her head. "Not from what he's told me. This has always been about my dad and stopping him from taking over. My grandfather is terrified Dad will somehow convince the pack to attack the witches."

"He's never said anything to you about me and James?"

"No, I swear it." Whitney pauses. "Well, maybe once."

I lean forward in my seat. "When?"

"It was just last night, before we went out. I heard him tell James to be careful. And then he told James 'make sure you treat her right, it could lead to something bigger.'" Whitney's impression of Ivan's deep voice makes me smile. "I had no idea what he meant at the time, but I guess I do now."

265

I sit back in the chair. Interesting…

"What was James's response?"

Whitney shrugs. "He basically brushed it off. He told my grandfather he doesn't play games, not even for the pack."

My heart lightens a little. She makes it sound like this has all been a huge misunderstanding. Whitney is a lot of things, but I don't think a liar is one of them. I can't see her looking me in the eyes and not telling the truth.

"Are you mad at me?" Whitney asks.

I walk over and give her a hug. "Not at all."

She squeezes me back. "I hated the thought of you being mad at me. I had to come talk to you."

We separate and return to our seats - she on my bed, me in the desk chair.

I look at the clock. 10:00 p.m. I killed more time on the roof than I thought. "Your brother will be home soon."

"I know. I talked to him before he boarded his flight home."

"Was he pissed?"

"No, not really. He sounded tired. And sad."

I nod. "That's what Willa said too."

"He asked about you. I told him I hadn't spoken with you, but everyone assured me you are safe. He is worried because you went out on your own this morning. He's afraid you'll do it again."

"I was upset. I shouldn't have run off like I did. It was stupid."

We sit quietly for a moment and Whitney changes the subject.

"Rawley called him today."

My stomach drops. "He did? What did he say?"

"My dad saw the pictures online. Rawley wants to meet with James again tomorrow at 10:30 a.m."

I rub my temples, the trace of a headache coming in. "At least something good came out of last night."

"I'm scared Chloe," Whitney admits. "My dad is crazy. Who knows what he has planned for you guys."

"Hard telling, but we'll be ready for it."

After Whitney leaves, I lay down in bed. I try to sleep, but instead I think about Rawley and what he may have in store for James tomorrow. Will he finally reveal Julian's location? Or will he have some other hurdle for us to jump over?

Despite my concerns, I doze off. I'm woken up by my bedside phone. My digital clock says 12:15 a.m. My heart starts pounding when I realize this is probably my "James is home" call.

"Hello?"

"Chloe, it's Frank."

"Yeah?"

"Werewolf in the house."

Just as I suspected.

"Where is he?" I ask.

"He's by the pool."

"The pool?" That's odd.

"Yep. The pool."

I sigh. "Alright."

"Go get him tiger," Frank says with a chuckle.

"You're ridiculous."

"Just part of my charm."

I hang up the phone and head for the bathroom. I splash my face with cold water to wake myself up. My hands shake as I dry them with a towel.

"Get it together girl," I say out loud to my reflection.

I take the elevator to the 12th floor and hold my breath as the doors open. I see James immediately. He is standing in front of the glass wall staring out into the night sky. Somewhere along the line he managed to change his clothes. He's now wearing a pair of dark denim jeans with a red t-shirt.

He doesn't realize I'm watching him until I say, "Cameras" loudly. I watch the red light go out on the camera closest to me.

James turns to look at me. He smiles sadly, then turns back to the window. I walk toward him and sit on the chaise lounge closest to him. I tuck my legs into my chest and squeeze them, just like I did the day I hid under the quilt tent with Chelsea in our old bedroom.

That seems like another lifetime.

I glance over at James. Neither of us says anything for a minute or two. I'm not sure where to start.

"Do you remember when I had to go back home and get my men?" James asks me. He doesn't turn away from the glass.

"Yes," I answer.

"I was gone for four days. I was less than thrilled to come back. You torched my watch and it seemed like you would be difficult to work with. I thought this was a horrible idea." He looks at me for a second, then back out the window.

"It was late when I came home. I showed my men where they would be staying and then found my own room. I was restless and couldn't sleep. I decided to go for a swim, I thought it might be relaxing, or at the very least, wear me out. I used the stairs, but when I walked in, you were already here."

He smiles to himself. "You were standing in this very spot with your hand against the glass." James raises his own hand to the glass.

Recognition dawns in my mind. "The night of the storm…"

He nods. "Yes. You stood here watching the storm. The lightning illuminating your face and body. I stood in the shadows and watched you. I'm sure it sounds creepy, but it was the most beautiful thing I'd ever seen. You were breathtaking."

I remember how I felt that night. Lost in the storm. I also remember for a second I thought someone was watching me. I guess I was right.

"I was smitten with you from that moment on. Everything I did after that was for you. You probably don't believe it, but it's the truth."

James pulls his hand off the glass and walks toward me. He sits across from me on the edge of a chaise lounge.

"Do you know the men I brought with me are the best fighters in our pack? They know more about combat than I ever will."

I shake my head. "I don't know anything about them."

"Because I didn't want you to. I didn't want you getting close to any of them. In the beginning, I couldn't trust them to fight with you in their Were forms. I was too concerned they would hurt you, so I did it myself."

James stands again and paces. "I told myself I couldn't get involved with you. We had business to take care of and when it was all over, I'd be heading home and you'd be here in New York. But then I started allowing myself little things. First it was combat training. Then it was group meals. Then it was our meetings in the library. I was letting go a little more each time."

"Why didn't you say something?" I ask. "I was driving myself crazy thinking I was imagining something between us."

James grimaces. "I never meant for this to happen. I was supposed to come here, catch my dad, and go home. I've had my life planned out since I was a kid. You were never part of the plan."

"What about the things your grandfather said?"

James sighs. "I made the mistake one night of confiding in him that I have feelings for you. I went to him for guidance, but instead he got excited. He played out in his mind what a union between us could mean. Since then, he's brought it up almost every day. What you heard this morning was another one of those talks."

"Okay, so what happened between us this morning?"

James stands in front of the glass wall looking out at the horizon. "I told myself last night I wasn't going to do anything inappropriate. I would stay close to you in the club so we would be seen together. Nothing more than that. But then I saw you dancing, and I couldn't stop myself. I had to touch you. I wanted to feel your skin under my fingertips. And then you kissed me, and told me you wanted me. When you bared your neck to me, I lost myself completely."

I get up and stand next to him near the glass, our arms touching slightly. I reach out my hand and take his. He grasps it, his touch warm.

"James, I meant what I said to you last night at the club."

He nods. "I know that now, but I wasn't sure last night. Then Whitney made the comment in the car about how smart you were for baring your neck to me. I thought it was all for show. I was angry. Really angry. As you could tell this morning."

"You didn't give me the chance to explain."

"I was too upset. When I heard you ran out of the building," his hand tightens around mine, "I was so worried about you. When I think about what could have happened to you..." his voice breaks.

I touch his face with my free hand. "I'm okay."

He gazes at me with sad eyes. "It would have been my fault if something happened to you. It makes me sick to think about it, even with you right here in front of me."

James looks back out the window. "I was frantic to see you. To be sure you were fine. As soon as Bane mentioned Florida, I was out of here." He snorts. "And to think you were under my nose the entire time."

I frown. "I wasn't a part of that plan. I'm sorry."

"No, it's okay. It forced me to slow down and think things through."

270

"Me too."

James shakes his head. "That Willa, she's a smart lady."

I wrap my arms around his neck. "I'm sorry about everything. I should have said something in the car last night."

James brushes a piece of hair out of my eyes. "No, I'm sorry. I shouldn't have overreacted and ripped you apart this morning."

"I probably shouldn't have frozen you and your grandfather either."

James laughs. "I guess we both acted poorly today."

"To say the least."

"How about this - I won't charge into your room at 5:30 a.m. and you won't freeze me and my loved ones. Deal?"

"Deal," I say with a smile. "I'm glad you're back. I missed you."

He raises an eyebrow. "Even though you were furious with me?"

"Yes." I look up into his eyes. "I don't want to rush things with you. I want to do this right."

His eyes are intense. "Me too. You mean so much to me."

I let go of his neck and take his hand. "Come on. Let's get out of here."

"Where are we going?" he asks as I pull him along.

"My room."

The next morning, I wake up with my head on James's chest. We climbed into bed together last night and passed out, both of us exhausted from the long day we had. Having James next to me in bed was the best I've felt in a long time.

I'm relishing the moment when my bedside phone rings. James stirs when I roll off his chest.

271

Hello?" I answer.

Frank's voice fills my ear. "Good morning sunshine!"

"What do you want?" I ask, chuckling.

"Tell your man it's 8:30. We need to discuss his meeting with Rawley and get him miked up."

"Alright. We'll be down soon."

When I hang up the phone, it hits me. Everyone in the building knows James stayed with me last night. They probably think we got it on.

If only they were right…

"Let me guess," James says stretching his arms and legs, "Frank telling me it's time to get back to work."

"Yep."

James lays on his side and props himself up on his elbow. "What do you say we forget the whole thing and lay in bed all day?" He runs his finger up my arm.

"Don't tempt me."

"Oh," he says with a sly grin. "So I shouldn't do this?"

He pulls on my legs and I slip down onto my back. He's on top of me in a second, holding up his weight with his hands. He leans down and kisses my neck from ear to ear.

It feels so good. I slide my hands along his back. I want to feel his body against mine. He kisses my lips...

And then my phone rings again.

James groans and rolls off of me.

"Frank!" I yell into the phone when I pick it up. "I swear to God…"

A female voice interrupts me. "Chloe, it's not Frank. It's me, Whitney."

"Oh. Hey Whitney. What's up?"

"I'm worried about James. He didn't come home last night."

I smack my forehead. Poor Whitney, always in the dark.

"Whitney, he came home last night."

She's not persuaded. "No he didn't. He's not in his room, and my grandfather said he never heard James come in last night."

James grabs the phone. "Hey Whit!"

I can hear Whitney stammer on the other end. "Um...hi James."

"I stayed with Chloe last night. Thanks for the concern though."

James hands the phone back to me. I look at him horrified. What the hell am I supposed to say now?

He grins at me and jumps out of bed. He whistles as he turns on the shower. I have to look away when he starts taking off his boxer briefs. I won't be able to handle it.

"See," I say casually, "he's fine."

"I guess you guys made up, huh?"

"You could say that." I'm distracted by James standing in my glass shower, his back to me. I'm captivated by the soap running down his naked body.

Whitney brings me back to Earth. "Chloe, are you there?"

"Yeah, sorry. What did you say?"

"I asked if James is meeting with Rawley today."

"He is. We're heading down to the Guard center soon."

"Is it okay if I come?"

"Absolutely! You should come."

"Okay. See you in a few."

I hang up the phone and head into the bathroom. James is already out of the shower and has a towel wrapped around his waist. A single bead of water runs down his chest and I have the sudden urge to lick it off.

"I'm going to run up to my room for some clean clothes." He gives me a quick kiss. "Meet you downstairs?"

I nod. "Sure."

I sigh loudly after he leaves. I can't help but wonder – does taking it slow mean no sex?

We follow the same protocol as the last meeting with Rawley and send James out with an invisible wire. I'm not a nail biter, but I find myself picking at them as we listen to James walking down the city street.

Rawley chose yet another coffee shop to meet in. This one a few more blocks away.

We hear James walk into the coffee shop and I relax a little. No way Rawley will attack James in a public place.

James speaks first. "What's up?"

Rawley's gruff voice comes across the mic. "James, good to see you. Sit, please."

"Did I do good?" James asks.

"Good? Brother, you did great! Your father is ecstatic. We never guessed you'd be able to get so close to her."

"I told you guys, I got this."

"Clearly. A picture says a thousand words and the pictures of you with the Verhena tell a pretty good story."

"What next? What do you guys need me to do?"

"How are her skills coming? Any big developments?" Rawley asks.

"She stopped training. She doesn't think she needs it anymore. She thinks she can rely on me and the Guard to protect her."

"Excellent." Rawley sounds thrilled. "It's all coming together. Thanks to you."

"I told my dad I will do all I can to help him. I meant it. If I have to put up with that scatterbrain to get him where he needs to be, I will."

I'm not even a little upset by the things James says about me. He's painting a picture that we need the rogue wolves to believe.

Rawley clears his throat. "Here's the deal kid. Your dad is ready to make a move. He's seen how much she trusts you and he doesn't want to wait any longer. I'll call you Wednesday morning at 8:30 a.m. I'm going to give you a location. Be there by 9:30 a.m. Bring the Verhena with you. Your dad will take care of the rest."

"Let me get this straight," James says annoyed. "You expect me to get her out of the building and to a location without the Guard on my ass the entire time?"

"Figure it out James."

"Am I finally going to my dad's hideout? I can't wait to get the hell out of that building."

Rawley laughs. "You're going to the big show kid. You'll meet our pack and see our new digs."

"Sweet," James says. "It's about damn time."

A chair scoots across the floor.

"Wednesday morning. 8:30 a.m. If the plan to get the girl out of there sounds legit, I'll give you the location. We don't want the Guard following you to the hideout, so you better come up with something amazing."

"Not a problem. I'll make it happen," James says confidently.

"Good. I'll talk to you Wednesday."

We're huddled in the conference room again, figuring out where we go from here.

"Obviously the location isn't far away if he thinks you'll make it there by 9:30, but it's probably not here in the city. That would be too close to our headquarters," Frank reasons.

275

"I agree," says James. "Maybe somewhere out on Long Island? Or upstate maybe?"

"Was there anything about Rawley's appearance that stood out? Any kind of clue there?" Ivan asks.

James shakes his head. "I don't think so." He pauses for a second, then his eyes light up. "He does have a woodsy scent to him."

A memory flashes through my mind.

"The wolves who were in my apartment at Leviston, they smelled woodsy. It was the first thing I noticed when I ran into the apartment."

Frank nods. "I remember that too." Frank stands and walks toward the door. "I'll be right back."

Frank disappears for a minute. When he returns, he's holding a stack of photographs.

"This," he says as he throws a picture of a tan SUV on the table, "is the getaway vehicle from Leviston. Look at the tires and the bottom half of the car."

We all lean over and examine the picture.

"It's covered in mud," Whitney observes.

Willa sums it up. "So they're in a wooded area within an hour of here."

"Who knows if they'll give me the actual location of their new hideout. They could be playing with me," James notes.

"This could all be a set-up," Ivan adds. "This whole thing could be a scheme to trap you and Chloe. There's no guarantee your father isn't trying to harm you James. You are the heir to the throne, so to speak."

I sigh. "We'll never know his true intentions. We can guess all day long what they're planning, but I think I'm Julian's main target. If he only wanted James, Julian would have given James a location already and killed James when he showed up."

"You're right Chloe," Whitney chimes in, "he wants you dead. He wants to be able to show everyone how strong he is by killing another Verhena. Plus, he's not worried about James being pack leader because he thinks James is on his side."

We all nod in agreement.

Pleased she made a valuable contribution, Whitney looks across the table to James. "You have to take me with you."

James shakes his head. "No Whit. You stay here."

"Dad will never believe you left me behind," Whitney insists. "He knows you better than that. If you don't take me with you, he'll be suspicious."

Everyone considers this for a minute.

"She's right," Ivan concedes. "Whitney needs to go with you."

Whitney smiles proudly.

But James is frowning. "This is getting out of control. Maybe I didn't think this through enough." He leans forward and puts his head in his hands. "I'm putting everyone I love at risk. It may not be worth it."

Frank crosses his arms. "If you want out James, tell us now."

"Hey," I say to James and he looks up. "We have to do this. We can't let your father get away with killing Barbara and my sister. He's not going to stop. Even if he never gets to me, he'll find some other target to take out. He could come after you and Whitney."

James straightens up after a moment. "You're right, I'm good."

"Alright," Willa says, "let's put our heads together and come up with the best damn plan we can."

This is the first time I've heard Willa curse. She looks hyped up, ready to go into battle.

Her energy pumps me up too. "First, we need to figure out a good story for how James is getting me out of here without the Guard following us. It has to sound legit."

277

"I think I've got something," James says. "The wolves look at the Guard as a bunch of blowhards."

Frank narrows his eyes.

James puts up his hand. "Sorry man, it's what they think."

"Go on," Frank says through clenched teeth.

"I'll tell Rawley I paid off one of the Guard members. A disgruntled guy looking for some dough so he can get out of here. I'll tell Rawley he's an IT guy who will shut the entire grid down for half an hour. Which should give us enough time to get out of the building and out of the city."

Frank rubs his chin. "That could work."

"What about a getaway car?" I ask. "We can't take a vehicle from here because Rawley will know they have trackers."

James shrugs. "I'll tell him the same IT guy disabled it for me."

We all ponder this story for a minute.

Ivan breaks the silence. "It's a simple story, but it's believable."

Willa agrees. "The simpler, the better."

Frank clicks and unclicks his pen as he considers the plan. "Okay, next issue. How do we follow you without the wolves noticing?"

James shifts in his chair. "That's a harder sell. I can only assume they will be following us and looking out for you guys."

"What about the method we used when we went to the funeral? Cars catching up with us on the route…" I stop myself, seeing the problem with this. "But we won't be able to get cars out ahead of us because we don't know where we're going."

Frank nods. "Exactly, we'll have to chew on that one for a while."

Nerves are setting in for all of us. If we can't figure out a way to have the Guard follow us, James, Whitney and I will be on our own.

We spend the next few hours discussing potential scenarios for our arrival at the pack hideout. What type of weapons will they use? How many werewolves will be there? Will they attack immediately?

The possibilities are endless.

Willa yawns and calls it quits. "It's been a long day. We're all tired and need a break. Let's get some food, try to enjoy the evening, and reconvene in the morning."

No one dissents.

"I hate that my sister is involved," James says when we're back in my room.

"She's stronger than you think. Give her a chance."

"I wanted to keep her out of all of this."

I sit next to him on the bed. "Whitney doesn't want to be held back, she wants to be involved. She wants to help."

James picks at his palm, jaw clenched. "We had a rough childhood. I hoped to spare her a rough adulthood."

I put my hand on his shoulder. "Keeping her in the dark doesn't make her happy. Whitney isn't the kind of girl who wants to be locked away in a tower. She wants to saddle up and ride into battle with us. Let her."

James leans forward and we touch foreheads.

I stand and extend my hand to him. "Now, let's go eat some pizza. I'm starving!"

James takes my hand and stands up. "Pizza?"

"Yep. I asked Jessica to order everyone pizza for dinner. No healthy stuff tonight."

James smiles. "You're the best."

I wrap my arms around his waist and give him a kiss. "I know."

Chapter Seventeen

The next morning I'm in the training center early. James is still sleeping in my bed. A smile crosses my lips when I remember how peaceful he looked wrapped up in my down comforter.

Willa walks into the training center. "Sorry I'm late. I had to deal with an issue from the Boston coven."

"No problem."

"When you called this morning, it sounded urgent."

I bite my lower lip. "I have an idea. I haven't talked to anybody about it yet. I need to know if you think it's possible."

I share my plan with Willa. "Do you think I can do that kind of magic?"

Willa's brow furrows. "I've never tried it myself under those circumstances. Rose, my mentor, knew a lot more about these types of spells than I do and she took a lot of notes. One of her journals may have the answer to our question."

I nod. "Okay then. Let's start with the library. We only have a couple days. We need to work fast."

Willa and I luck out. A few hours later, we find what we need in one of Rose's notebooks. If Rose is right, my plan should work.

Willa and I return to the training center and work together until I'm completely zapped.

"You need to rest Chloe. We'll pick it back up again tomorrow."

"Do you think I'll be able to do it?"

Willa nods her head. "Yes, I do."

Tomorrow is Tuesday and we're supposed to get the location Wednesday. If I don't have the spell down by tomorrow, I'll have to come up with something else.

When I get back to my room, James isn't there. I'm disappointed, but I'm too tired to track him down. I kick off my shoes and climb under the covers. I fall asleep almost immediately. By the time I wake up, the sun is down. I can't believe I slept all afternoon. I roll over and see James sitting at the desk, flipping through a stack of photographs.

"Whatcha looking at?"

James glances up from the photos and smiles. "It's aerial photographs of the surrounding area. Frank and I are narrowing down the possible hideout locations."

"Any luck?"

"A few possibilities."

I sit up and stretch. "I have a plan, but I need to know about the man in quarantine first."

James puts the pictures down. "Daniel? Why do you need to know about Daniel?"

"I just do. I promise I'll explain why."

James rubs his chin. "Daniel is a problem child, to say the least. Frank asked us to bring a rogue wolf with us, and Daniel was the only one in our possession. I didn't like traveling with him, but at the same time, I didn't want to leave him behind either."

"Frank said Daniel was caught stealing some of Ivan's documents. Is that his worst crime?"

James grunts. "I wish. I'm sorry to say we didn't give Frank all the details because we were afraid he wouldn't let Daniel in the building. But in reality, your quarantine is the most secure place for someone like Daniel."

Although I don't like it, I ignore the fact that we weren't given full disclosure about Daniel upfront. "Tell me. Tell me what he's done."

"Daniel was a high ranking member of our security personnel. We had no idea he was affiliated with my father." James sighs.

282

"Daniel came into headquarters one night and started mowing people down with an automatic machine gun."

I gasp. "No!"

James grimaces. "He killed five people. We found him in my grandfather's office trying to steal documents." James stands and walks over to the bed. "He's an awful person Chloe."

I nod. "Good. That's exactly what I needed to hear."

After I tell James my plan, we call Frank. Frank comes up to my room and I share my idea with him.

"I don't like it. It's too dangerous," Franks says when I'm done.

"It's risky, but I've thought it through. Willa and I discussed all the necessary magic, and we think it can be done."

"What about the Guard? How are we involved in this?"

I hesitate, then say, "You're not."

Frank shakes his head. "No. We can't send you out on your own."

"You have to," I plead. "It's the only way this will work."

"What if you end up getting killed? What then?"

I clasp my hands together. "Well, you better hope the next Verhena is as cool as I am."

Frank scolds me. "I'm not in a joking mood Chloe."

I sigh. "If you come up with something that allows the Guard to be involved without compromising the plan, let me know."

Frank stands. "I'll share this with a few of the guys. We'll reconvene in the morning."

As agreed, the three of us are together again in the morning. Ivan and Willa are with us as well. I purposely didn't invite Whitney to the meeting.

"I talked with the guys last night and we've come up with a game plan on our end." Frank pulls over a work board covered in notes and the aerial photographs James was looking at yesterday.

Frank puts his hand on a group of photographs. "Judging by these aerial photographs and information about the rural properties available in a fifty mile radius, one of these six locations is likely Julian's hideout."

"Only six?" I ask.

Frank nods. "Yes. We ran all possible locations through a database using searches for recently sold or abandoned properties. We then narrowed the search down based on proximity to the road, available out buildings, etcetera. We also compared photographs of the properties from a year ago to today to see if there has been any recent development on the properties."

Frank and the Guard are so smart it blows my mind.

"Bottom line is Julian is at one of these properties."

"Why don't you go raid those properties?" Ivan asks. "Then we can leave my grandkids and Chloe out of this."

"No," James says firmly. "We have a way to get inside. The rogue wolves will let me and Chloe on the property, they don't expect us to attack them. If we send in the Guard, we risk Guard members being harmed."

"Your plan is based on the assumption that your father is being honest. That's a risky assumption to make," Ivan argues back.

"Ivan," Willa says gently, "you and I are passing the torch to the younger generation. Let them handle it."

Ivan tears up. "I don't want to lose my grandchildren. I can't bear it."

I reach out my hand and place it on Ivan's. "You won't lose them. I promise."

It takes him a second, but Ivan meets my eyes and nods.

I get back to business. "Okay. You've got the possible locations nailed down. What next? We can't send surveillance teams out there. It will be suspicious."

"We will have teams set up within two miles of each property. Once Rawley gives James the location, we'll put the necessary team on high alert."

This can't be the entire plan. "What else?" I prompt.

"James will tell Rawley the vehicle isn't being tracked, but we'll have a tracker on it anyway. If Rawley calls at some point to change the location, we'll see the car change direction. We'll keep a close eye on the route your car is taking the entire time."

"Anything else?" Willa asks.

"Yes. Our teams will stay back, but we'll be ready to descend upon the property if we get a distress call."

"A distress call?" James asks.

Frank holds up a silver watch. "This watch is equipped with a distress button. The wearer simply pushes in one of the side cogs, and we'll be on our way."

"So you want me to wear the watch?" I assume.

"No," Frank says to my surprise. "It's for Whitney."

When we all look at him confused, he continues, "They'll be paying less attention to Whitney. She can hit the distress button more discreetly than you can."

Makes sense.

"Speaking of Whitney, what are we telling her?" James directs the question to me.

"I say we tell her ninety-five percent of the plan."

Everyone agrees with me. I feel awful not telling Whitney the entire plan, especially after I lectured James about how he needs to give her more responsibility, but I need an honest and true reaction from her.

I sigh. "Whitney's going to be mad at me."

"Sometimes difficult decisions have to be made," Willa says. "Whitney will forgive you. She loves you."

I know Willa is right. I just have to live long enough to be forgiven.

"How did your training with Willa go?" James asks when I lay in bed next to him.

My hair is still wet from my shower, but I'm too tired to care. "Really well. I'll be ready for tomorrow."

James leans over and kisses my forehead. "Just think, in twenty-four hours, this will all be over."

"Or we'll be dead."

James strokes my face. "Don't talk like that."

"It's true though," I whisper. "This isn't a fairy tale. We've already lost good people."

He hugs me tight. "No more good ones. Only the bad ones."

His body heat warms me.

"James," I say as I consider my impending doom, "there is one thing I'd regret if I die tomorrow."

"Yeah, what's that?"

I tilt my head back and press my mouth against his. As our kisses intensify, James rolls on top of me. I spread my legs so his body can press against mine in all the right places. The energy builds as we explore each other's bodies.

He breaks our kiss. "I thought you wanted to go slow," he says with a smirk.

I smile back. "I don't have time for slow."

I pull his mouth to mine. His strong hands move up my body. I sigh as his hand cups my breast. I tilt my head back and expose my neck.

James stops. "What are you doing?"

I look in his eyes. "I want you. In every way. I want to be your mate."

His eyes are on fire. "Are you sure?"

"Yes."

He leans down and touches his tongue to my collar bone. I moan as he slowly makes his way to my jaw line. He whispers in my ear, "Are you mine?"

In between breaths I whisper, "Yes."

"Say it," he commands gently.

"I am yours."

He licks my neck again. Electricity shoots through every nerve in my body. We slowly undress, both of us naked under the blanket.

"Say it again," he whispers in my ear.

"I am yours."

He thrusts inside me and my back arches in pleasure.

"And I am yours," he growls.

Chapter Eighteen

Whitney

My bedside alarm goes off at 7:30 a.m. I want plenty of time to get dressed and ready.

"Whitney!" my grandfather yells from down the hall. "Are you up?"

I roll my eyes. "Yes! I'm up!"

He doesn't even trust me to get up on time. It won't surprise me if he demands I stay home at the last minute.

I take a quick shower and blow dry my dark hair. I put on a pair of black leggings, a long silver sweater and my black leather boots. No heels though, they might get stuck in the mud.

Chloe came to see me yesterday and told me the details of our plan. We'll be leaving promptly at 8:30 a.m. under the ruse that the Guard's grid is down. We will travel to my dad's compound and hope to God everything goes okay.

When I asked what my role in the whole ordeal is, Chloe basically told me it's to stay out of the way.

Oh, and to wear the Inspector Gadget watch Frank gave me.

I meet the group in the Guard conference room at 8:15 a.m. James and Chloe are standing together next to Frank. Chloe looks amazing. Her blonde hair is pulled into a bun and she is wearing skinny jeans with ballet flats and a beautiful white pea coat. I question whether wearing a white coat to a fight is wise, but keep my opinions to myself.

We are anxiously awaiting Rawley's call. A part of me hopes he won't give us my dad's location. I'm in way over my head. I talked a big game about wanting to be involved the other day, but now I wish I had kept my mouth shut.

289

My nerves increase when Willa brings Daniel into the room. I knew he was coming on the road trip with us, but my stomach still rolls when he walks in. He's grown a scraggily beard since the last time I saw him. He's dressed in jeans and a black hooded sweatshirt, the same outfit he was wearing the day we brought him here.

The main difference is the look in his eyes. They are empty and vacant. Nothing at all like the crazy eyes of a wild man. Willa is pulling him along behind her like a zombie. Chloe told me Daniel would be under hypnosis, but seeing him is unsettling. She claims we need to bring Daniel with us as a showing of goodwill. The ruse will seem more believable to my dad if Daniel is with us.

Hypnotized or not, the guy gives me the creeps.

At 8:25, James excuses himself and steps into another room so he can take Rawley's call. He is wearing a wire, so we all know when the phone rings. We stand around the monitors like statues and listen to the call.

"This is James," my brother answers.

"Good morning James. What have you got for me?"

James tells Rawley the story about buying off an IT guy.

Rawley falls for it hook, line and sinker. "Ah, greed. One of my favorite deadly sins."

"I prefer lust myself," James quips.

Rawley laughs. "I'm sure. You ready for the address?"

"Yes."

Rawley rattles off an address. Frank writes it down on a piece of paper and heads back to the conference room. Chloe and I follow behind him. Frank walks up to his work board and pulls off one of the aerial photographs.

He puts it on the table. "This is it. This is the hideout."

I look at the picture. It's an old farmhouse set back about half a mile from the main road. The dirt road leading up to the house is completely surrounded by trees. A large red barn sits on the property. Probably where all of the rogue werewolves are hiding.

James walks into the conference room. "Let's go." His face shows no sign of nerves. How can he be so cool under pressure?

"I'll have my men shut off the exterior lights now, that way it looks like our power has gone down," Frank says. "We'll turn it back on in thirty-two minutes."

Chloe nods. "Sounds good."

Frank gives Chloe a hug. "Good luck girl."

After she returns Frank's hug, Chloe grabs my hand. "C'mon. We've got this."

I'm glad she's confident. I feel like I might pee my pants.

James calls out to Daniel. "Daniel, follow me."

"Do we have to bring him?" I ask Chloe as we ride in the elevator down to the garage.

"Yes. Willa has him in a trance. The only person he'll listen to is James."

"Are you sure?"

"One hundred percent."

"What if he wakes up?"

Chloe shrugs her shoulders. "I'll just set him on fire."

When we get to the garage, James points to a white Cadillac. "That's our ride for the day."

We climb in. James and Chloe in the front, Daniel and I in the back. James starts the car and drives out of the garage. I keep my fingers crossed there is no traffic. We don't have time for it. We'll be cutting it close to Rawley's deadline as it is.

Luckily, we cruise through the city with no issues. It's a crisp March day. Gloomy, but no rain. James and Chloe talk quietly up front. They don't make an effort to include me in the conversation and I don't interject. There's nothing I want to talk about anyway. I'm too stressed out.

I check my cellphone to see if Brandon has texted me. Nope. It's been two days since I talked to him. He's probably out on one of his adventures, but he could at least send a text to let me know he's okay.

He and I are due for a serious talk when I get home. If I ever go back home. I like New York City. I've been reading about their different fashion schools online and would love to attend one. The only thing holding me back is Brandon, but I need to be honest with myself about our relationship. I'm not a priority to him, and I need to move on.

I put my cellphone away and steal a glance at Daniel. He is staring straight ahead, not moving. I skootch closer to my door anyway. We cross a bridge, I'm not sure which one, and we are out of the city. I keep checking my watch to see what time it is.

"Will we make it on time?" I ask when my watch says 9:15.

"Yes. We're almost there," James says. "Our turn should be coming up any minute."

Chloe glances back. "You ready?"

I want to scream, "No! How can I be prepared for the completely unpredictable?!"

But instead I say, "Yes."

A couple minutes later, James turns off the main road and onto a dirt path. The car bounces as we make our way through the thick trees. Once beyond the trees, we come to a clearing.

An old farmhouse sits to our left. Its once-white paint is chipped and peeling. The wraparound porch is missing several planks and leans awkwardly. The house shows no sign of life and appears uninhabitable. The large red barn to the right, however, looks brand new.

Two men walk out of the barn as James stops the car. Neither of them is my father.

"Is that Rawley?" I ask from the backseat.

"Yes," James confirms. "I don't know the other guy."

We look around for a second to make sure there aren't any more wolves coming out of the barn or from the woods behind us.

"It's show time ladies," James says. He and Chloe hold hands for a brief second and exchange a loving glance. Then they move for their doors.

"Daniel, get out of the car," James instructs. Daniel does as he's told and opens his car door. Once outside, James tells him, "Shut the door Daniel and follow me."

I watch from the other side of the car as Daniel shuts the door and walks behind James. I swallow a huge lump in my throat and shut my own door.

From ahead of me, I hear Chloe say, "James? Where are we? I thought we were going to Vermont to ski?"

"Just a pit stop sweetie," James answers back.

They are already playing their parts. All four of us walk up to Rawley and the other man.

"James. You made it," Rawley says, pleased.

"Where is my father?" James asks.

Chloe feigns shock. "Your father? Your father is here? Are you crazy? He wants to kill me!" Chloe turns on her heels and runs for the car.

"Daniel, grab Chloe," James says without turning his head away from Rawley. Daniel does as told and grabs Chloe by the arm as she tries to run past us. He drags her back to James.

Chloe is kicking and screaming. "Get off of me you loser!"

Oh, she's good at this. Chloe can stop Daniel easily, but the rogue wolves would never know it watching this show.

Once Daniel drags Chloe to his side, James says, "I'll ask you again, where is my father?"

"He's watching," Rawley answers.

James flexes his jaw. "Seriously? He still doesn't trust me?" James puts his hands on his hips. "He asked for her, and here she is. He still won't come out here?"

Rawley starts to talk, "James, I assure you…"

James puts up his hand to interrupt him. "Fuck this. I'll kill her myself. Maybe that will be enough to earn his trust."

"Wait? What?" Chloe asks, her eyes wide. "James, no! This isn't the plan!"

James gets a shark-like grin on his face. "You never knew me sweetheart, but it was fun while it lasted."

James pulls a large knife out of his coat and walks toward Chloe.

I gasp. What is going on? Chloe never mentioned a knife to me. Or my brother acting like he was going to kill her.

Chloe struggles and zaps Daniel. Daniel drops his hands, but doesn't fall to the ground. Chloe runs away, sheer panic on her face. My heart is pounding. Chloe isn't pretending anymore!

I step in front of my brother. "James! What are you doing?"

He gives me a menacing look and throws me to the ground. "Get out of my way bitch!"

I land hard on my hands and butt, cringing from the pain. I reach out to grab James's ankle, but he is too fast.

"James! Please!" I plead with him.

He growls at me, his eyes wild. He turns his attention back to Chloe. "Daniel! Get her! Now!"

Daniel takes off and tackles Chloe from behind. I hear her grunt as she slams to the ground.

"Get off of me!" she screams when Daniel pins her down. She zaps him again and he lets go momentarily. Just as Chloe is about to get up, Daniel grabs her throat and squeezes. Chloe is strong enough to fend him off and the two start wrestling. They roll around on the ground.

"Use your magic!" I yell.

Chloe struggles to keep Daniel pinned to the ground. "I can't! Willa's spell is too strong!"

Huh? Oh no... Willa's hypnotizing spell. It must be blocking Chloe's magic!

Chloe and Daniel continue to roll around on the ground, both covered in mud. For a second, it's hard to tell what is going on. James circles the two of them until Daniel is on top of Chloe. Daniel sits on Chloe's midsection and pins her wrists to the ground.

"Do it now James!" Daniel yells.

I see James raise the knife, a wicked grin on his face.

"No!" I scream. I jump up and run for them.

"James, what is happening? Don't!" Chloe pleads, "Please don't! Wait!"

I watch in horror as James plunges the knife into Chloe's stomach. He pulls the knife out, then stabs her in the chest. Blood spews from Chloe's mouth and runs down the side of her beautiful face. Deep red stains spread across her white coat. Daniel stands and looks down at Chloe's body, a satisfied smile on his face.

I fall to my knees. I can't breathe. My stomach turns and I throw up. As I'm wiping my mouth on my jacket, I see the silver watch. The Inspector Gadget watch! I press the panic button a few times before realizing it's useless. I'm too late.

James hands the knife to Daniel and walks back toward Rawley. I don't recognize the sinister look on his face. I stand up on shaky legs and go after him.

"You monster!" I yell as I launch myself at him.

He turns just in time and grabs my arms. I kick my foot and connect with his shin. He winces in pain, but throws me to the ground again.

295

"Daniel!" he yells. "Come get my sister. Put her back in the car. Don't let her leave."

Daniel comes up behind me and grabs my arms. I push myself hard against him, but he squeezes me in a bear hug.

"Let go of me you piece of shit!" I kick my legs into the air and try to get loose.

"Hey!" he protests. "Cut it out Whitney!"

I continue struggling as I watch my brother, Rawley and the third man walk into the barn. I throw my head back and connect with Daniel's nose. Daniel loosens his grip. I take advantage and break free, running for the tree line. My feet pounding the ground as I run as fast as I can.

When will the Guard show up? Will they even want to help me when they see what's happened to Chloe?

"Whitney! Stop!" Daniel yells.

I make it to the tree line and dive into the woods.

"Whitney!" Daniel yells again.

I find a hiding spot between a tree and a small bush.

Daniel walks by me. "Whitney, please! It's not what you think."

I huddle against the tree and try to control my breathing.

"I know you're here Whitney. Come out!"

I close my eyes and pray the Guard will get here soon.

"For the love of God Whitney!" Daniel shouts. Then mumbles to himself, "I should have told her everything."

I open my eyes and look out at Daniel from behind the bush. What did he just say? That he should have told me everything? Hold on a second...Daniel isn't supposed to be talking at all. He's hypnotized.

While I'm processing all of this, Daniel closes his eyes and moves his lips silently. Suddenly, he's no longer Daniel. He's Chloe!

Without thinking, I mumble, "Chloe, is that you?"

Chloe rushes over to me. "Whitney! I'm so glad you're okay!"

I step back. Chloe is alive? I need to test this, make sure it's truly her.

"What is Bane's real name?"

Chloe looks surprised by my question but quickly answers, "Sue."

I come out from behind the bush and grab her. I give her a big hug. "Oh my God! I thought you were dead!"

She squeezes me back. "It was glamour spells – one on me, and one on Daniel. Willa and I weren't one hundred percent sure it would hold after Daniel died, but it did. He still looks like me."

Chloe's white coat has grass stains, but it isn't covered in blood. She holds the bloody knife in her right hand.

"So James really killed Daniel?" I ask.

Chloe lifts the knife and looks at it. "Yep. This is his blood, not mine."

"And James was in on it the whole time?"

Chloe nods. "I'm sorry we didn't tell you. It had to seem as real as possible."

I let out a huge sigh of relief. "Thank God you're okay."

Chloe grabs my hand. "Come this way. We have to watch the barn."

Chloe crouches down and I follow suit. "What are we looking for?"

"As soon as your brother comes out of the barn, I'm going to blow the place up."

"So that's the big plan?" a deep voice asks from behind us.

The voice is so familiar. I look up just in time to see my dad bringing down a giant rock over Chloe's head.

297

"Chloe!" I shout, but the rock connects. It makes a sickening noise and Chloe falls forward onto me, a small trickle of blood coming from her forehead.

Four werewolves in their human forms surround us. Crap! What do I do? The Guard hasn't shown up yet. James is in the barn. Chloe is passed out on top of me. It's all on me. Think Whitney, think!

Then it comes to me. I'll do what I do best.

A huge smile crosses my face. "Daddy!"

"Hello baby girl," my dad coos. "It's been a long time."

I move Chloe off of me, laying her flat on the ground. I stand up and brush dirt off my clothes. "Ugh, I'm so dirty," I whine.

Dad shakes his head and turns to one of his men. "Go back to the barn. Get my son. I knew this was too good to be true. He's always been a disappointment."

The wolf takes off for the barn. Dad turns back to me. I start talking before he can say anything.

"It's so great to see you Dad! I had no idea where you went! You didn't leave a note, or your number. I have to say it really hurt my feelings when you reached out to James, but not me."

I ramble on and on about how much I missed him. He's watching the barn, but he occasionally looks my way and says, "Uh huh."

He doesn't suspect a thing.

I smile wide. "Can I get a hug Daddy?"

He shifts his eyes from the barn to me, then back to the barn. "Yeah, sure."

Chloe

The good news is Whitney gave me enough of a warning to start a protection spell. The bad news is the rock still hit me pretty hard.

When I land on top of Whitney, I do my best to lay lifeless and pretend to be knocked out.

I help Whitney a bit as she lifts me off of her, but no one seems to notice. I'm confused at first when she starts talking sweetly to Julian, but quickly realize she's buying us time. I crack one eye open to survey my surroundings.

Julian looks a lot like his children. The dark hair, brilliant green eyes and attractive features. He is shorter than James, but they're built the same. As I watch him, I notice a darkness in Julian's eyes, an underlying insanity.

"Can I get a hug Daddy?" Whitney asks.

What is she doing? She shouldn't get anywhere near this man!

Julian mumbles, "Yeah, sure," but his attention is focused on the barn.

Whitney lifts her arms from her sides and I see something shimmer. What in the…she has the knife!

Julian isn't paying any attention to Whitney as he opens his arms to her. His gaze shifts back and forth between me and the barn. Like everyone else, he has underestimated his daughter.

Whitney reaches for her father, but instead of giving him a hug, she shoves the knife as hard as she can into her dad's stomach. Julian's face twists in shock, and then pain. His eyes wide and desperate. Whitney uses both of her hands to pull up on the knife. Julian tries frantically to free her grip, but it's no use. The knife is so deep in his stomach, all I can see is the hilt.

The other wolves are watching the barn and have their backs to Julian. They are completely oblivious to what is happening until Julian says, "Help…" in a feeble voice.

The wolves turn just as Julian starts coughing up blood. I sit up and freeze them in place before they can spring into action. Disbelief on their faces.

Whitney lets go of the knife and Julian collapses to his knees. He reaches out to Whitney, but she steps back. Without Whitney there to catch him, Julian falls forward. When he hits the ground, the impact forces the knife even further into his body. The back of his leather jacket sticks up like a tent.

Whitney stands over him quietly. I get up and walk over to her.

"Damn Whitney."

Tears spill from her eyes. "Think he's dead?"

"Oh yeah. He's dead."

"Make sure."

"What?"

She turns to me. "Make sure he's dead. I don't want to take any chances."

I nod my head. I shoot fire from my fingertips, careful not to set the nearby trees ablaze. Julian's body ignites into flames. I stop the fire when he is unrecognizable.

I'm about to say something comforting to Whitney, she did just kill her father, but she speaks before I do. "Alright, let's get moving."

I'm shocked by her indifference, but Whitney's right. We have to get back to James.

Whitney pauses next to the frozen wolves. "What about them?"

I'm not sure what to do with them. I don't know anything about them. They could be harmless henchmen. Or teenagers who lost their way.

"They'll be okay like this. We'll come back for them later."

Whitney nods in agreement.

As we run toward the barn, black Escalades roar up the dirt drive.

"It's the Guard!" Whitney exclaims.

"Did you hit the panic button?" I ask, not breaking my stride.

"Yes! As soon as I thought you were dead!" Whitney yells back.

The SUVs stop short of our Cadillac sedan. Frank jumps out of one of the cars and runs to Daniel's body. Except it still looks like me. Frank falls to his knees next to my fake body.

"Frank!" I yell, running toward him.

He can't hear me. He picks the body up and cradles it in his arms.

"Frank!" I yell again, waving my hands in the air.

This time he looks up. He glances down at the body confused, then back at me again. He sets the body on the ground and stands, relief on his face.

Frank jogs toward me. "Chloe?!" When we meet, Frank grabs me in a big hug. "Man you freaked me out! I knew the plan, but I was still afraid it was you."

I stare at the body and remove the glamour spell. Instead of a fake version of me, Daniel is now laying in the grass. Frank squeezes me again.

"We have to get James," I tell Frank. "He's in the barn."

Frank yells to the rest of the Guard, "To the barn!"

I holler back to Whitney before following Frank. "Take a few of the guys into the woods. Show them what we left there."

She nods and pulls aside two Guard members.

"What did you leave in the woods?" Frank asks.

"Julian and two of his men."

Frank smiles. "Nice."

We're about to enter the barn when the doors fly open. Frank and I retreat fifteen feet and take our fighting stances. Two werewolves have James, one holding each arm. Walking directly behind them is Rawley.

I lunge forward, but Frank grabs my arm. "He has a gun Chloe."

Frank's right. Rawley is holding a gun to the back of James's head. The group comes to a stop ten feet in front of us. The men holding onto James let go. They stand on either side of him with their arms folded across their chests. Rawley stays behind James, using him as a human body shield.

Wuss.

"Well, well, well. This just got interesting," Rawley says over James's shoulder. "Looks like the Guard showed up for our little party." James winces when Rawley presses the gun further into this skin. "You really had us. Your dad will be so disappointed James."

I square my shoulders. "Julian is dead."

"Sure he is," Rawley says unconvinced.

"His charred remains are in the woods, right next to two of your other men."

Rawley lowers the gun enough to lose contact with James's skin. I take a step forward.

Rawley raises the gun again. "Not another step. I'll pull the trigger."

"Go ahead. I want you to."

Rawley smirks. "Don't call my bluff princess."

I roll my eyes. "I'm tired of this."

I shoot electricity from each of my hands and hit the wolves standing on either side of James. They fall to the ground and flop around like fish out of water.

Rawley stares at them, terror in his eyes. He looks back at me, teeth clenched and eyes filled with rage. "You bitch!"

"You guys keep making that mistake. I'm a witch, with a 'w'."

Rawley cocks his gun and aims for James's head. "This is on you."

James closes his eyes and prepares for the worst. I pray my plan works as Rawley pulls the trigger.

In a flash, Rawley is on the ground. A bullet hole in his forehead.

"What just happened?" Frank asks with disbelief.

James opens his eyes and lets out the breath he was holding in.

"When Rawley lowered the gun, I put a protection spell on James. When he pulled the trigger, the bullet ricocheted off the protective bubble I made and hit him instead."

Frank is impressed. "Nicely played."

James runs over and sweeps me off my feet. Literally. He spins me around before setting me down.

He kisses my lips. "My hero."

"Um, guys," Frank says from beside us, "I don't mean to break up the reunion, but we have trouble."

James and I turn to see wolves rushing out of the barn. Some of them are in their Were forms, mouths snarling and ready for a fight. The wolves in their human forms are carrying guns.

"Stay close to me!" I yell to Frank and James.

I throw a protective shield around us as the gunshots start firing. Members of the Guard come running up and fire back at the wolves.

"Take cover!" I shout at them.

I gather all of my energy and shoot fire at the barn. A huge fireball hits the door and explodes. The force of the explosion sends werewolves flying everywhere. Many of them are injured and those in their Were forms transition back into their human bodies. Guard members immediately grab them and drag them out of the way.

The entire barn is consumed by flames within seconds. The wolves who were hiding inside run out of the exits on either end. They are captured by the Guard without much of a fight. They realize they are outnumbered. While it's hard to tell in the chaos, I'm guessing Julian assembled fifty to sixty rogue wolves.

When the coast is clear, I drop my bubble.

I turn around to check on Frank and James when Frank yells, "Chloe! Look out!"

I glance over my shoulder and see a wolf in human form aiming a gun at my back. Before I can do anything to protect myself, Frank jumps in front of me and takes me to the ground. I hit the grass hard as multiple gunshots go off. A loud boom goes off near me, Frank's gun taking out my would-be assassin.

Frank lands on top of me with a heavy thud. James runs over and rolls Frank off of my body so I can breathe. I lay on my back taking deep breaths, still dazed. When my eyes focus, I see James huddled next to Frank. Frank is laying on the ground, motionless. His arms splayed out next to him.

"Frank!" I crawl over to Frank's body. His eyes are closed and he doesn't respond when I touch his face. "Oh my God! No, no, no!"

I lay my head and hands on his chest. My healing skills are not the best, but I put all I have into it. "Please Frank! Please!"

After a few seconds, Frank opens his eyes. "Chloe?"

I cry out, "Frank!" and give him a big hug.

"Chloe?" he asks again, his voice gritty.

"What is it Frank? What do you need?"

"I...I can't breathe."

I'm hysterical. "Did the bullet hit a lung?" I look up at the other Guard members. "Is there another healer here?"

"Chloe, you're squeezing me too hard," Frank murmurs.

"What?"

Frank smiles. "You're crushing me."

"Oh." Apparently my frantic energy made my bear hug feel like an actual bear hug. I let go of Frank and help him sit up.

"Where are you hit?" James asks.

"The vest." Frank pulls off his shirt to reveal a black bulletproof vest. A lone bullet is stuck in the mesh over his heart.

I slap Frank on the arm. "You bastard! I thought you were dead!"

He laughs. "Is that the thanks I get for literally taking a bullet for you?"

I grin. "You're the best Frank."

James and I help Frank stand up and he surveys the damage. "I'll help the guys round up the rest of the werewolves. We need to call in more vehicles to get them out of here." He kicks a pile of ash that may or may not have been a werewolf five minutes ago. "And a cleaning crew. You guys head on home. We've got it from here."

James takes my hand as we start to walk away. I think of something and stop. "Hey Frank?"

"Yep?"

"How did you get here?"

He smiles. "I waited ten minutes after you left, then I got in a car and drove up. I met the guys at their surveillance location. No way I was sitting this one out."

I run back to Frank and bury my head in his chest. "I love you Frank."

"I love you too girl," he says when he hugs me back. "Now go home and get some rest. You did good today."

James and Whitney are waiting for me by the car. I grab Whitney and squeeze her.

"You were amazing Whitney. I'm so proud of you."

She gives me a half smile. "I killed my dad."

"You did?" James asks, eyes wide. He turns to me. "She did?"

"She did," I confirm. "Whitney, I'm sorry you had to kill him. I never intended to put that on you."

"He was an awful person. It had to be done, and I was in a position to do it. I would do it again." Whitney has dirt all over her face and leaves in her hair. She's never looked so strong.

Whitney opens her car door and sits down. "I'm ready to go now."

"Me too," James says.

"Want me to drive?" I ask.

"Nah. I can."

I grab his hand. "I was scared to death when I saw the gun against your head."

"I wasn't."

"Of course not. You're cool, calm James."

He shakes his head. "No. I wasn't worried because you were there."

I touch his face with my hand and look up into his eyes. "We did it. We're still alive."

"I told you, we're not losing any more good ones. Only the bad ones."

James pulls me into him and we stand together in a tight embrace. Eventually we pull apart and get into the car. Whitney is laying down in the backseat. Her eyes are closed and her breathing is slow. If she's not asleep, she's close.

As we pull away from the property, I watch the smoke from the barn rise into the sky. The Guard is gathering the remaining wolves and loading them into vehicles. I'm sure the fire department will be here soon to put out the fire. Who knows what the Guard will tell them to explain the situation, but I'm sure they're on top of it.

On our way home, I tell James what happened in the woods. He tells me about the chaos in the barn when the wolf from the woods ran in to say the Verhena was still alive.

After we're done sharing our stories, I call my parents on James's cellphone.

"Hello?" my mom answers.

"Mom, it's me."

"Chloe! I haven't heard from you in days, I was worried."

"Sorry Mom. I was working on a project."

306

"Oh, okay."

My voice cracks. "I kept my promise Mom."

She doesn't have to ask me which promise. She starts crying and my dad gets on the phone.

"Chloe? Is everything okay?"

"Yes. More than okay." I repeat what I told my mom.

He asks for the details, but I'm tired. "Dad, I'm coming to see you in a couple days. I promise to tell you all about it then."

We end the call after each of us says, "I love you."

I put James's phone back in the center console. "You up for meeting my parents?"

He smiles and takes my hand. "I've survived worse."

I squeeze his hand and hold onto it.

I lean my head back against the headrest and look out my window. The sun breaks through the clouds.

I hope somewhere Chelsea is watching.

Acknowledgements

Branded was the first full-length novel I finished. I was insanely proud of myself when I was done. I shared it with some friends and they loved it. I loved it too. There was still more to this story though, so I immediately sat down and wrote *Torn*, the sequel to this book. Yes, there is a sequel ;)

Once both books were done, I set them aside for almost two years. I worked on other projects and improved my writing skills. When I felt ready, I came back to *Branded*. And you know what – I still loved it. It needed rewrites, lots and lots of rewrites, but I loved the characters and the story.

A very special thank you to my friend Jill, to whom this book is dedicated. I asked her what she would like to see in a paranormal book. She is an avid reader and loves the genre. She told me she wanted a story that brought witches and werewolves together. Here you go bestie!

I also want to thank Melanie. She read this book, and my others, as they were being written. I'd send her a few chapters at a time and she encouraged me to keep going. Mel, for real, I would not have completed these projects without your encouragement.

To my readers, I appreciate you spending time with me. Feel free to reach out to me at nevabellbooks@gmail.com or on Facebook and Instagram - @neva_bell_books. If you enjoyed *Branded*, please check out my other full-length novels and poetry collections.

Made in the USA
Las Vegas, NV
07 November 2021

33931438R00184